GOOD GOD, JOHNNY

GOOD GOD, JOHNNY:
A Christian Journey to the Third Millennium

By *JJ Spankston*

Wonderful teachers taught this English Swede to read. An Englishman from Africa taught me to write (well, the library helped a bit, too.) Although we have never met nor spoken, sir, your pen has been a good pal to me (and one mustn't meet his friends to simply have them be.) Warmest thanks and highest regard for the Hemingway of Africa - Wilbur Smith.

This book is also for my fine friend, Fallyn. Thanks for always being there for me Fay.

*More to me than all the other
Colors running light and true
Words can only task and sully
Shining stardust that is you*

For a good many men, taking chance is a sin -
frightening sadness, poor luck, and dismay.
They fail very rarely, and therefore just barely,
enjoy the great things life throws their way.
They hardly succeed spouting caution's poor creed,
avert risk and avoid life's disasters...

For a great fewer men, snubbing chance is a sin -
inherent gifts, bold success, and hoorays.
They fail very often, but attitudes soften,
when that risk swells to glory untold.
Living hell strengthens steel, while heaven can't feel,
all the good for the chance that it shatters...

For me and my friends, these are classes of men –
We shall bet on and chill with the latter.

GOOD GOD, JOHNNY

"I knew you had that goofy lookin son-bitch," Matt spoke sly, sprawled out in his backseat of the bus. "When I saw yer face, I knew ya had im."

"Shut up, dude." Johnny chided him, not unkindly. He knew from years of experience with his best friend that his predictions were usually voiced in the past tense and heavily influenced by the outcome. Staring out the window at the starless sky, Johnny's thoughts had already moved on past his win. In lieu of the usual weekly chapel, tomorrow was senior appreciation day. As the senior class president and valedictorian he was expected to give a speech to his peers and juniors. He had written it days previously and was silently rehearsing his lines.

"Honestly, I was kinda surprised that'cha beat him. Jesus Johnny, that dude had a forty yard lead on you if it was a foot. Dan ran a pretty shitty third leg. I mean, sweet Jesus that was bad, dude. He always looks like such a puss on that last hundred. Like he's gonna cry er somethin. I heard coach bitchin about not runnin him in the 4by8 at state. A 2:05 won't cut it there even with you pickin up the slack. I can't believe you ran a 1:53 man. Aint that your PR?" Matt didn't hide his adoration as he shook his head in wonder. It was hard for him to fathom running farther than a quarter mile without stopping.

Johnny didn't respond immediately as he looked out the window. The light was really going now. There weren't many stars yet. He could faintly see Orion's belt, but only Venus really twinkled this early.

"Maybe you could take his spot," he said.

Matt's eyes flew wide, horrified. "Huh-uh! No way, dude. That's *way* too far for me."

"I bet we could get you down to a two-flat in time for state." Johnny was grinning at him. "I'll talk to Coach Casey. We could have you and Dan do a time trial together. I bet you could take him. We won't know unless you give er a try."

"No way in hell, dude. Like my uncle Bob says, 'you don't gotta own a dog to know what dog shit smells like'."

"Matthew! How many times do I gotta tell ya? Watch yer mouth back there!"

"Sorry Coach Casey! I'll try."

"Don't try, son, just do it!" Their coach's eyes were serious but he had the faintest smile on his lips.

Matt lowered his voice - all conspiratorial. "I forgot about ol owl-ears up there. How the heck could he hear that from the front-a the bus?"

"He probably planted a bug in that seat a yours to keep track-a ya." Johnny smiled as his buddy started feeling around for anything unusual.

"How's that gold medal feel, John?"

"Feels like lead covered in gold paint."

"You shoulda seen coach hootin and hollerin on that last hundred. I thought he was gonna have a heart attack. He was just screamin, 'Now! Now! Now! Take him now!'"

"Well, I was tryin as best I could. That guy had a kick like a lop-eared mule." His lungs still ached and he coughed after he said it.

"When was the last time you lost a race anyways? I really can't remember, dude. It's been a while."

"Matthew, I've told ya a thousand times. The last time I lost is the last time I won." Johnny smiled at his friend, and Matthew did the like at the familiar expression.

"Man, did you see that little blonde *chica* I met at the end-a the meet? She was a flat-out fox. She wanted me bad, dude. I mean *real* fuckin bad. You shoulda seen the way she was lookin at me all dreamy and evrathin."

"She wasn't *that* little. Looked pretty thick to me. I can't imagine what she'll look like when she stops runnin." Matt looked hurt and immediately went to her defense. Johnny smiled at how easy it was to rile his friend and looked back out the window of the bus.

Johnny had never been consciously scared of anything besides snakes. Public speaking did not daunt him. What often bothered him, however, was the feeling that he must always surpass others' expectations of whatever he did. Whether it was sports, school, or accomplishments, his record of success had become both a boon to his esteem and a hurdle to his creativity. It was like his life itself had become a race. The faster he ran the more dramatic would be a fall.

"She didn't say so or anathin, but she was just fawnin up at me. All I had to do was glance at her, and she would swoon, man. I thought she had a nice goddamn body. Built like a brick shithouse." Matt pouted to himself a bit.

Johnny's speech was good, but it wasn't great. It wasn't what they were expecting. Though spring was in its infancy and the butterflies were still tucked in their cocoons, this thought set them aflutter in Johnny's stomach.

"Dude, remember in second grade when we goosed Emily Foster at the same time? I took the left cheek and you took the right. You didn't wana do it, didja? But everyone thought we were studs after that. You looked so scared when we were walking down the hall to get paddled." Matt laughed and Johnny looked up at him annoyed. He remembered the paddling but not being scared. Matt had talked him into a lot of things over the years that had got them both into trouble. That one had been worth it though.

"Yeah, what about it, man? I'm goin over my lines." Matt sighed with pleasure at the memory and looked out his window.

"That was awesome." He spoke more to himself than his friend. Johnny rolled his eyes and looked back out the window. The stars were beginning to show now.

"You wrote that speech yet, dude?" Matt knew as he said it that his question was rhetorical. As best friends since kindergarten they knew each other's moods better than their own. He could tell from the creased brow and slight frown that Johnny was far away in introspection. Johnny's incessant tugging on his left ear lobe helped to tattle-tale the hunch.

Looking across at him now, Matt let his thoughts delve into the pool of affection he had for his best friend. Back to that first day of kindergarten when the seed of their friendship had been watered by this then stranger's actions...

"Matthew, you're more than an hour late to class!" He could still hear the condescension in the woman's voice. "You have interrupted the classes' mathematics lesson. Come up to the front and dutifully explain your reason to the class." At the time he wasn't sure what dutifully meant. He knew what duty was. His father had explained to him on multiple occasions that his duty was first and foremost to God, then to country, and finally to family.

He didn't know it then, but there would be many occasions in the future that he would be tardy to class in the morning. All he knew right now was that his mother had been very hard to rouse out of bed that day, and that she tended to drink from a bottle that was off-limits to him in the afternoons. He knew that the teacher was mad at him. He needed to come up with something good to protect his mom.

His shoulders slumped and he hung his head, "well, Mrs. Anderson..."

"It's *Miss* Anderson, Matthew!"

"Oh," he said, "does that mean ya aint married *Mizz* Anderson? Like, if ya was married, ya'd be called *Mizzus* Anderson, right?" He seemed proud to know the difference.

"That is correct, Matthew!" she screeched. Her eyes glared at him.

"Is that why ya aint got a ring on that finger too?" He poked her finger a few times.

"Yes, that is exactly why I don't have a ring on that particular finger, Matthew!" she said all mad and loud. She wasn't even close to finding a husband, and she had been having a good morning until the problem had been so grossly brought to her attention again.

Matt looked up at this beast of a woman now. She seemed so huge. He saw her greasy hair and furry mustache. He smelled her musky smell and heard her shrill voice. He looked at her, nodded once, and knew why it was so.

9

"Well, *Mizz* Anderson... ya see... it wasn't my mom's fault or anathin. She was up all night beatin on these big rats with her big ol broom."

"Oh really, Matthew? I must say, that is an extremely believable tale you've come up with there. As impressed as I am with your excuse, it still does not account for why you are late, and why you have interrupted your more punctual peers' mathematics lesson!"

"Well, that's not all, *Mizz* Anderson. Ya see, when she was swingin the broom, cuz there was so many rats and all, and it really was a big broom, and my mom don't like rats at all in the house ya know, and she was swingin it like a wild *Kamanchee*, and it was purdy dark so she couldn't see real good, and she um, accidentally knocked over a candle, and um... our whole house burnt down." Even though being lied to was one of Ms. Anderson's multiple pet peeves, she couldn't help but let fly a guffaw at this ridiculous story.

"Well, well, it appears we have a veritable Shakespeare in our midst, children. Though lacking in poetry, your classmate, Matthew, is not only a great storyteller but a greater liar. If you were in my shoes, what would you all recommend for punishment of this little lout?"

At this outburst Johnny looked up for the first time from his assignment. He had been so busy tallying the difference between apples on the ground and those on the tree that he'd missed the majority of the inquisition on display.

He looked at Matt, chin lowered and eyes downcast, tears forming on the lower lids. He not only felt sorry for him but was angered by his new teacher. She seemed nice while handing out their assignment, but now he knew in his simple way that she was both talking over Matt's head and down to him at the same time. She was humiliating him in front of his classmates. She was being disrespectful and mean, and Johnny didn't like it.

He had been taught to respect his elders. This early lesson had always come with a motherly addendum, however. '*Your respect is yours, not anyone else's, Johnny. Give it freely, but it's always yours to take away. Don't you ever, ever let anyone talk down to you – no matter what the situation.'*

It was pretty obvious Matt was lying to the teacher, but she was being really mean and that wasn't right either. It was out before he could stop it. "It's true, Ms. Anderson. I drove by Matt's house this mornin on the way to school. It was all the way burned down, and just the chimney was left. I saw Matt outside with his family..."

Looking at his new teacher, Johnny could tell he had really stepped in it. He had seen that look before on his mother's face. Two months previously when he punched his big brother in the nose for using his freshly broken in baseball glove without permission.

But he glanced at Matt then and knew it had been worth it. Matt raised his chin and perked up as they made eye contact for the first time. Smiling his thanks at the unexpected ally, his face shone with a kind of brotherly love; by virtue of its scarcity, hardly found and rarely given. He had already made a good friend.

What the heck, Johnny thought to himself, *might as well back him up all the way*. "And I saw his mom too... She had a big ol broom."

"Ow'd the meet go today, son?"
"Pretty good, Dad. I got four golds and PR'd on the 4by8. Ran a 1:53."
Mr. Daniels scowled to hide his pride. "Well damn my eyes. Yeah, I'd say that's pretty good, John. You definitely got that speed from your momma. Hey, throw me the clicker, would ya?"

"Here ya go, Big Boy. It's called a remote, by the way."
"Shad-ap."
"Hey Pops, did you ask Mr. Lewis if you could get a few days off to come watch us at State? Coach Casey said he thinks we've got a real shot on that relay this year. I might even have a shot to take the 800 open, too. That

McDaniels kid will be in it, though. That guy's got a kick like a mule, but I reckon I might be able to sneak up on im if I'm feelin it that day."

"Reckon, huh? God, your uncle'd kick my ass if he heard that southern lingo comin outta his nephew like that."

"I like that word."

Mr. Daniels rubbed the back of his neck and exhaled through his teeth. He wasn't a large man, but he was put together well. He had big shoulders and forearms and a crooked nose he acquired in a bar long ago. His work kept him physically fit, but it was hard work and his body suffered a lot of aches and pains. It had been a hell of a day, and he was still sore. He was a pipefitter by profession and a damn good one too.

"I'll see if I can work it out, bud. We've been busy as hell down at the plant, and that bastard's got me workin doubles more often than not. And whenever it slows down a bit he sends me over to the goddamn weldin house." (He was a damn good welder, too.) "And whenever *that* slows down he's got me dinkin around with them goddamn electricians."

"Your neck crampin up on ya again, Dad?"

"Nah, it's nothing, bud... just a little sore. But I shouldn't complain bout havin the work. Lotta guys in my line been hit bad with the recession. I hate ta say it, but that tornado really helped us out down at the plant. Lotta orders been comin in lately."

Johnny and his father had been out of town the day the tornado hit. He had felt bad about it often, but it had been good for his dad's work and pay.

"Lotta times I wish I'd never moved us outta South Dakota, bud. Pays a hell of a lot better down here, but I really miss it up there sometimes." Johnny's father had moved the family a few states south when Johnny was five. His family and Johnny's mother's family were all still there. They made it up there to hunt and fish at least once a year, but if you're born in South Dakota your heart will never leave.

"Me too, Dad." Johnny loved it up there just as much as his father. "Spose you gotta work all day tomorrow? I got that speech thing round noon if you can make it."

"Aww hell. Sorry, bud, I completely forgot about that. I doubt I coulda got off anyways. I'm savin up my vacation days for that fishin trip we got planned for Pierre this summer. I dunno why I even take you up there, though. I always out-fish ya. I don't think I ever even seen you catch a walleye."

Johnny laughed polite at the well-worn slight. "Yeah right, Dad. I out-fish you ever time up there in those dang tailraces. I caught more fish in a few days last year than you've ever even laid eyes on. And what you do manage to catch I could use for bait! And don't even get me started about salmon fishin, creek chub. I caught twelve last year, and you got like, two!"

Mr. Daniels grinned at his son. He looks just like his mother, he thought. He was smaller boned like her and had her eyes and smile. She'd been gone for ten years now along with Johnny's older brother, but he could still see them sometimes when he looked at Johnny.

"You think there'll be anybody that'll tape that speech a yers for me, Little Man? I'll watch er tomorrow night when I get off."

"I'll ask around. I'm sure someone will."

"You've done one helluva good job at that school, son. It's a tough school, but that's why your mother wanted you to go there. I'm proud of ya." Johnny's mother had insisted he and his older brother went to Almighty Wonders Christian School. It was the only private school in their medium sized town, and the public school wasn't known for its scholastics. Tuition was about ten thousand dollars a year, but they had felt it was worth it.

"You have supper yet, bud?"

"Not yet. I was hopin Jennifer would come over and cook somethin up."

"Not tonight. She's busy gradin tests and things."

"Oh. That's OK. I'll have a couple *Hot Pockets* or somethin."

"Alright, Little Man. Sorry I aint much of a cook."

"That's OK, Big Boy."

"Well, good job today, bud. I think I'm gonna turn in."

"It's only 8:00 though, Pops."

"Yeah, I know. I'm one pooped pup, though. I gotta get up at 4:30. Nuther double. See ya tomorrow, Long-John."

Mr. Daniels got up and rubbed the back of his neck again. He walked all stiff to the stairs that led up to his bedroom. He put a hand on the rail and Johnny held him up.

"Hey, Dad... I love ya, Big Boy."

He nodded at his son before heading upstairs. "I'm proud of ya, son."

Johnny smiled to himself. He didn't need to say it back.

T he raucous applause along with the student body jumping to its feet brought Matt out of his amorous reverie. Johnny's speech had obviously gone well. His concentration had managed to find a new focus, moments into the speech. A pretty little underclassman had whispered something about her geometry lesson that he took way the hell out of context. *I'll give her a real lesson later tonight*, he had been thinking to himself.

"Great job, man. I knew you'd beat it up." He could see from Johnny's expression as he took his seat next to him that he was pleased to have the ordeal over with. "Yeah man, I think they really liked it."

"Ya think so, Sherlock? Geez, everyone is still staring at you and on their feet. Take a bow!" The generous applause was causing him a good deal of embarrassment, and Matt was rubbing it in pretty good.

"Great job, Johnny. That was really something I think we'll all remember for a long time." Almighty Wonders Bible teacher, Mr. Tyson, had taken his place at the mike and given Johnny one of his standard winks. He was a big man. Not many a plate had retained its food for long after he sat at his supper table. Completely bald, he had a face that smiled easier than it frowned and a laugh that could be heard from distance even easier.

"Well, gang, that pretty much sums up our senior appreciation day."

"God I hate when he says gang," Matt whispered to Johnny. Johnny concurred with a nod. He hated it too.

"Although today has been a break from your usual chapel, I'm not going to let you all off that easy." Johnny knew what was about to come. Attending weekly chapels at Almighty Wonders since their youth, they all knew what was about to come.

At first he had been embarrassed by his classmates' private revelations. But after so many, he had come to enjoy the entertainment. Neither he nor Matt had ever taken part, but they both smiled in anticipation. Everyone knew this was the last one at Almighty Wonders for the year.

"Hopefully we'll hear some good juice today, bro," Matt rubbed his hands together and whispered to Johnny.

Mr. Tyson intoned the familiar refrain. "James 5:16 says, 'therefore, confess your sins to each other and pray for each other so that you may be healed. The prayer of a righteous man is powerful and effective.'

"Today is the final day our seniors will have to speak in front of you all. God knows we are all sinners in His eyes — myself included. But I encourage everyone with a heavy heart that has sinned. Anyone that has fallen short of God's glory and wishes to come clean to his peers. Come forward and make your sins known. As we know, Matthew 18:20 says that when two or three come together in my name, there I am with them. God is here with us, gang. Come forward, seek God, confess your sins, and let the blood of Jesus wash you clean."

With his trademark wink and carefree smile, Mr. Tyson stepped down and the usual silence ensued. Most had their chins lowered slightly, reflecting on their own shortcomings and deciding whether they merited public attention and forgiveness.

The minutes dragged by; the seconds slowed by the silence with which they were coupled. Mr. Tyson never let it go for more than five minutes, and he didn't press for mandatory confessions of the students.

Johnny admired that in him. And although he didn't relish this time, like any human being he couldn't help but enjoy watching a public confession. Sitting contentedly out of the spotlight while another lanced his soul of guilt and shame; silently taking the pleasure of superiority over another. Thinking the age-old thought, *I've sure done some bad things, but I would never do that.*

The soft rustle of moving cloth and creaking of a pew brought him back to the present. Someone close behind him had stood up. He could hear his classmates shifting their knees with alacrity to allow the poor soul better access as he sidled toward the aisle.

He would not look around and gawk. Whoever was up was likely receiving sufficient stares from the boisterous lower classmen farther back. Seniors always sat in front. He kept his head down out of respect. He would wait until their voice broke the silence. Even then his eyes wouldn't be necessary to identify the spokesman. Most of those in his class had been together for years. There were only fifty people in the class, and he would know their voice before the first word was completely out.

His best friend, however, was far less patient, and spun around as soon as movement was detected. "Sweet Mother of God, I don't believe it. Little Davy is finally takin the walk of shame," Matt whispered more to himself than to Johnny.

Johnny looked up as Davy stepped into the aisle. His face was pale, and he moved as if only half present. Johnny noticed his hand shaking as he touched the corner of the pew. Aside from himself and Matthew, Davy Jones was the only other senior never to have made a public confession at chapel. They had been classmates since he entered Almighty Wonders in the fifth grade.

Even the strangest of those in Johnny's class had their niche. Unlike at most public schools, no one really got picked on at Almighty Wonders. People's houses were often tee-peed, and cars were sometimes egged, but it was usually out of fun rather than meanness or spite.

Unlike a lot of young boys that must earn their way into a clique with sporting prowess, physical size, or a witty tongue, Davy Jones had found his quickly and without much adieu.

In middle school almost all the boys would convene a game of kickball or soccer during recess. At that age Davy had found himself much happier with a certain group of females that preferred four-square or board games. He was a good student but really stood out in English class. He loved Wilde and Yeats, Steinbeck and Twain, Tennyson and Dickinson.

In high school, after the trumped up cooties myth had been dispelled for most, he could often be found aloof and chattering with various rings of girls, discussing with playful disdain the bold but inexperienced attempts at love by the likes of Matt and Johnny.

Johnny fondly recalled a recent rebuff from a girl that brought out Davy's poetic flare as they walked away. 'Walk on young gentlemen, for these lovely lilies shall not be sullied with boorish lines and bawdy display. Walk on young gentlemen, and task yourselves with these dreams another day!'

"Shut up, Davy." Matt grumbled as they walked away, but they both grinned in sympathy when they heard his distinctly spaced tenor laugh, "ah-ha-ha-ha-ha-ha-ha!" He didn't have a mean bone in his body, and they grudged him this rare display of dominance.

Everyone liked him because of his gentleness and seeming vulnerability. He was nicknamed Little Davy simply because he was the smallest boy in the class. His nose and ears were too large for his head which was usually cocked at an inquisitive angle. He had neatly parted, wavy blonde hair and a little pink birthmark on his left cheek. But his eyes were the most noticeable thing about him. Wide-spaced and framed with long lashes they were very dark blue. Like a deep, clean pond they were pure and very blue.

Looking at him walk up to the podium in his light blue jeans and oversized sweater, Matt couldn't help but speculate. "It's gonna be porn. Sweet Mother Mary, this shit's gonna be fuckin hilarious."

This was the most common male affliction at Almighty Wonders. Snorts of incredulity and gleeful snickers followed any details the speaker decided he must specify. Watching their Christian teachers squirm at lewd words and unbelievable acts was, in fact, a rare treat.

Johnny had a different premonition, though, and tried to will his classmate down from the altar. He was trying to telepathically send him a message of discouragement from what he knew in his guts he was about to do. *We're almost done Davy, don't do it. Please, for your own sake, you don't have to do this, bud.*

Davy walked up the steps and took his place behind the podium on the high altar. The microphone whistled as he lowered it to his height. He looked around at the congregation for many moments before he spoke - back and forth, back and forth.

"I have had the privilege to know you all for the greater portion of my life," he began wistful. "I think most of you would agree that I have led a life marred with my share of sin, but it's been a life in which I have been happy and content. Many would be proud of such a life. But after much reflection, I cannot say this is true for myself. For as long as I can recall I have been telling a lie.

"I cannot say it is a traditional lie. When one thinks of a lie, they imagine telling their teacher they didn't cheat on their homework. They imagine telling their parents a better story for why they scraped the fender of their car. A traditional lie is deceiving with words."

"My lie, though," Davy bowed his head in thought. "My little white lie has lacked words entirely. I have held it close to my heart for as long as I can remember. But my deception has been none other than my own. As my life trundles by, day by day and breath by breath, I feel as though my little white lie gains color and size."

"Come on Davy, just spit it out," Matt mumbled into his cupped hand.

"I have not been honest about who and what I am. As my friends and classmates, I owe you all better. Throughout my life I have struggled with something that I feel is so much a part of who I am that to deny it or fight it is simply to deny myself and fight myself." He looked at Johnny then and pursed his lips in an expression of pain.

Johnny was the leader of the class and the student body for that matter. As the leader, it seemed as though he were apologizing to Johnny personally for what he was about to do. That little gesture of seeming insignificance was so indicative of Davy's caring and compassionate nature. The pain that Johnny saw in his eyes choked his breathing.

He tried to scream at him, *you don't have to do it, Davy! Come down, please don't do this!* but nothing came out. He was frozen along with everyone else in the student body. Even Matt's total attention was directed at Davy's face. The import of his disclosure was so obvious from the pain and suffering on display.

"I..." Davy took a deep breath, and like a cliff diver about to give himself to gravity, let it out of his control in a rush, "am a homosexual..."

In Hollywood movies and tall tales there is a standard moment of silence that always follows a monumental revelation or disclosure. At that moment, in that church, for the congregation of students, teachers, family and friends at Almighty Wonders Christian School, these words hit like a sledgehammer on a thumbtack.

With human beings relief is accompanied by a sigh. But at that moment, the immediate and incredulous inhalation of breath could have sucked the air out of a fleet of hot air balloons.

"Holy fuckin shit, dude!" Matt exhaled everyone's sentiment the best. Davy was in tears at the altar. Everyone's shock was displayed in lifted eyebrows and slack jaws. No one said a word. The chapel was as quiet as if no one were there. Davy couldn't handle the scrutiny any longer and ran out of the chapel sobbing.

It had been a hell of a day. Johnny loaded up his backpack with homework and slammed his locker door harder than necessary. School was almost finished, but he still had a large paper to write for American History class. The topic of his essay was to be the realization of liberty during the Civil War era. It was a difficult topic, and he was worrying over where to begin.

As he walked down the hall, he registered snatches of conversation from various cliques of students and teachers. Everyone was discussing chapel, but all had forgotten his speech. *"I can't believe he did that." "I feel so embarrassed for him." "I should talk to him." "I totally wasn't expecting that." "How awkward."*

All wore worried expressions, but they were tinged with excitement and intrigue. It annoyed Johnny, but he didn't say anything as he sidled past. He walked out the double doors with relief and smiled up at the gentle spring sun. The sweet scent of dogwoods and rose bushes filled his nostrils, and he began to feel better.

A spunky little breeze brought a subtle *Clang! Clang! Clang!* to his ear. Johnny looked up and smiled again. The flagpole at Almighty Wonders stood in the center of the parking lot, and the halyard straps were hitting the aluminum. The school couldn't afford a track so they always did workouts in the parking lot. Johnny and his teammates had run repeats around that flagpole thousands of times over the years. It was very tall and flew extra-large flags that were a point of pride for the school. It doubled as a meeting place of sorts for special events that were held outside. It always flew the American flag above the Christian flag. Johnny looked around again and smiled. It was all very pretty, he thought.

He began walking toward his vehicle parked underneath the pole. All of a sudden, a little butterfly wobbled in under his nose. It surprised him, and he made to swat it away. He looked down at his shirt and frowned at the accident. He'd smashed the little winged animal, and there was a yellow smudge over the left breast of his white polo. He tried to rub it off but only smeared the remnants of the yellow wings in deeper.

Clang! Clang! Clang! hit the halyard.

Johnny walked on and continued brushing at his polo. He looked up toward his vehicle and kept the frown. There was a group of individuals close to where he had parked. After a few paces, it became obvious what was going on.

Davy was in the center of the ring. There were four or five of the most religious kids in the school surrounding him. A mother of one of Johnny's classmates, Lisa, was with them too. She was wearing a floral dress that was probably expensive but looked cheap. Shorter than them all, but stoutest of the bunch, she seemed to be the ringleader. They all were holding Bibles and laying hands on Davy. They seemed to be praying. Davy was hanging his head with them but more out of humiliation than reverence.

Johnny walked around to the driver's side of his truck. He put his backpack in the bed and studied the group for a moment. "Hey, Lisa, what are you guys doing?"

Lisa had been a fixture at Almighty Wonders for years. Her husband was a doctor, and her job, therefore, was to volunteer for any activity that called for parental help. She was at their final chapel, and Johnny had seen her unconcealed dismay after Davy's confession.

Substitute teaching or help in the kitchens were just a couple of the activities she helped out with on a regular basis. But of all the nice things that she did for the students, Johnny suspected she thrived more on the gratitude from everyone than the good works themselves.

There was no doubt she was a nice woman with a nice résumé, but she'd turned Johnny off a few months previously on a field trip. Their class had traveled to a large city to visit a downtown museum. Lisa volunteered to come along and help, of course.

Although it had been a normal field trip day, an incident in the afternoon had stuck with Johnny. He and Matt were at the back of the file walking up to the door. Lisa was a few paces back. As they turned a corner, they came upon a homeless man lying on the sidewalk. He held up a hand in the universal sign for help of any kind. He looked as if he hadn't eaten in a week or bathed in a month. "Help of any kind is appreciated," he drawled with the despondence of a man without hope.

"Don't touch me you filthy animal!" she'd screeched. The tone was even harsher than the words and dripped with disgust. Johnny shot Lisa a dirty look, but neither he nor Matthew had said anything.

Lisa looked up at him now with the humble countenance of a person that is so often called to do the work of God. "Hello, Johnny. We're laying hands on David and asking God to help rid him of his sin. Would you like to help us pray for Jesus' forgiveness and healing of David's homosexual desires?"

Clang! Clang! Clang! hit the halyard.

Johnny studied the group again and scratched the back of his head. "Umm, no thanks, Lisa. I need to get home. I got a lotta stuff I need to do."

Lisa's pious eyes slithered over Davy as she stroked the back of his head. "Davy is not evil, Johnny, but he is caught in something he doesn't understand. I am afraid for him, and you should be as well. I understand if you do not want to lay hands on him in public, but he needs your prayers tonight. His heart is full of lust and sin. He needs to be cleansed, and only we can do that through the power of the Holy Spirit."

Lisa nodded at her noble wisdom and continued stroking Davy's wavy hair. "Davy has sinned in the eyes of the Lord and His son Jesus Christ. It is not his fault, but the devil has a hold on his heart and mind. His desires are perverse." Lisa pursed her lips with pain and suffering for the young man while the others nodded in agreement. "Davy has been corrupted by sin. We must pray for him. His desires are disgusting in the eyes of the Lord, and only we can help him. We must do all we can to help him back to the straight and narrow."

"Therefore, confess your sins to each other and pray for each other so that you may be healed. The prayer of a righteous person is powerful and effective. Davy needs your prayers, Johnny. We need your help," intoned one of the most religious students.

Davy looked up at Johnny then. His eyes were puffy and red. His sweater was wet with perspiration and tears. The pain was there. The plea for help was in his eyes. Johnny could feel the beast again. He felt it breathing down his neck. It made him light-headed and raised goose bumps on his arms as he looked over at Davy. And it whispered things that he did not want to hear.

Johnny dug the keys out of his pocket and unlocked the door. As he opened the truck, Davy spoke for the first time.

"Johnny!" His voice was strangled with tears and emotion. Johnny looked over at him again. There was no anger in Davy's face. There was no trace of hate or resentment in his dark blue eyes - just pain. There was pain and fear and uncertainty in his old friend.

Johnny knew exactly what he should do as he looked at Davy: *Walk past those guys - put my arm around Davy - tell them to piss off - tell them Davy is my friend, and my friend is gay - tell them to leave Davy alone - tell them all to go to hell...*

Johnny cleared his throat and looked down at his shoes. "I'll see ya tomorrow, Davy."

Clang! Clang! Clang! hit the halyard.

Johnny climbed into his rig with the beast on his back. He put the truck in reverse and backed out of the parking spot. As he drove off, he looked in the rear-view mirror at the little group. Lisa and the religious kids had heads bowed and Bibles clutched. They gripped Davy's shoulders as they spoke to the Creator of the Universe. Davy was watching him go; still no resentment - just hurt and pain.

I can still turn around and go back... It's not too late... I can still walk past those guys - put my arm around Davy - tell them to piss off - tell them Davy is my friend, and my friend is gay - tell them to leave Davy alone - tell them all to go to hell...

But Johnny Daniels did not go back that day.

And the beast roared like hell. It choked his throat and made it hard to swallow. It brought tears to his rapidly blinking eyes and slithered around his guts like a poisonous snake. But the beast wasn't pain this time. It wasn't fear, either.

It was just shame.

D avy slowly picked his way home from the parking lot. Lisa and the others had prayed on him for well over an hour. His house was only about a mile from school, and he decided on the way that he did not want to go back. Of course he would have to tell his parents what had happened. His mother would be fine, but his father was another story. He felt nauseous with guilt and shame for himself. He thought it would be a relief to get it off his chest, but he was wrong.

God, he felt alone. He had many friends at school, but none would want to talk to him now. Now that he had told

his secret he doubted anyone could even look at him
without being disgusted. He shouldn't have told everyone
like that. He thought it would be a relief. As he walked
down the grass covered alley he saw an old woman in her
backyard tending her plants. She wore a big straw sun hat
and an oversized slip-on dress that old women tending
gardens seem to be so fond of.

"Your rosebushes are lovely, madam. Are those
Carolineas?"

She looked up, surprised and constipated at the same
time. "Well how'm I sposed ta know what they're called?
They're just roses!"

"Well, they're very beautiful, whatever they may be.
You've done a good job with them. I can smell them from
here. I think they're quite wonderful."

"I know that. I don't need you telling me that I'm a
good gardener. What do you want? What are you doing in
my alley anyway?"

"I was just walking to the park and noticed your
garden. It's very beautiful. Have a nice day, madam."

"Well... the park is that way." She pointed her spade
north and continued with her work. Davy frowned at his
shoes and continued up the alley. His hands were clasped
behind his back as he worried his situation. His father
would be angry. No, he wouldn't be angry; anger would be
easy to assuage. He would be humiliated and disgusted. He
would be so disgusted with his only son. His friends at
work would give him such a hard time, and this made Davy
even sadder.

*Everyone's going to say I'm a fairy. Everyone is going to laugh at
my dad. They're going to say he raised a faggot and a fairy. He will be
so ashamed...*

Davy adjusted his backpack as he turned the corner of
the alley. He brushed his sweater absent-mindedly and
smiled a bit at the feel of the material. It was his favorite
sweater. It had been a gift from his mother the year before.
She was so sweet. She had given it to him for no apparent
reason. It had some cashmere in it and felt soft and warm

when he touched the sleeve. Sometimes she would get him
things just to say she loved him.

A few years ago, he had walked into his bedroom and
found a brand new, blue cashmere quilt on the bed. They
could hardly afford it, but she was always sacrificing for
him. She loved him so much. She told him every day, but
some days she would surprise him with nice gifts like this
one. She was such a sweet pea. She really was.

A blue jay swooped down and lit on a branch above his
head. Davy paused to admire it. He loved the color blue.
The bird wore it with such pride, he thought. As they
looked at one another, the bird screeched in its strident
manner. Davy cocked his head, and the bird did the like. It
screeched again. He looked around to make sure no one
was watching.

"Have you been a bully to other song birds today, Mr.
Blue Jay?" He looked around again. He knew it was strange
to talk to a bird, but he needed to talk to someone. He was
screened from most houses by the low-hanging oak, and the
bird was looking right at him, after all. He knew from
watching birds over the years that blue jays were bullies of
the sky. The bird screeched at him again. It said, *ehyyyyya!*

"You shouldn't pick on other song birds. Robins are
bigger than you, but you still bully them, don't you, sir?
And why do you pick on cardinals? Is it because they are
more beautiful than you? You will not feel any better after
you do so. It will not make you more beautiful, either." The
bird screeched again and flew to another branch that was
even closer. Davy could almost touch it now. It cocked his
head to study him again. *Ehyyyyya!* it cried.

"But why do you pick on the little sparrows? They are
so small and they don't do you any harm. Why can't you let
them be without screeching at them? Why can't you let
them be peaceful? Why do you invade their nests? Why are
you so cruel to them?" Davy looked around again, but no
one was out and about. The blue jay fluttered down and
flew away up the alley. Even he didn't want to talk -

probably had a little bluebird to pick on in that old lady's yard.

Davy watched him go. "Maybe someday a big bald eagle will teach you a lesson, sir," he muttered to himself. Even the pretty plumage of the blue jay could not hold his mind for long. He felt so alone. He thought of his father again, and his shoulders gave a shudder.

Everyone's going to say I'm a fairy. Everyone is going to laugh at my dad. They're going to say he raised a faggot and a fairy. He will be so ashamed...

Davy continued up the street. After some time he reached the little park that was right by his house. It was large enough to be open but small enough to be cozy. He came here often when he was little, but it had been some time since he was last here. He sat in the old chain swings and began to pump his legs. He swung for a long time like that but felt no better. He looked around the park as his feet slowly scuffed him to a stop.

No one was around. It seemed strange at this time of day. Usually the elementary kids were running all over the place in the afternoons. On a nice day like this there should be more than a couple people walking around. There wasn't even anyone walking their dog. That was too bad. Petting a dog would be nice right now, he thought. It would be nice to pet a big friendly dog. Labradors were amiable, but golden retrievers seemed so regal and proud. Their coats were so shiny and flowed so pretty when washed and combed out.

Davy sighed. He looked around for songbirds, but even they were absent his surroundings. Not even a red-breasted robin hopping around looking for worms. That old blue jay bully probably scared them all off, he thought. As the sun began to set he knew he would have to go home soon. His mother would be worried, and he didn't want that. Davy hung his head.

Everyone's going to say I'm a fairy. Everyone is going to laugh at my dad. They're going to say he raised a faggot and a fairy. He will be so ashamed...

"Well, I always knew he was a bit fruity." Mr. Daniels spoke around a mouthful of roast beef. "Hell's bells, just watching that boy walk across a room I could tell he was gay as a bag-a butterflies."

"Hey, what time is that meeting-a yours, Dad?" Johnny didn't feel like talking about Davy's revelation. Although any conversation around the dinner table that didn't center on his father's new political furor was a welcome relief, he didn't feel like talking about Davy.

"Well, son, it's a town hall meetin actually. Round eight or so, down at the legion. You really should come with me. You might learn somethin."

"I'm gonna go for a run. You readin anythin good in that paper for a change?" Mr. Daniels always read the paper at dinner.

"Same ol, same ol - nothing but fear and shame. That's all these fellas that call themselves journalists can whip up. Look here, page three. Down in Atlanta a bunch of fourteen and fifteen year old African Americans, or whatever the hell they wanna be called these days, *stomped* another one to death just for talking to a girl. Rib pierced his heart." He exhaled sadly and shook his head. "Damned animals."

"Did you hear about that white guy that raped a six year old girl to death a couple days ago?" Johnny added.

"Yeah, just read that, too. Don't know what this world is coming to. Don't know what this country is coming to, either. That's why meetins like this are so important. I'd really like ya to come with me, son. Just once to see what it's like. I want ya to meet a few of my new friends."

"Well, I guess I could run afterwards," Johnny said.

"Great John-John! That's just great. We gotta take back what's ours, son. We gotta take our goddamn country back."

T he Daniels climbed into the old man's rig and drove toward the edge of town. They chatted and smiled about hunting and sports along the way. Mr. Daniels began talking politics, and Johnny listened with little interest. It was a bit of a relief to reach their destination.

The building was a nondescript white color with splotches of brown where paint had chipped away. The American Legion symbol was proudly emblazoned on its front siding. For any Tea Party newcomers, a rent-a-sign on the lawn stated simply, 'Patriots park here'.

They parked and walked up to the door. The energy of the attendees felt bubbly and garrulous, dour and skeptical. As Mr. Daniels crossed the threshold, his brain began registering snatches of conversation from assorted rings of individuals.

Just not right... Completely and utterly unconstitutional... Children and grandchildren's debt... Liberal bastard. Mr. Daniels felt an instant camaraderie and acceptance. These people were on his wavelength, and he enjoyed it.

The interior appeared larger than the building. Folding chairs were neatly set into rows, and the dominant colors on the walls were various fabrics in red, white and blue. It smelled like the cafeteria at an old folk's home - a remnant of some potluck lunch.

A fat man in a cheap suit called the town hall meeting to order. He stood behind a plywood podium at the end of the hall on a raised platform. A white Christian flag stood at the back of the stage (flanked by its American offspring), and a matching banner also draped the podium - just in case the attendees forgot who the hell they were and where in the hell they came from.

"Have a seat everyone. You're too kind. Man it's good to be an American aint it? Thank you for coming here tonight. Hey, do you all love your freedom? Any of you here that've served in uniform, now or before?" A few attendees raised their hands.

"God we thank you for your sacrifice. We thank you for your service. God bless you. We salute you and honor you. Thank you. Let's get pumped up tonight like we should be guys! Do you remember how vitalized this movement was when Scott Brown won that Senate seat in Massachusetts?" A few people clapped.

"I mean geez laweez; he was just a guy with a truck that really represents this powerful movement. He saw how messed up things are in Washington right now. He thought, hey, I'm gonna do my part to put the government back on the side of the people. It took a lotta stuffing and a lotta hard work, but Scott Brown won that seat, fair and square."

Everyone in attendance remembered the significance of winning that seat. It had been in a very blue state and liberal hands since the early sixties. The win had been the start of something big for sure.

"And who do you think Barack *Hussein* Obama blames for that loss? Himself?"

'No!' Chorused the crowd. Someone in the back yelled, "That liberal bastard's a socialist rag head!"

Hilarity broke out all over. The speaker made a mental note of the joke for future use.

"Nope, he blames George Bush for everything!" The fat man lifted his voice to reassert his authority.

"The only place he hasn't laid blame is on his own liberal agenda! He blames Bush, but Barack *Hussein* Obama has only himself to blame for this mess we're in! Himself, and Frisco Nancy, and Dirty Harry Reid, and that socialist agenda a theirs! That agenda that leaves us and our children less secure, more in debt, and more accountable to big government! They're outta touch and just don't get it y'all!"

Raucous applause - he was getting warmed up now.

"This is about the people. This is the people's party. It's bigger than the leader of the Tea Party and it's a hell of a lot bigger than some charismatic guy with a teleprompter." He had stolen that line from Sarah Palin.

"It's about everyday Americans who grow our food, and run our small businesses, and patrol our streets, and fight our wars. People in small towns all over this great nation are having town hall meetings like this one. They're running for office like Scott Brown did. They're standin up and speakin out, and they're tellin Obama hell no, we won't go! Hell no we won't be flushed down the toilet of your liberal ideals. Our vision of the future values conservative principles and common sense solutions.

"This president's ideas are dangerous, just like we were endangered on Christmas day by Abdulmutallab. That Nigerian bastard walked right through security with a bomb. He trained with al Qaeda in Yemen, and his visa wasn't revoked until after he tried to kill hundreds of innocent passengers. It was only because of brave passengers he didn't succeed, and that, my friends, is a shame!

"And how does our president wanna look at it? The same way he wants to look at any act of terrorism - like some sort-a crime spree and not as an act of war. We are in danger, y'all. Your kids and mine are in danger. You can see it now in Washington as we speak. They wanted to treat it as a law enforcement issue. But I tell ya true, that's not how radical Islamists look at it. They know this is war, and I'll give em credit for that. They know a leader should represent his country's best interests, not its best intentions. To win a war you need a commander in chief with the sand to stand up to em. Not some law professor debatin with em!"

The fat man was rolling now. His face was glistening with sweat, and his furor had everyone rapt to attention. The American flags everywhere emphasized the importance of what he was saying. Mr. Daniels was glad he had remembered to button his American flag pin on his chest.

He noted his son's naked lapel and was sorry he hadn't an extra.

"You can see it every day in our president's actions. He writes chummy letters to his dictator buddies, apologizing for our behavior. North Korea has nukes and could bomb the hell outta the South at any moment and what's that damned Harvard professor do? He bows down real low and says, hello friend, konichiwa!

"Hell, look at our erstwhile ally, Israel." Erstwhile was an uncommon word, and he said it with relish. He'd heard Glenn Beck use it on his show, and, after a quick trip to dictionary.com, had made sure he used it as well.

"I mean geez laweez guys, they are possibly our greatest ally and sure as hell are our greatest ally in the Mideast. And what does Mr. B.O. tell em? Stop buildin settlements in the West Bank!

"These poor people have been kicked around for thousands-a years. Now that they have their country back and the means to defend themselves, what does he tell em to do? 'Stop building on land that is rightfully theirs.' Who knows what's goin on behind the scenes with Iran? Who knows when they'll drop a nuke on Israel? I tell ya what guys, it is just beyond the pale.

"I mean, it's so obvious this land belongs to Israel. And whose side does Barack *Hussein* Obama take? The damn Moslem's side that's who. He says he's a Christian all the time, but whose side is he really on? Ours, or them Moslems? I'm not accusin him of anathin. I'm just saying the proof is in the pudding!"

A few attendees stood up and began clapping violently. The man next to Johnny yelled, '*yaaaah!* Git er done, brother!' Mr. Daniels was nodding his head emphatically and clapping along with the crowd. Johnny appeared uncomfortable.

"We need to get back to an administration that distinguishes our friends from our enemies again. We need to get back to our roots in a strong national defense like that great patriot Reagan stood for." The applause here was hearty as ever but expected.

"Peace through strength was his creed. I'll give Barack credit for sendin more troops into Afghanistan, but we just gotta spend less time bowin to our enemies and more time buildin up our allies. I'm sick and tired-a all this professor talk. When he's not talking he's just playing the blame game. And who's he blaming? This guy could take one piece-a advice from JFK. When he was in office he said that the problems of the world aren't his predecessor's fault. And that's the truth if I ever heard it."

Mr. Daniels turned to his son flushed with excitement. "Well isn't this something, Johnny? What do ya think, son?"

"It's good, Dad."

"This president is simply ignoring our Constitution, y'all. He has a complete disregard for the principles of limited government. Look at all the companies and industries the government has bailed out and taken over the past couple years. First it was the banks and the mortgage companies and financial institutions. Carmakers came next, and then came student loans, and now our health care! We got the best health care system in the world, and he wants to run it right into the ground!"

Everyone was up off their feet at the mention of health care. A general roar of anger went up from the crowd. The man next to Johnny yelled, 'yaaaah! Git er done, brother!'

"I tell you the truth, he won't be happy until our taxpayer dollars are wipin the asses of every illegal Mexican baby born on our side-a the fence. Next he'll wanna be buildin orphanages in Tijuana and abortion clinics in Juarez. How much are we going to take?"

For the first time since walking into the building, Johnny was annoyed. He had a few friends that were Mexican, and he had never met a Mexican he didn't like. He enjoyed their language and the friendly manner in which they always treated him. Johnny only knew a few Mexicans, but they were his friends.

"Look at our budget and where this president's priorities lie. We are in debt trillions of dollars. Christ, trillions-a dollars! Instead-a cuttin back and tryin to get this ridiculous number under control he goes and passes a goddamn stimulus." The word rolled off his tongue with the aplomb of a fur ball covered in excrement.

"After giving Wall Street 700 billion dollars, they go and throw another 800 billion that they don't have at the problem. This money was simply intended for the feds to gain more control over states' rights. Thank God people like Governor Palin were in there at the time and courageously refused some-a those dollars."

Everyone in the crowd was on their feet again. The mention of Sarah Palin was assured a hearty applause in this environment. Johnny's father whooped all hearty. The man next to Johnny put his hand in his pocket and smiled to himself.

"So the feds then threatened lawsuits if they refused some of this money. Can you believe this? This federal government threatens to sue these states that don't want or need these printed and invented dollars. This is debt that must be shouldered by our children and grandchildren, and they're throwing it around like a buncha drunken sailors around a sweaty stripper pole."

Johnny chuckled along with his father at the analogy. It was a little funny.

"We are floundering in our debt, gang." *God why do people say that word out loud*, Johnny wondered to himself.

"And what does our president do? He presents a budget for three trillion some dollars! He keeps printing money we don't have and borrowing from other countries. We are completely in the thrall of foreign countries that do not have our best interests at heart. As the great Sarah Palin has said, that is not only generational theft, it's not only unconscionable, it is simply immoral. And I won't stand for it much longer!"

"Jesus, I wish this man was our president right now," Mr. Daniels sighed to himself during another episode of raucous applause. Johnny turned to look at his father with lifted eyebrows of incredulity. Sure, he was saying some good things about the debt, but the speaker gave Johnny the impression of a man who would launch a nuke on a goddamn whim.

"And being in debt to other countries makes us less secure. It taxes our freedom and ticks me right off. We need private creation of jobs, not more government jobs. We need a pro-market agenda that encourages competition. We need lower taxes for mom and pop stores, and a government that supports innovation and that don't reward laziness but rewards good hard work.

"Do these things, and keep it simple, and then get the hell outta the way, Washington. If they would just do these things our economy would bounce back in a heartbeat. On this health-care takeover, for instance; this needs to be repealed yesterday, and instead pass market based reforms that incorporate steps with bipartisan support. Use the best ideas from the right side-a the aisle for a change and not this back room bull crap we've had to put up with. Simple things like purchasing insurance across state lines and tort reform will really make a positive difference for our country."

"We are the defenders of the Constitution. We are a force for what is right in this country. We will be counted, and we will stand up! Our vision for the future is not of our making but merely a reflection of our past which has made us great. As Sarah Palin says, 'we know that the government that governs less governs best.'"

The fat man bellowed his creed toward the audience. He was beginning to crescendo and Johnny hoped this indicated the finale of the speech. It was hotter'n hen pee in the legion. And the man next to him was sweating profusely and kept rubbing his arm against Johnny's. The son of a bitch hadn't worn deodorant, either.

"Our freedom is our God given right, and it is worth fighting for. Our men in uniform are a force for good in this world, and that is nothing to apologize for. Don't let the liberals label you as extreme and intolerant. Don't let the elitists denounce what we represent. We are the Tea Party. We are the patriots of this great nation, and we will not sit down, we will not give up, we will not shut up!

"God shed his grace upon us, and I believe he has ordained the Tea Party to convey his message. We are the Tea party nation, and we will fix this nation because our best days are still to come! God bless you, and God bless the United States of America!"

Mr. Daniels stayed longer than Johnny would have liked. They shook many hands and drank coffee with the fat man for a bit. When they finally got outside, Johnny breathed a sigh of relief. It was a clear spring evening, and the night seemed very still, he thought. The western rays of light had kissed the stars goodnight, and now they trembled lonely in the sky.

"Wasn't that great, Johnny?" Riding back home in the truck, Johnny's dad was still bubbly from the town hall. He seemed happier than usual and had a satisfied smile on his face. He was hanging his arm out the window and patting a beat on the truck door to some song that was going through his head.

"Yeah Dad, it wasn't bad."

"Wasn't bad? Man, Johnny, I know yer more into science than politics, but I can hardly sit still after listening to that man speak. I tell you what, he could light a fire under a fish's ass in a rainstorm. Now that's a true patriot."

Like most young adults at that age, Johnny had adopted his father's view toward politics. His father had always been a Republican, so he was a Republican. His exposure to political issues was funneled and processed almost exclusively through his father. When he disagreed with certain views it was much easier to just listen and nod.

Some of his dad's more extreme views occasionally caused him to wrinkle his forehead and inhale through his teeth. Mr. Daniels usually confused his dissension for uncertainty, though, and would always expound on his comment for Johnny's sake. His dad was easily riled when challenged, and he usually didn't care enough to do so.

He was now eighteen and eligible to vote when Obama was up for re-election. He wouldn't vote for him, of course, but he had heard some things that evening he didn't like hearing about the president.

"You gonna come with me again next week, son?"

"We'll see, Big Boy. I'd like to hang out with everyone from class as much as possible. A lotta my friends are shippin out for college soon, and who knows how often I'll get to see em." It was a damn good excuse, and he knew his ol man wouldn't pout about it.

"That's fine, John. You come when you want... Man, I love them town halls."

A good relationship between a father and his son is more common than not. Johnny and his father were quite close. His dad worked hard and Johnny enjoyed seeing him in a good mood. He had little reason to spoil it with his opinion about some of the things he had heard that night.

There's always a time for disagreement, he thought to himself. *Being right or being wrong has nothing to do with being happy.* And they smiled at each other on the car ride home.

"**M**an dude, I can't believe we finally made it." Matt looked down at his well-polished dress shoes after the remark. It sounded hollow to them both.

High school is often portrayed as a time of uncertainty and gangly confusion for people. High school for Matt and Johnny had been nothing short of a blast, and now they were venturing into the unknown.

They had been the jocks and big fish of their small world and graduating from it had never been a goal for either of them. But they had been there for four years, and now it was time to move on.

"Welp, I guess all good things must come to an end." Matt tried to glaze over his insincerity with some philosophy.

"You know, Matthew, that's why I hang out with you. Not because you'd wail on anyone that screws with me, your good looks, or even your way with the ladies. It's because you're just so wise."

"I got skills you haven't even heard of, bro," Matt said as he smiled at his buddy. "Man I feel gay in this dress."

"Yeah, well everyone's gotta wear them, dude. I'm sure everyone and their mothers know you're not gay."

"I guess that's true," Matt conceded. "This hat does look pretty fuckin good on me." Matt studied his reflection in the glass doors of the lobby.

Parents and friends had already filed into the gymnasium where the ceremony was held after greeting the graduates. Fathers and relatives had taken the standard ridiculous amount of photos. Mothers had cried while wearing smiles in the feminine way.

"I guess Mr. Sanders forgot to give me one of those cord things you've got around your neck," Matt mumbled while looking down at his chest. The golden honors cords were given to those graduating with at least a 3.7 GPA and a 30 or higher on the ACT. Their class was very smart and hardworking, and those without the gaudy accoutrement were in the minority.

"Here you go, Cinderella, put mine on." Everyone knew Johnny was smart as hell and the valedictorian anyway.

"That's very sweet of you, Johnny." Their classmate, Laura, had seen Johnny drape his cord around Matt's neck and took the opportunity to join their conversation. She was a bit plain but in a pretty sort of way. She had a fine porcelain complexion and well-proportioned eyes and mouth. Her brown hair had been curled for the occasion, and she had donned an appropriate amount of eye shadow that always makes a woman more attractive. She played soccer and ran track, and her lithe, athletic body reflected the attention.

"You look very pretty today, Laura." She had possessed a violent crush on Johnny for years. When they were freshmen, she had scored an impressive goal during a pick-up soccer match, and Johnny had given her *be*hind a couple of pats to show his approval. Ever since, just being in his presence caused her heart to race and trip on itself. It was obvious from his half-cocked smile and gaze that he was being sincere but teasing her as well. She blushed like a rose.

Their class was cliquey as any other, but these were fluid associations. Everyone was more or less comfortable with one another. Matt put his arm around her in a brotherly gesture.

"What my dearest friend here is trying to say, Laura, is that he would love to see you at the party tonight." He lowered his voice conspiratorially. "Maybe see what you've got underneath these robes."

"Matthew, you are nothin but a big ol animal!" She feigned indignation as she squirmed out from under his muscular arm, but they all laughed together.

"I swear you'd hump a pile-a sticks if you thought there were a rabbit inside!" Laura's family was from Louisiana, and some of her stranger expressions were just assumed to be southern in nature. Matt and Johnny laughed a little harder at this one.

"Laura, do me a favor and take a head count to make sure everyone is here already. I guess we shoulda taken our seats by now cuz Mr. Tyson is giving me the eye up there." Mr. Tyson had put Johnny in charge of keeping the class together for the ceremony. Johnny kept peeking his head through the double doors to receive a hand signal on the time remaining.

"Why don't you do it yourself, Long-John?" She raised her chin as she said it and looked him straight in the eye. Matt's comments and the excitement of the evening had made her bolder than usual.

"Well aren't we sassy this evening, little lady? Do as I say before I have to slap that little caboose-a yours again."

His lopsided grin told her he had liked her challenge. "And save that sauce for later tonight, honey."

Although he was still a virgin, Johnny had the confidence and self-assuredness that can easily assail a woman's resistance. Laura whirled around to do his bidding, disconcerted by the ease with which he had lowered hers.

"She wants you, dude." Matt used this phrase on a daily basis but was as stoic and sincere as if he had just coined it. They both watched her glide away, ticking off the count with her forefinger.

"I don't think I've seen Davy yet, John."

They hadn't talked about Davy's revelation in the week since that last chapel. Seniors didn't have to take finals, and their classes hadn't been much more than a study hall. Everyone had just mingled and talked to one another, reflecting on memories and good times. Davy Jones, on the other hand, had completely withdrawn himself.

The first two days he hadn't come to school at all. Mr. Tyson informed his parents that he needed to come the final days if he wanted to receive his diploma. It was obvious that he was extremely embarrassed and ashamed. Johnny had tried to amuse him with some purposefully terrible rhymes he made-up but sensed his attention was just causing more discomfort.

One day Matt called a movie 'gay' in a loud voice which drew silence and stares. Davy was horrified and tried to cover his face with his hands. Johnny noted their literature teacher smirking at Davy's embarrassment.

Davy had been his best student by far, and he often bragged about producing the next Edgar Poe. Mutual interests and small classes meant certain teachers and students were uncommonly tight at Almighty Wonders. The two had been good friends just a week before. Johnny could interpret his disgust for Davy with ease; it was as if Davy were receiving some sort of divine justice for his sin. His dad had always said that fair weather friends are as common as spring-time rain.

"He's still pretty embarrassed about everything, yo. I saw him the other day in the parkin lot. He was cryin and gettin preached to by Lisa and her little group," Johnny said as he paused and scratched his chin and looked down. "They were torturin the hell outta him. God, I shoulda said somethin to em... You think I shoulda said somethin to em?"

Matt looked down with Johnny and coughed into his hand. "Hell, I dunno man."

"You think I shoulda said somethin... Don't cha?"

Matthew looked Johnny square in the eye. "You're goddamn right you shoulda said somethin, John. I can't stand them bastards."

Johnny winced and looked down again. "I don't know why he had to tell everyone like that."

"He felt guilty about it, I guess," Matt reflected.

It was obvious Johnny was upset about not sticking up for Davy. Matt smiled at his friend, and his eyes kindled a bit. "Member how we used to play kickball in third and fourth grade during P.E.? Member Little Davy running the bases?" They chuckled together, not out of meanness, but fondness. If Davy would have walked up at that moment, Matt would have put him in a friendly headlock and told him exactly what he had said.

Men and women tease each other in completely different ways. A woman will often tease another along the edge of her periphery in order to create confusion and distress. A man's affection for another is usually proportional to the harassment heaped upon him. "Boy, he could scoot pretty good, but man would he swing them arms!" Matt rounded out the laugh and caught his breath.

"I guess I always kinda knew he was gay," he said to himself and scratched the back of his head.

"Yeah, I guess I did too, man." They lapsed into silence as they thought about it. Laura sidled up to Johnny with the air of a job well-done.

"Well, what's the word, *chica*? We gotta get goin here."

"Forty-nine, Johnny. We are one short."

"Who's missin?"

"It's Davy, Johnny... Davy is gone."

The rope was of the single braid variety and composed of twelve separate strands. Constructed of synthetic nylon, it had been woven at a factory in Hangzhou, China, two years previously. A cargo ship then brought it across the Pacific Ocean into harbor at Long Beach, California. From there it had been cut into hundred foot sections, formed into loops, and stored in cardboard boxes at a warehouse in East Los Angeles. It was purchased in bulk by a large home improvement store and shipped by semi-trailer to a medium sized town in the Midwest. Davy's dad had purchased the rope a year earlier for no particular reason. He was a bit of a handy man with a large garage filled with a lot of tools. Any man in this situation will have some rope lying around for whatever reason.

Davy looked down at it again.

His parents were out to dinner together that night. They had been looking forward to the graduation ceremony but understood his reluctance to attend.

Lisa had called Davy's mother on the day of his confession before he arrived home from school. After relating the event in detail (and her pious acts in the parking lot with the religious kids), she let Davy's mother know what the best course of action would be. They should organize a few pastors and some of his more wholesome classmates to convene a prayer meeting for Davy's temptations and sins.

She let Davy's mother know that she was free on Friday evening and would be more than happy to make the necessary phone calls. Knowing Davy for so many years and being so fond of his loving and gentle nature, she even volunteered to bring a casserole and 2-Liters of Coke as refreshment. She was a good Christian and took no pleasure in this work.

She had been justifiably irked when Davy's mother said she appreciated her concern but didn't think it was a good idea. Davy was sweet and shy like his mother, and she knew that the attention would be traumatic for him. Lisa completely understood; but as she hung up, the shortness of her tone implied she didn't appreciate such a rebuff of her generosity.

That night, after Davy had gone to bed, his mother stole into his room like she used to when he was little. As she kissed his cheek she felt his salty tears and muffled sobs. She held him to her chest and rocked him, back and forth, back and forth, and cried along with him; whispering love and hope of sunshine in the way that women do so beautifully. That had been the only time Davy had felt anything but anguish since his revelation.

A loving mother will readily share sorrow by sharing tears. He knew his mother was crying not because he had told his secret but to help dull his pain. They rocked and cried in a quiet lullaby.

Due to a lack of any mutual interests, Davy and his father had never been close. Davy had gone fishing with him a couple of times because of the pleasure he knew it would give his father. Mr. Jones, on the other hand, was never excited about doing things Davy liked. Six months previously, Davy had begged him to attend a traveling Broadway show with himself and his mother, but Mr. Jones wouldn't be caught dead at one of those. He was difficult to drag to a movie, even, unless he was assured of some kill scenes.

His mother told him about Davy's confession that very first night so that no one else would have the displeasure. Davy could not meet his father's eyes over breakfast the next day. His mother was overly bubbly. In her feminine way she protected her son from paternal wrath with her mood and her eyes. His father couldn't even look at him, scowling at his orange juice and coffee. He didn't say a word during the entire breakfast, but when he walked away from the table he muttered, "Now everyone knows I raised a goddamn fairy." And he punched the cabinet with his fist.

Davy had expected such a comment, but it still cracked his heart like a whip. He hadn't spoken to the man in the week since. Davy knew he wasn't mortified so much because Davy was gay, but because everyone now knew. Davy had disgraced their surname and family, and that was the utmost contemptible act.

Davy looked down at the rope again. It felt smooth and cold to the touch. The garage where he stood smelled of gasoline and fresh cut wood. There was a small oil stain where his father's truck usually sat. A long work bench ran along the far wall. It was about four foot off the ground and was littered with blueprints and tools. The ceiling was about ten foot high. A rafter would probably hold him, he thought. His shoulders gave a shudder and he shook his head at his fate. He felt alone.

Adrenaline heightened his senses so he could smell the moisture on the cement and the metal tools. The air even seemed to have a taste to it. It tasted like dirt and oil and pain. He shuddered again as he ran the rope through his fingers. "I can't believe what I've become... I can't believe the things I've done," he mumbled to himself.

As Davy fondled the rope he contemplated his sins and fate. He had never been with a man or had hardly even touched one for that matter. He had seen on a daily basis the way that men roughhoused in sports - an arm around a shoulder or a slap on the backside after a goal.

Matt would sometimes put him in a headlock and rub his hair with his knuckles. Davy would keep his hands behind his back, terrified that any contact he made would be misinterpreted. He knew from school that masturbation was a sin. His Bible teacher called it the sin of Onan. While in the shower, he had let his guard down often and eventually allowed other men into his fantasies. Though he had initially resisted, over the past year he had completely given in to his desires. There was no longer any pretense of women in his lustful thoughts.

When left to nature, his dreams would betray him as well. The crusty stains on his morning bedding caused him shame. When he could recall the unnatural things he had done with men in those dreams he was nauseated with disgust for himself.

As Davy's thoughts delved deeper and deeper into despondency he began to fashion a knot. There was pretension in a noose, he thought, and he didn't know how to tie one anyway. His heart began to race as he tightened the knot, but he could not fathom a way out. He had never been introduced to drugs or alcohol and had the pure mind that struggles to shirk logic. There was simply no way out of his thoughts and desires and future.

The wooden rafters in the garage were exposed. Pink insulation rested atop. The garage seemed very still, he thought. Davy grabbed a metal step-stool resting along the wall. It pinched his palm as he opened it, but he hardly felt the sting. He took three steps up to the work bench. *One.. two.. three.* The height and the fear made him giddy as he looked down at the floor. As he stood on the bench, his foot nudged one of his father's wrenches.

Davy's mind flitted to happy memories with his dad. Though never close, he loved his father, and was sorry for the shame he had caused him. Davy rucked up his sleeves and smiled softly at the feel of the material. He wore his favorite blue sweater. The cashmere was soft and warm like his mother. They could hardly afford it, but she was always sacrificing for him. She loved him so much. She told him every day, but some days she would surprise him with nice gifts like this one. She was such a sweet pea to him. She really was.

His mother had been his shield and protector, and he loved her more than inadequate words could express. But he would not think about his mother now. Right now he was all alone.

He reached up through the itchy insulation and threaded the rope over the rafter. He tied a childlike knot and checked its hold with a *tug-tug*. There was only a few feet of rope between the two knots as he slipped the loop over his neck. He cinched it up tight and looked down again.

The excess rope draped onto the floor. His breathing came shallow and fast. He hadn't planned for this to happen. It was as if his subconscious had led him to this workbench in his father's garage.

He was overwhelmed with sadness. His life was hopeless. His soul felt hollow and cold. He looked up to heaven and whispered, a tear escaping his eye, "I'm so sorry. I'm so sorry."

Davy knew if he didn't do it he would eventually consummate his sin. He had to get out. He began to hyperventilate in fear of what was in his power to do; quick and shallow breaths, in time with his heart. He looked down at the oil stained floor, and Davy prayed his favorite prayer:

"The Lord is my Shepherd; I shall not want. He maketh me to lie down in green pastures: He leadeth me beside the still waters. He restoreth my soul: He leadeth me in the paths of righteousness for His name' sake. Yea, though I walk through the valley of the shadow of death, I will fear no evil: For thou art with me; Thy rod and thy staff, they comfort me. Thou preparest a table before me in the presence of mine enemies; Thou annointest my head with oil; My cup runneth over. Surely goodness and mercy shall follow me all the days of my life..." But he couldn't finish the prayer, for he knew he was all alone.

Davy glanced up at the garage door. He thought he had heard gravel crunching and he waited for the automatic door to open. He listened, all intent. If his father saw him like this he would change his mind about everything. If his mother saw him she would help him too. Davy strained to hear. He thought he had heard something. Maybe someone was coming to save him.

He waited and listened and waited some more. As he stared at the door, he knew someone was about to save him. The minutes dragged by; the seconds slowed by the silence with which they were coupled. Someone had to come. Life shouldn't end like this. Someone would come to save him.

But as he stood there on the work bench at that moment, Davy knew he was being a coward. He knew deep down that no one was there.

Davy hung his head. He took a big breath and closed his eyes.

And then he gave himself to gravity, and let it out of his control in a rush.

His feet left the bench. The rope came taut with a hum. The immediate pressure was unbelievable, as though his head had been plunged to the bottom of the sea. His legs kicked at the lancing pain in his skull. It was like a firecracker had exploded in his mouth. He swung and gasped. Lights and stars exploded his vision. Vivid colors cart wheeled away into a black abyss. Pictures and forgotten memories flew behind his eyes.

Blood suffused his head as the rope cut into his throat. It choked away his breath. All his senses were screaming. The pain was a roaring beast - he could taste it and see it and hear it and smell it. Davy swung and kicked and grunted, but he kept his hands clasped in the attitude of prayer. *Dear God the pain. Oh God the pain!*

And he could faintly hear the rafter groaning. *Please don't break!*

Now the pain was at its crescendo. It was a lightning hot hammer behind his eyes. It scorched him like a thousand suns and froze his painful thoughts. It siphoned his life away, and it was a horrible thing. Swinging and writhing in agony his hip bumped into the bench and sent a wrench clattering onto the cement with a *Clang! Clang! Clang!*

And it was almost over. Davy's struggles slowed as his breath left him. His eyes were already closed. His limbs came to rest. His head cocked back into its natural, inquisitive angle. The rope had forced his chin up towards the ceiling, giving him a confident air that he'd rarely felt in life.

A neutral expression formed on his lips - a mixture of hope and pain. A shoelace dangled freely and made him look innocent and vulnerable like a little boy.

The rope moaned in sympathy to the weight of his grief, and the rafter creaked protest at the life that was there. The body had ceased struggling, but something was there. Davy was there. Life was still there.

And then it flew from his thumb with a twitch.

The swinging body slowed, but he was no longer there. And it slowed more and more before it came to find rest.

Moments later, a susurration was present. Like a standstill breeze it kindled the air. Something was there that was conscious of self. A soft sigh from the sky - photons of time - the last thought of the dead perhaps. The body was dead, but something was there. There was something in the garage that man does not understand. Something in the air, looking down...

And then it was gone.

And the garage was still again.

"**O**h stop it, Johnny. I know you could have run circles around me."

"Nah, Laura, I'm serious. That last mile was six-minute pace. You really gave me a run for my money." Laura could never tell when Johnny was being serious or sarcastic. It was his way of giving a compliment while teasing at the same time. Some people would find it annoying, but Laura loved it. She stuck her little pink tongue out as a way of saying thanks.

"How come we don't run together more often, *chica*?"

"Probably because you never invite me to do so, Mr. Daniels."

"Whatever. You're always too busy playing with dolls or curling your hair or something. You're such a girly girl, ya know?" They had run a loop around town and finished back at Johnny's house. It had been an unusually cool summer day, and the dusk light filtered soft and warm through the windows. The pair walked into the kitchen to get a drink. Laura punched him in the stomach at the insult, and Johnny smiled.

"You want a Gatorade, John?"

"How bout a bottled water, honey bunny. They're in the bottom drawer-a the fridge there."

"Whatever you want, John." She lifted one corner of her mouth and lowered her voice. "You can have whatever you want, mister." The exertion from the run had colored her cheeks, and her perfect teeth looked even whiter than usual. And her eyes took a sassy slant that Johnny hadn't seen before.

He experienced a giddy rush and a tightening of his torso. She opened the fridge and bent way over searching for a bottled water. Johnny made no attempt to look away. She was wearing tight black biker shorts that could have passed for swimwear.

As she rummaged around the fridge, Johnny noticed for the hundredth time that day how shapely her legs were. Her calves were slim, knees small, and her thighs were long and perfectly proportioned. As his eyes found her perfect little rear he cleared his throat and sat down.

She stood up with the bottled water and smiled that same smile again. Her eyes screamed, *come and get me if you dare*, louder than her mouth ever could. Johnny's focus wandered down. She wore a bright pink sports bra that failed to conceal the perky breasts underneath. He knew she was watching him, but he let his eyes go further, to her lean stomach with its little belly button, then along the flare of her hips, and down to the mound of her pubic bone.

"What time does your dad get home, Johnny?" She had one thumb hooked in her shorts as she smiled down at him.

Her voice was low and sweet and husky as she bit her lower lip.

"Umm, not for a real long time. It'll be a lot later. Like way later tonight for sure." Johnny's voice didn't crack, but it was a little squeaky. He didn't have a slice idea when his dad was getting home. All he knew was he couldn't stand up at the moment in his flimsy runner shorts. Laura took another drink and put her hands on the front of her hips in a wonderfully feminine manner. She looked around again and shook out her hair.

"You wanna go up to my room, Laura?" It was out without thought. Johnny placed his hands over his most private part, but this did little to hide his arousal. Laura took another drink and looked down at his lap. He blushed. She smiled. Laura reached out to him, and Johnny put his hand in hers.

"*Come* with me, Johnny." Johnny gulped and stood up. Laura pulled him as they walked up the stairs to Johnny's bedroom. She pushed the door open and led him in. He made to kiss her, and she laughed and pushed him across the room. He fell on the bed and began appreciating her body again. She closed the door softly and locked it with an overt flourish.

"Take off your shoes and socks, sir." Johnny thanked God Almighty that his feet never stunk and immediately did as requested. He also gave thanks that he had the presence of mind to rub one out before the run.

Standing in front of the door Laura kicked off her shoes. Her little pink socks matched her sports bra perfectly. She was still wearing that wry little smile, and Johnny thought he had never seen anyone so beautiful.

"Now you take off your top." His breathing was becoming ragged and desperate.

"You can't tell me what to do, Long-John," she cooed in a little girl voice. Now she was the one teasing. She hooked her thumbs in her shorts and twirled in a circle. Facing away from him she slowly pulled them to the floor. She wore nothing underneath. Johnny gasped, and she smiled again. Laura grabbed the base of her top and pulled it over her head.

"Do you like me, Johnny?" The dusk light filtered through his high windows and outlined her body. Her breasts were the size of grapefruits and topped with perfect little nipples. She had shaved herself save a little brown line that ran down to the pouting lips of her sex. Johnny couldn't speak. He only groaned and nodded like a bobblehead.

"Now your turn, mister." Johnny's shirt was off before she had finished her sentence. Laura shook out her curled brown hair and slowly began walking toward the bed. She moved lightly and took the hair tie off her wrist as she stood before him. Her skin was a creamy colored brown. As she put her hair in a ponytail Johnny reached around and squeezed her firm rear and began kissing her hip bones. He kissed her sex and stuck his tongue in her belly button. Laura giggled.

"Johnny, that tickles." She straddled him on the edge of the bed and kissed him full and hard on the mouth. They groaned into each other's throats as their tongues sparred and slid around themselves. They kissed for many minutes like that until Laura broke off and touched her forehead to his. They were panting harder than they had during the run.

"Laura, you're so beautiful." And she could see in his eyes that he meant it. "You smell so good." Johnny had never smelled anything more sensual as his hands squeezed her breasts and her sides and her smooth legs and her lower back. His heightened senses could smell her flowery lotion and her mushroomy breath and the sweet musk of her arousal. She looked down at his now and giggled again.

"It looks like your boy there was too big for his shorts," she whispered as she bit his earlobe. Johnny looked down and laughed with her. He was still wearing his runner shorts, and his arousal was up to his belly button. Laura raised herself up on her knees, and Johnny lifted his bottom off the bed. She grabbed the shorts and pulled them down to his knees, and Johnny kicked them across the room. Now there was no barrier between the young couple. She kissed him again slower and deeper as she sat on his thighs.

Johnny broke off again and grabbed her face firmly in his hand. He looked her straight in the eye. "Laura, are you sure you want to do this?" She gave him that look with her eyes again and kissed his forehead gently. She raised herself onto her knees and brought her pelvis into his stomach. Johnny clenched her bottom tightly and helped guide her as she lowered herself onto him.

They gasped as he slid into her. Their eyes were huge and surprised as they both breathed, '*whoa*'. The first thing that struck Johnny was the warmth. It seemed to scald him as they each cried out together. Then nature's rhythm overtook them both, and all they could say were their names.

"Oh Johnny, Johnny!"

"Oh my God, Laura!"

Her arms were wrapped around his neck, and she drew his mouth onto her nipples and he suckled them, fierce and hungry. She began screaming his name as the tension rose up to highest ecstasy. The rhythm built to a crescendo as she bobbed faster and faster on his lap. Up and down, faster and faster, she took him into the warmth and the wet and the love and the life and the joy.

Faster and faster she ground him into the bed as his hands directed the speed of her hips. Suddenly, she was on the precipice. A moment later her head flew back. Her eyes shut tight, and her mouth opened wide. Laura cried out as she was flung into the hazy clouds of her climax. She screamed his name to heaven.

As she fell woozy back to earth, she saw Johnny wasn't far behind. "Sweet Mother Mary! Laura, I'm gonna come!" And her womanly instincts kicked back to practicality. She wasn't on the pill, and they hadn't used a condom. She seized him by the wrist and put his hand around her pony tail. Then she kissed him once more for good measure – deeper than ever.

She pulled away and smiled at him like Johnny had never been smiled at before. It was a smile of excitement and pride and sheer bliss all wrapped together. When he grew old and all the details of his first time became hazy and blurred, that was the picture Johnny would so fondly recall. That smile of that beautiful girl.

Laura hopped off and dove down. Johnny still had a grip on her ponytail. She was only just in time as her mouth closed around him. As he pulsed into her mouth he groaned aloud. Laura was grunting along with him as she took him in.

Long afterward they lay together on the bed and smiled at each other. They kissed each other's cheeks and necks and lips and eyelids.

"Johnny, I feel guilty about what we did. We shouldn't have done that."

"I don't. I'm glad it happened."

"Really?"

"Yeah, really cutie."

"If I were you I'd feel guilty about not feeling guilty."

Johnny smiled at her and kissed her forehead and said, "I always hoped my first time'd be with you, Laura." She knew he was fibbing but it made her feel good, and she smiled back.

"Johnny, I'm leaving for college in a few weeks."

"I know."

"If you want me to stay, you can ask me to."

Johnny faced her and said, "I'm not going to ask you to stay, Laura. You worked hard to get into that school." Laura looked away but nodded in acceptance of his answer. At that moment she wanted him to ask her, but she knew him too well to expect it. They continued chatting and giggling together like they had so often before. Laura glanced at Johnny's bedside clock.

"Johnny, I have to get home. I told my mom I'd help her with supper."

Johnny kissed her on the cheek and said, "Okay, tootsie." He grinned at her, and she punched him in the stomach again as they stood up.

"Hey, that hurt."

"Don't call me tootsie, mister."

Johnny pulled his shorts on and gave her another half-cocked smile. "Don't tell me my business, devil woman."

"Oh you are so dead." She jumped at him in mock anger, and he caught her and they kissed again. That's when they heard it for the first time.

"Good God, Johnny! The TV's on downstairs! John, the TV!" she whispered. The horror of being caught was undisguised in her eyes.

"He probably just got home. Don't worry about it, *chica*," Johnny whispered back.

"Johnny, don't call me *chica*!" she whispered with a passionate fire. Her eyes flared at him.

"Geez Laura, what the hell do you want me to call you?" Neither realized how ridiculous it was to be whispering after the racket they had just raised.

"Don't call *me* what you call *other* girls."

"Oh God, here we go. Boy, that didn't take long."

Laura drew herself to her full height and gave him a look that could have melted an ice cube in Antarctica. The threat was completely lost upon Johnny as he stared all dreamy at her naked chest. She realized this was not the time and tossed a perfunctory hand gesture in the air. They both redressed and Laura smoothed out her hair. She threw on one of Johnny's old T-shirts and checked her appearance in the mirror on his bedroom door.

Johnny led the way down the stairs and turned toward the front door. Mr. Daniels was sitting on the couch in the living room watching TV. He looked up as the two came around the corner.

"Hello, Laura!" He boomed all genial. Laura blushed like a rose.

"Hey, Mr. Daniels. We just got done with a run, and I needed to change. Have you been here long?"

"Nope, just got back." Laura said, *"whew"* under her breath as she bent down to re-tie her shoe. Mr. Daniels smiled big at Johnny and gave him a hearty wink. Now it was Johnny's turn to blush. He wondered how much the old bastard had heard.

"Well Mr. Daniels, it was good to see you. I need to get home and help my mom cook supper."

"Okay Laura, you too. Tell your parents I said hello."

Johnny walked Laura outside and gave her an awkward hug. He kissed her cheek and she smiled at him.

"Johnny, I just want to say that I don't want you to feel like you have to act a certain way around me now. Just be yourself, and I'll be fine with that." She paused and looked down. "Just don't act like you owe me anything, OK?"

"OK, Laura." Johnny kissed her cheek again, and she turned down the sidewalk.

"Hey, Laura." Johnny held her up and jogged across the lawn. She smiled at him again.

He lowered his voice. "I'm glad that my first time was with you."

She smiled from ear to ear. "Me too, Johnny. Me too."

Now to explain to my dad, Johnny thought with a bit of dread. He opened the front door and strode inside. His chin was lifted, and he still had a bemused grin on his face as he scratched the back of his head. Mr. Daniels smiled back at his son. There was a new swagger there. If he hadn't been looking for it he wouldn't have noticed. But what was done was done, and that Laura was a damn fine girl. He couldn't help being proud of the little bastard.

"What's up, Pop-ason?"

Mr. Daniels tried to scowl, but the smile couldn't be contained as he shook his head. His boy was a boy no more.

"You look pretty cocky tonight, John."

"Well Dad, a man's got a goddamn right to be cocky every once in a while."

"That's true, son. Now be a good man and grab me a beer outta the goddamn fridge."

"You got it, Big Boy." Johnny walked into the kitchen and opened the fridge. His father shouted from the living room, "Hey, Johnny! Grab yerself one a them too, Little Man."

It was a night of firsts. Johnny grabbed a couple *Tecates* and smiled.

J ohnny was expecting the long ball from Matt. They had played soccer on the same team since they were kids, and Johnny knew all of his strengths and weaknesses on the field. Matt was very fast once he got up to speed, had the type of personality that didn't hesitate at decisions, and at well over six foot, he was usually the first to get to a header entering the box. With his average ball skills and mellow attitude he was well suited to play central back.

A couple of snappy South Americans had corralled him into his corner and were nipping at his heels. This position on the soccer field is the least threatening to the opposing defenders, and they involuntarily crept up with their midfielders to lessen the space. Any good coach teaches this to an extent and will cringe at yards of green between his lines.

As Matt shielded the ball the Brazilians pinched him off, looking to steal. Many in this situation will sneak a quick glance for help in search of their fellow team-mates' position. Matt had a habit of playing with the ball in pick-up games and getting himself into this pickle. Johnny found a hole in the center of the pitch and yelled his name.

"Now, Matthew, now!"

At the sound, Matt leaned back into his opponents to create space, stepped over the ball, and spun his body in turn. While falling back he put his entire body into the kick and sent the ball sailing through the air. Johnny had seen him do it countless times, but it still always surprised him how far Matthew could kick on a dime.

The team they were playing was composed solely of Latinos - Brazilians, Argentineans, and Mexicans mainly. They played a beautiful form of the game that emphasized possession and short passing. Kicking the ball far and hoping for your team to maintain possession is not a winning strategy in most cases. One can see this type of soccer if he so wishes by watching children play. Johnny was captain of their rec team and emphasized a game of possession like the Latinos.

But the defense had cheated up and weren't expecting the long pass. Johnny sprinted just past the half line and turned with perfect timing to field the ball off his chest. As it fell at his feet, he turned toward the two Mexican defenders just yards away.

Since his youth Johnny had been a gifted soccer player. He was the first in the state to become an All-State team member as a freshman; and he tallied sixty-one goals in his senior season, another first. He had quick feet and simple tricks that moved the defense and helped to score goals. He was a natural scorer, and at all times his first instinct was to go at the goal. His soft touch had been developed from countless hours juggling the ball by himself.

The first of the last two approached him with speed. Johnny knew he could have approached faster but had already developed healthy respect for Johnny's skills. He moved the ball with the outside of his right foot to open up the defender's legs. As the Mexican stepped out, Johnny rolled his boot back over the top of the ball. The defender responded as desired by closing up his stance. Johnny repeated the move and rolled the ball to his right with the outside of his foot. As the Mexican lunged for the take away, Johnny stepped on the player's left foot. It was the defender's plant foot, and as he turned to run with Johnny he lost his balance and sprawled to the ground. *One to go,* Johnny thought to himself.

The final defender was, as such, more wary. It was his job in this position not to over-commit. He would stall Johnny by backing with him and wait for help. Johnny could still hear his soccer coach in his mind; *time is with the defense, not you, John.*

He could sense others coming fast behind him. Johnny's skill gave him the confidence to go straight at the man. Short taps in stride with the outside of his boot, he watched the defender's waist, not the ball.

His favorite player was Cristiano Ronaldo, the Portuguese national. As Johnny drove at the man, he crossed over the ball with his right. He had practiced to look like Ronaldo - short, quick crossovers that are pretty and simple. Another crossover with his left, and then right again. The defender was back-pedaling furiously, and each crossover was confused as a possible move to the flank. One more crossover and his stance was wide open. Johnny tapped the ball between his legs and blew by the defender, entering the box.

He glanced up at the keeper. He was from Argentina and very good. He made himself as big as possible and rushed at Johnny to shut down his angle on goal. Johnny made as if to strike the ball left which caused the Argentinean to overcompensate his right arm and right leg. With the adieu of contemptuous ease, Johnny poked the ball through his legs into the old onion bag, a proud smirk on his face not from the goal but the humiliating nutmegs. Putting the ball through a defender's legs is rewarding - doing it twice is showing off.

He jogged back to the Mexican he had downed. He was rubbing his ankle and grinning all rueful. "*¡Tú pisaste mi pinche pie, carepicha!*" He lamented having his foot stepped on.

"*Yo lo aprendí de ti, güevón.*" Johnny let him know where he had learned the trick. Like it or not, Latinos play the game dirty - but Johnny did too. He had had his jersey pulled, arms held, ankles nipped, and legs taken out from under him multiple times during the game. In any sport, though, it's only a foul if seen. A crook gets caught, an artist does not.

The Mexican laughed at the jibe in his own tongue. "*Pinche güero,*" he laughed to himself as Johnny helped him up. Johnny's Spanish was only about forty percent and he took every chance to improve it.

Matt ran up to join the goal celebration carrying a wry smile. He'd seen him do it countless times, but it still always surprised him how easy Johnny made it look to score goals.

"Nice pass, dude."

"Nice goal, dude."

They feigned humility for the benefit of the opponents that had gathered around Johnny by shaking hands. Johnny's coach had taught them that the only thing better than a good celebratory dance is a humble handshake.

"We'd better get goin to class, bro." Matt had begun his cordial haranguing of the Latino gents and Johnny attempted to rein him in. It was almost two o'clock, and it was time for Biology class.

Their summer had passed in a blink. They spent it mowing lawns and hanging out with friends that were leaving in the fall. Their new university was medium sized and located in their hometown.

Johnny had been accepted to much more prestigious schools, but this one was a great deal cheaper, and he could live at home. His plan was to attend here for two years and then transfer to a better school to graduate. He had received many offers for soccer scholarships, but he turned them all down. He loved the game but wanted to focus on his education. He didn't expect to play professionally after school and resigned his talents to the rec league.

When it came to scholastics, Matt had implored him to ease up their first semester, but Johnny had taken twenty-one hours. Matt stuck with twelve because 'that was his favorite number, goddammit.'

"I don't suppose you got your biology homework done, creek chub?" Johnny smiled at his friend.

"I looked at it. Can I look at yours to check real quick, though?"

Johnny was more nervous for his biology class than any other. Science had always fascinated him, and he had enjoyed studying it since he was young. What scared him about this college class, though, was that he knew they would try to force evolution down his throat.

Johnny's teachers at Almighty Wonders had always been difficult, but he liked being challenged. His first science teacher had done well to emphasize the importance of the scientific method. There was little that was contentious about anatomy. Chemistry was universal as well. But Biology had always been Johnny's favorite. Every year at Almighty Wonders the senior science class would stage a debate for the high school congregation. The topic of the debate was creation versus evolution.

Since the eighth grade the students at Almighty Wonders had been exposed to the inherent flaws of this theory that secular scientists constantly purport as fact. Throughout history, creationist Christians have dutifully taken it upon themselves to debase theories from the scientific community with simple truths that cannot be ignored. Needless to say, there usually weren't many volunteers to support team evolution on the stage. Johnny had the type of personality that didn't revel in argument and hadn't participated in the debates. Though he hadn't taken part, he always enjoyed the show from the audience. The evolution team always got trounced and usually didn't put up much of a fight. Johnny didn't blame them.

In their classes the word evolution was treated with contempt and disdain. The shock of even hearing it plausibly defined was similar to hearing one curse. Charles Darwin was not a scientist but a veritable demon out to tear down the truth of Scripture; a big bang out of nothing was simply ludicrous.

Johnny's teachers said that it was the job of creationists to poke holes in the theories provided by secular scientists. Their platform of beliefs that had firm roots in the word of God wasn't up for discussion. From this solid foundation they would snipe at secularist untruths, shooting down evolutionary theory. Johnny's high school Biology teacher, Jennifer, had received her Master of Science in microbiology from a large Christian university and had done well to emphasize the legitimacy of the controversy.

When Johnny was ten years old both his mother and brother died in a car crash. His dad said afterward that he would never touch another woman as long as he lived. He had kept the vow for years, but after meeting Jennifer at a science fair his resolve wavered. They had been dating ever since.

She was a sweet and affable person who ate dinner with them often. She was a good cook, and Johnny liked her company. They often talked science at the table, and although his father had little interest in the subject, he would smile at her logic and the sound of her voice. She made his dad happy and as a good son this made him happy as well.

Johnny and Matt walked into the science building. Matt found a nice spot and plopped down Indian-style on the carpeted hallway. He began copying the homework assignment. Johnny glanced at his watch as Matt stuck his tongue out the side of his mouth in a fury of concentration. Johnny saw their Biology teacher walking down the hall and snatched his paper back from Matt.

"What the hell, dude, I gotta get that last answer down for Chrissake."

"Don't copy it word for word, dumbass, or the teacher'll know what's up."

M att and Johnny entered the Biology classroom and found their own seats. They were close as friends could be, but they didn't sit next to each other in every classroom. They were both extroverts, Matt being more so than Johnny, and they were eager to meet new people.

The professor was a smaller man with a weathered looking face. He smiled a lot and seemed eager to teach. He always wore khakis with a sweater, and his sleeves were constantly being pushed up past his elbows. His thick glasses and sandy gray hair gave him a scholarly air that seemed appropriate at a university. His wrist had some sort of dolphin tattoo that Johnny thought looked out of place on the man but intrigued him as well. He spoke intelligently, and like any great teacher, was constantly pausing during his lesson to assess the faces of his students.

Johnny took a corner seat in the tiered, semi-circle classroom. He gave his full attention to the professor, and, noting his obvious interest, the professor gave him a great deal of eye contact in return.

During his multiple pauses in the lesson, Johnny studied his classmates along with the professor. After a few weeks of college he had come to know the usual suspects that attended the classes. There were the country boys that wore camouflage jackets and talked real loud - present for credit. There were the dolled up ladies that smelled great and always seemed to be at attention. Johnny guessed after speaking to a few of them after class, however, that their stares at the professor were most likely blank, thoughts on outfits and gatherings crowding out the present moment.

Then there were the students in the front that did not seem so interested in their own apparel. These were the most familiar type for Johnny from high school. They hardly looked at the teacher to digest the lesson. Their noses were kept inches from their notebooks, aiming to record every word the professor said. Johnny had never needed to take notes in high school and he kept the habit in college. He found it more rewarding to listen to the teacher and enjoy the lesson. It is almost impossible to write and think critically at the same time.

Johnny noticed from the outset how the professor relied so heavily on the theory of evolution in class. In the past few weeks, the man had said evolved, or change throughout time, or speciation, or population dynamics in every single class.

Johnny learned early on that Matt wouldn't be much of an ally in his stand against the brain washing. The first few times the teacher said 'evolve', Johnny quickly looked to his Christian friend for assistance. They would have rolled their eyes, scowled a bit, and shook their heads in sympathy for the disillusioned man. Matt, however, couldn't seem to care less.

He had planted himself next to a girl from the first day of class from whom he would only momentarily divert his attention. Matthew had always exhibited a palatable taste in women, and Johnny had never seen him go after such a mutt. She was ugly as hell but made up for these shortcomings well enough with her chest. She also had that little slant to her eyes that when coupled with a particular grin says silently, *come hither big boy*. Johnny left him to it.

He was therefore resigned to a silent duel with the professor. Whenever he said something that went against Johnny's Christian education, Johnny would wrinkle his forehead and squint an eye at the teacher. At first he didn't notice, but once Johnny started shaking his lowered head at the *e*-word the man got the damn hint.

The time was 2:52, and the professor wrapped up the lesson. Johnny stood up as everyone began gathering their things. He stretched to the ceiling and yawned with a bit of pleasure. He was sore from that game with the Latinos. They had beaten him up pretty good, but it was the pleasant pain of hard exercise.

"Mr. Daniels, may I have a word with you in my office, good sir?" The professor's high and unexpected voice brought him out of his next thought.

"Is there a problem, sir?" Everyone in class had looked at Johnny after the professor's request, and he had to stand his ground a bit.

"Not at all, Mr. Daniels. It will only take a couple of minutes if you can spare the time."

"Of course, Dr. Likins."

Johnny shouldered his back-pack and stepped into the hall, waiting for his escort. Matt walked out of the classroom with his arm around the mutt. His huge smile was all out of proportion to the package in tow. He apparently thought he had himself a real trophy. Johnny figured he was getting desperate for a consistent release and smiled back at his best friend.

"Let's kick the ball around later, Matt. Meet me down on the field round seven. Dinner at my place at eight."

"You got it, dude. I think I'll have my dessert before then though. Just scream for me if you can't handle the good professor." Matt winked in a good-natured way at their teacher, and the girl giggled delightedly as they walked on. Johnny reckoned the choice of vocabulary was for her benefit.

"Follow me please, Mr. Daniels." The professor was genial and so non-confrontational that Johnny smiled back. They walked down the carpeted hall and entered a room that had the name Len Likins, Ph.D. on the door.

The desk was covered with papers that consisted of student's exams and research articles. There were dozens of small animals and worms and only God knows what pickled in mason jars on shelves. There was a large poster that said *Save the Rainforest* on the wall. As Johnny shut the door, he noticed another that said, *Save the Whales*.

"So Dr. Likins, how are the whales and the rainforest doing?" He laughed politely at the humor.

"They'll be fine, Mr. Daniels. Don't worry about them too much."

"Well sir, what can I do for ya?"

"Well Johnny, eh-hem, I'm sorry, may I call you Johnny?"

"Of course, sir. I like my name just fine." Johnny grinned at the man. He didn't know what in the hell was coming, and he was a little nervous.

"Well, Johnny, I'll come straight to the point. I'm sure you have things to do. I have noticed in class that you seem to have a bit of an issue with a few topics we've covered so far."

Johnny knew what he was talking about, of course, but didn't show his hand.

"What do you mean, Dr. Likins?"

"Well Johnny, I've done some asking around about you, and I know you are a very gifted student and come from a good school here in town."

"Yes sir, I attended Almighty Wonders Christian School my whole life." Johnny's chin came up, and his chest swelled a bit. Not simply from defiance, but pride in what he considered a part of himself.

"Well Johnny, let me just say that I have no desire to step on your toes or berate your beliefs. I am familiar with the science curriculum at the school. I studied the textbooks when deciding where to send my youngest daughter for high school next year. I know that they teach you that evolution is inherently wrong, Johnny, and I just want to let you know that what you believe, no matter what you believe, is completely fine with me."

There was a humility to the man that Johnny liked, and he seemed to have very little ego involved in the matter. Johnny couldn't help but like his directness and candor. "Well sir, I appreciate that." His voice trailed off as he said it. He was embarrassed now for all that damn head shaking he had done in class.

"Johnny, do you have any classes immediately after this one?"

"No sir, my next class is astronomy, and that isn't until five o'clock."

"This is just a suggestion, Johnny, and of course you don't have to come here if you don't want to, but I would like it if you came to my office after class from now on and we can talk about any questions that you may have. I hope I am not embarrassing you, Johnny, and I don't want you to feel obligated, whatsoever, but I have been watching you in class, and I can tell that you are very interested in the material we cover. I have a syllabus that I must keep to in class, but I would really enjoy your company afterward, and we can iron out anything that you may not have already learned about evolution. Any questions that you have about Biology or science in general are fair game.

"In my investigations I also heard you are quite the hunter, sir. Hell, we can talk about that or even girls if you like." The ice in their conversation had had little time to develop, and they both laughed comfortably.

"Well, Dr. Likins, there has been a lot covered so far that I can't say I agree with or completely understand as you present them, I guess."

"That's excellent, Johnny! Science is about asking questions and testing the answers. Get on outta here now, and I'll see you in class Thursday – and afterward if you still wish." Dr. Likins smiled and they shook hands over the desk.

Johnny smiled back. "See ya later, Dr. Likins."

"Johnny, if I use your Christian name, then you may use mine. Call me Len, OK?"

"Alright Len, we'll see ya later."

As Johnny walked out the door and down the long aisle, he felt as good as he had in a while. Like most athletes, he enjoyed a challenge and knew he was up for a mental one with Len. He walked out of the building into the bright, cool sunshine of early fall.

Johnny Daniels was on his way.

"So I don't know what the hell she wanted me to say. I was just sittin there in my boxers on the bed, and she wanted to talk about feelings all of a sudden."

"Well, Matt, chicks like talking about that stuff. You know that."

"Course I know that. How the hell do you think I got to the bed in the first place, dude? So anyways, we had been makin out for hours it seemed like. My lips were gettin chapped as hell, and I was gettin blue balls like no other.

Fierce blue balls, yo – like I'd been punched in the gut. God I hate it when you hear chicks say that blue balls aint real. So anyways, I start takin her shirt off real slow. Luckily it was a button-up top. I can peel those off way easier than when you have to lift it up over their heads. The necks on girl's shirts are so fuckin small that sometimes it gets stuck. And that's just awkward as hell."

"And that's when you hit the wall."

"N-n-no, I got her bra off, and that's when I hit the wall. I think it scared her that I got it off so smooth. Remember when I used to make my little cousin wear one so I could practice gettin it off one-handed? We'd stuff it full-a socks and I'd practice while we played Mario Kart. Damn I got good at it. You gotta pin that one side with your thumb real good then pinch the other side over it with your two fingers. Unhookin it aint that hard if you plant your thumb good. Most guys try to just pinch it together or unhook it with the thumb. That aint the way, man. You'll end up having to use two arms, and reachin around like that will make you look like a real twat-waffle. You gotta plant that goddamn strap between your thumb and her back real good."

"I know about your rule of thumb, bro. You've made sure that I remember all your wise teachings over the years. Maybe you'd a got further along with her if ya used two arms this time."

Johnny smiled over at his best friend. They kicked a soccer ball around almost every day. They didn't always talk about girls, but it was the norm. Sometimes they played catch, but usually they kicked the ball.

Matt ignored the jibe. "Right when she felt a breeze on her chest she locked up cold, dude. I tried to warm em up, but as I laid her back she did that thing where she locked her elbows to her sides. God I hate it when chicks do that. They can pin their arms stronger than a goddamn bear trap when they want to. I was kissin her neck and started whisperin to her, but it didn't work. I finally had to ask her what was wrong. I shouldn't a done it, but I had no choice.

Then the emotional floodgates opened up, and she started tellin me about her family, and how her cousin was abused as a child, and all this other crap. God, it was torturous. I mean, it really fuckin was, dude."

"What were you whisperin to her?"

"You know, man, normal stuff. I said evrathin was gonna be alright, and she was really pretty, and how she smelled so good. She was still actin all stiff, so I told her I loved her. Then she looked at me really weird and said, 'I know.' It kinda freaked me out to be honest with ya."

Johnny laughed at his friend's desperation. "I can't believe you're messin around with that *chica*, dude. You can do better than that, man, you're a good lookin bastard."

"Ya, I know," Matt said, "but it takes a lot more time and I just kinda wanna get laid, man. I'm horny as hell all the time and it's gettin pretty fuckin annoying actually. I can't think about anything else, or when I do it just pops into my mind all of a sudden. God, did you see that little soro girl sittin in the front today in class?"

"Oh ya," Johnny said all dreamy.

"I'd fuck the shit outta that little cottontail," Matt said, all serious. "Chicks like that are right in my wheelhouse, dude. You really gotta take yer time with super fine felines like that and do evrathin right. You gotta take it real slow with em and make sure they're just lovin it. That's what you always hear these old dudes that really know their shit about chicks always say - take your goddamn time, but finish like a boss. You can never start too slow or end too fast. That's how I like to do it, John... I like to fuck em long, bro. And I like to fuck em good.

"By the way," Matt said, "that reminds me, bud. I've been meanin to tell ya somethin, and it's not as perverted as it sounds, but I just have wanted to tell ya just in case I die in a car crash or somethin and don't get a chance to later on. I got an amends ta make, dude."

"What's that?" Johnny asked.

"Sometimes I think about you when I'm havin sex with a chick, dude. It's really not in a perverted way, man, but I just do it if I think I'm gonna splode too soon and it helps me not end on a low note, ya know?"

Johnny said Jesus real slow.

"Sorry, dude. I swear it's not as bad as it sounds, man. I can't lose my reputation dude, and if it works, don't fix it, right? I mean, I can't fuck around when my prowess is at stake, bro. Thinkin bout you helped me get an extra three minutes sack time with a chick a couple months back. I know *she* turned out happy. I don't do it all the time, dude, sometimes I think about baseball too. But anyways, I just wanted to tell ya and get that off my chest, man. Whew, that feels good. Thanks for listenin, bud." Matt smiled real big and looked around like he hadn't a single care in the world. As if his last one he had been holding onto for God knows how long had just been dealt with, and now, he was free.

Johnny shook his head and said 'Jesus' again even slower this time. It didn't really bother him that much, but it would have been weird to act like it didn't. "God, you're a real perverted son-bitch, Matthew. You know that?"

"Ya, I know," Matt said.

"Jesus," Johnny said, "you'd prolly pork that huge beast that sits behind that fine ass soro *chica* if you were desperate enough."

"I don't think so, man," Matt said. "She's like three hundred pounds, dude, and her face aint much better than er body. I don't think she bathes much either. Her hair's all greasy, and I caught a whiff a her walkin outta class the other day. Bout blew my fuckin socks off."

Johnny winced and said '*dyaaayz*'. Matt was pretty tolerant of such things. For him to say it was bad meant it must have been pretty goddamn bad.

"But hell, you can make it work with a chick like that if you hafta," Matt said and smiled at his buddy. Johnny was a little skittish of foul smelling people, and Matt liked to gross him out every once in a while. "There's plenty a ways to do the deed and not have to look at her face. And I don't mind the smell of a full-bodied woman every once in a while, either."

"You start messin around with chicks like that, and I'd hafta kill ya, man," Johnny said. "I wouldn't even let her go down on me for a thousand bucks," he said and shivered dramatically. "I hope you wouldn't either."

Matt smiled real big at his buddy. "Good God, dude," he said all slow and serious, "I'd eat er out for a thousand bucks."

"God, you're a real perverted son-bitch, Matthew. You know that?"

"Ya, I know," Matt said.

On a whim Johnny changed the tack of the conversation. "You think about Davy much, bro?"

Matt scratched his chin and looked down. "Yeah I kinda do, man. Not all the time, but I think about him quite a bit. I know I couldn't a really done anything to keep him from doing what he did, but sometimes I like to go back in my mind and pretend I'm walking into that garage right before he did what he did. I like to think about savin him, I guess."

"You think he went to hell, bro?"

Matt grabbed his crotch and spit. "Jeez Christ, Johnny. I don't fuckin know." The two rarely talked about such things. It wasn't that they were uncomfortable talking about them with each other. They were just more inclined to keep such matters resigned to thoughts. Talking about serious issues rarely changes them, and they had heard heaven and hell talked about enough already growing up.

"Obviously I know that you don't fuckin know, dumbass. I asked you what you think."

Matt cocked an eyebrow and grinned. Johnny had begun cussing on an infrequent basis, and Matt liked the change. He put his hands on his hips and a foot on the ball. He looked at the sky before he replied as if seeking his answer in the clouds.

"My dad says that hell is a buncha bullshit. When I was little he used ta say we'd have to do our chores there if we didn't do em here." Matt laughed at the memory. "Then one day we were in the car and out of the blue he said that hell is a made up place that doesn't exist. He said talkin about hell is the only time that Jesus ever sinned. It's one of those childhood memories for me that you remember real clear for some reason. We were on our way to church, and I can still see his eyes in the rear-view mirror as he said it. He said that it's used as a fear tactic to get people to believe in Jesus. Then he mumbled somethin about the offering plate." Matt laughed again.

"S-o-o, you don't think Davy went to hell?"

"Johnny, how long did you and I know Davy?"

"We knew him for a long time, man; a long time."

"Member that one day in sixth grade when Jessica had her period for the first time?"

Course he remembered that day. He smiled as Matt told the story.

"We were just sittin there in Mr. Winston's science class listenin to him go on and on about photosynthesis or whatever. God, he was a boring teacher. Jessie raised her hand and almost yelled at him, 'Mr. Winston, I gotta go to the bathroom!'" They both laughed together.

"She was wearin that white dress she always wore on chapel day. I thought she had diarrhea or somethin the way she jumped up. Then Mikey started screamin, 'Jess is bleedin, Mr. Winston! Mr. Winston, Mr. Winston! Jess is bleedin, Mr. Winston!'" The two were almost rolling as they remembered the panic in their old classmate's voice. Everyone in their class could see the large red stain on her bottom where the dress was stuck to her backside. She had run out of the room completely mortified.

"Mr. Winston looked just about as panicked as Mikey. That's when ol Davy jumped up and asked to be excused and walked out the door. Then someone said something about her havin her period, and that's when Mr. Winston really got uncomfortable. Member how scared he looked? He thought he was gonna hafta give us the birds and the bees talk. I don't think any of us really knew what a period was, but it sure seemed funny at the time.

"Bout thirty minutes later, Jess and Davy walked back into class like they just conquered Rome. They both had their chins about a mile high. She had a new skirt on, and Davy was right behind her. He obviously gave her one hell of a pep talk and gotten her all cleaned up cuz she looked confident as hell. Everyone started laughin again like crazy, and that's when ol Davy gave the look of death. Everyone shut their mouths right then. Member that, John? I can still see his face; real fire-breathin face. He was about half the size of anyone, but man-oh-man, he looked like he coulda whooped the daylights outta Holyfield that minute." The boys laughed again at the memory.

"I was still kinda snickerin when Davy sat back down next to me. Then he turned to me real slow and whispered, 'Matthew, if you carry on like that I will tell everyone that I caught you makin out with Brandi Smith in the communion room.' He had the fire in his eye, man, and his lip was quivering a bit. That was the only time I ever thought Davy could beat me up. I shut the hell up right then and there. I knew he'd do it, and I couldn't afford that kinda stain on my reputation."

Johnny looked so surprised it was almost comical. "You made out with Brandi Smith in the communion room?!" he screeched.

"Yeah, man... I never told ya bout it, but she was my first kiss." Matt grimaced while he scratched the back of his head. He looked down as though he were still embarrassed. Johnny cracked up again so hard the tears were rolling down his cheeks.

"How come you never told me, bro?"

"Why would I tell that to anyone," Matt asked rhetorically. "She was so ugly, man; so goddamn ugly." Matt shivered and squinted at the pain of past transgressions. The boys smiled together at shared memories and continued passing the ball. A few minutes later, Matthew grabbed his crotch and spit and spoke again.

"So I guess my answer is no, John. I don't think Davy is in hell. Davy was a real good guy. I know he killed himself and was gay, but I don't give a shit. Pastor Jennings thinks he's in hell, I'm sure, but I don't care what that son-bitch thinks. Davy was little, and Davy was shy, but Davy had bigger balls than most anyone I ever met. Tellin everyone he was gay like that took a shit-ton a guts, man; it took a lotta fuckin pluck, and I respect that. Davy was a good shit, man." Matt paused to reflect once more.

"Like I said before, Johnny, I don't know where Davy is right now. If people say he's in hell, then I say they can fuckin go to hell. If we all have an immortal soul that goes someplace after we die, then so be it. You'd think an old soul would give us a few memories or make us a bit wiser in this life. If I got a soul, I wonder what he was up to before there was me." Matt looked up a bit abashed.

Johnny grinned at his friend. Matt very rarely talked on such a personal level. Johnny knew it would be some time before he did so again. He brought him back to more comfortable territory, and Matt nodded his thanks.

"So what happened with your new little *chica*? I gotta be honest dude, she's almost as ugly as Brandi, but she does have a hell of a rack."

"No she isn't!" Matt feigned outrage, and Johnny smiled at how easy it was to rile his friend. "She's at least a five. I told her I'd take her out to eat at *Olive Garden*, and that settled her down pretty good. She'd already ruined the mood, though, when she started cryin."

"Better luck next time, Romeo. It's almost impossible to get some after a chick starts cryin."

Matt beamed at his friend's unintentional compliment, and Johnny read him like a book. "After all that you did her anyway, didn't ya, Matthew? Didn't cha?" He jogged up to him and prodded him all proud in the ribs.

"Is that the kinda guy you think I am, Long-John? She was in no condition for making love, but I had to let her know that I still cared. I respect all women, John, and their emotions." He had an aloof and humble air as he said it. "I consoled her with a blowie."

Johnny belly laughed with delight. "Well, at least you got a fish on the hook. Make sure you got another before you throw er back."

"I dunno if I'll hang out with her too much from now on. Off and on prolly. Hell though, man, I'm fine without a chick anyways. There's always another one around the corner. I've spent way more time in my life without chicks than with em. Way more time in the sack too actually. There aint too much better in life than gettin lifted and takin a shower and havin a nice little date with yourself. You just finish your shower and then you can go about your business. You don't hafta fuck around with the cuddlin stuff afterwards and hafta lie to em bout your feelins and shit. I prefer the real thing a course, don't get me wrong. But hell, dude, I've had some-a the best sex of my life when I was all by myself," Matt said.

Johnny nodded and smiled and glanced at the setting sun. Fall was his favorite time of year. It reminded him of hunting and being outside. He inhaled the clean smelling air and looked around again. It was all very pretty, he thought.

"It's gettin dark. I think Jennifer made lasagna tonight. Why don't ya come over and help us clean it up. You know how Dad hates having leftovers. Let's kick this pig, yo."

Matt put an arm around his buddy's shoulders and kicked the ball ahead of them. He smiled in anticipation as they walked to Johnny's house.

"Israel is in great danger, my friends. Iran threatens to wipe them off the map with nuclear weapons. These Persians of old already have two armies engaged and ready for action. Hamas and Hezbollah are currently camped on the borders of Israel in Gaza and Lebanon, and they are ready for war."

The three letter word brought Johnny's mind out of his thoughts and back to the present. He had much to ponder thinking back on the past few months. His talks with Dr. Likins had troubled him at first but had molded an analytical nature that Johnny had always possessed but rarely expressed. He had a great deal of topics that he wanted to discuss with his old science teacher. She would be coming over again soon to cook dinner which would present a good opportunity.

His surroundings now were familiar as any. He and his father had attended Almighty Wonders Christian Church for over thirteen years. The pew in which he now sat was the same in which he had sat for Davy's final confession. The chapel for school and the auditorium for church were one and the same. His former Bible teacher, Mr. Tyson, and the man glowering from the pulpit, however, were very dissimilar.

 He glanced over at his old teacher who had taken his seat in the blue carpeted pew across from him. He was smiling up at the preacher like he always did. He was the type of man who could smell roses from a septic lagoon without much effort. Most folks in silent thought will adopt a neutral bend to their lips or even a frown. Mr. Tyson always appeared to be in a happy state, as if he were constantly retelling himself a humorous joke.

Matthew's classroom antics probably had the record for outbursts provoked of the man. He would always follow him into the hallway afterward and tell Matt he loved him. Matt would laugh and tell him the like. It would have been strange from any other man. It was a difficult task to break his smile.

Their preacher, Mr. Jennings, on the other hand, usually chose to adopt a more lemon sucked skepticism that Johnny was beginning to find irksome. He had light blue eyes, was tall and lanky, and had thin lips that can come from too many years with braces. His dress was always immaculate. He wore suits of every hue from the finest cloth, and Johnny had heard him joking to a few mothers once about how all his shoes spoke Italian.

His sermons were always negative. If the rapture weren't tomorrow, well then, by God, it'd probably be the day after. Doomsday collection plates are always heavier than happy-go-lucky collection plates, and the church was doing quite well despite the recession.

Since the election of that liberal Obama, his sermons were getting darker and more judgmental by the week. The simple love that Jesus taught was pinched out more and more by current events of the end times. The United States of America was officially in the proverbial hand-basket and on the downward slide into flames. Johnny knew his father had noticed. His attendance was picking up, and he had never heard him speak so highly of the man.

Mr. Jennings had studied under the modestly famous TV pastor from Texas, John Hagee. He was a common fixture on various Christian broadcasting networks. Johnny had watched part of a sermon just days before with his father and Jennifer at home. Much like the town halls Johnny had attended over the summer, the colors red, white, and blue were copiously present. And by God, that Hagee wouldn't be caught dead without a good ol American banner on his lapel. Who needs a birth certificate when you got a goddamn pin? Mr. Jennings was proud of his tutelage and would often re-preach Hagee's sermons to his congregation. Johnny recognized this as the same exact one he had heard days before.

"Intelligence confirms that Hamas and Hezbollah have over 40,000 long and short range rockets ready to launch in attack on Israel at any moment. Folks, this is three times the number of rockets they had in their war of 2006. Many of these rockets can hit every major city in Israel, including Tel Aviv and Jerusalem. Today is the day, if there was ever a day, to pray for the peace of Jerusalem, my friends.

"Ahmadinejad's chief of staff just recently said, 'the annihilation of Israel should be a global goal. If the Zionist regime of Israel attacks Iran, the Zionists can be exterminated in a week. King David commands believers to pray for the peace of Jerusalem. History proves that when Jerusalem is at peace, the world is at peace. When Jerusalem is at war, the world is at war. When we pray for peace in Jerusalem we pray for peace in America.

"Why is this true, my friends? It is true because Israel is unlike any nation on the face of the earth. Israel is the only nation created by a sovereign act of God. In the beginning, God created the heavens and the earth. The earth is the Lord's and the fullness thereof. It belongs to God. God came down and entered into a covenant with Abraham, Isaac, and Jacob, and gave the land of Israel to them and their seed forever in Genesis 17:7.

"Israel was not born in 1948 by an emotional response of the United Nations to the Holocaust. Israel was born 3500 years ago when God Almighty made a covenant with Abraham. A covenant that is still valid because the God that we serve does not break a covenant.

"Mr. Hagee tells of a person he met in the media once that said that this was just something that people believed as truth a long time ago. Well friends, truth doesn't cease being with the passing of time, but becomes more true with the passing of time. And the truth is that Israel has a Biblical mandate for its land. It is not a vassal of the United States but a holy land created by God for the Jewish people.

"When God gave the boundaries of Israel and placed it in the Bible, he was saying both to the Jews and to the nations of the world that they can't just live anywhere. He was saying I want them to live exactly here, and I want them to live there forever. Therefore, Mr. Obama has no authority to tell Israel where they can and cannot build! Especially in the city of Jerusalem!"

Just mentioning the name Obama in a negative context got Mr. Jennings his biggest applause of the morning. His father grabbed the pew in front of them and looked around all eager for others willing to stand up. Mr. Daniels was no follower, but he was no leader, either, and chose not to stand for his hearty ovation. Mr. Jennings continued on the buoyed adulation.

"Jerusalem is the capital of Israel. It is not a desert outpost. Why is it important for the president not to pressure Israel to divide Jerusalem? Why is it important for America not to use its influence to divide the land of Israel that they call the West Bank and the Bible calls Judea and Samaria?

"The prophet Joel makes it very clear that any nation that tries to divide the land of Israel will face the judgment of God. This includes the United States of America. Speaking of Israel and the Jews, he that touches you touches the apple of God's eye. The word apple translates as pupil. When you intentionally offend Israel and persecute the Jews it is like sticking your finger in the eye of God.

"Keep it up Obama. You are going to get His undivided attention very soon. America is now sticking its finger in God's eye, and it won't be long til God pokes back.

"President Obama is using his influence to put pressure on Israel to divide the land of Israel." Johnny looked over as his father booed. "He's coming up with a zero building in the settlements policy. He's stating that Israel cannot build 1600 apartments, as they wish, in Jerusalem. The fact is, where Israel chooses to build is none of Obama's business. Jerusalem is the capital of Israel, not a settlement." Johnny thought his father was about to lunge to his feet, but he just clapped all feverish and yelled something unintelligible.

"Does Obama tell Russia where to build or China or maybe Iran? He has as much authority in Russia as he has in Israel. Why is he picking on Israel? President Obama's abusive treatment of Netanyahu when the prime minister visited the White House is simply inexcusable. The president refused to be photographed with the prime minister. It was a planned insult. It wasn't spontaneous, it was planned. The president left the prime minister there all alone and went to eat dinner with his family. This has never been done in the history of the United States of America. These actions were premeditated, and they were calculated.

"Why? Because Obama wanted to send a message to the leaders of the world, and especially to the enemies of Israel that I do not support this man, and I do not support the government that sent him. That's the very clear message he was sending to the enemies of Israel and to the enemies of the United States of America.

"Why should that matter to you? Now listen closely, friends. If America does not defend Israel, God is not going to defend America. Now it has meaning. The radical terrorists that are among us smell America's weakness. They see America as a declining global power - all talk and no do. They see Iran, China, and Russia as the bullies of the world, as the forthcoming super powers. And they have no respect for the United States of America because of what we are doing now..."

At the end of the sermon, Johnny sidled into the aisle and made his way to the front door. There were many exits, and Johnny knew them all, of course, but his father insisted on filing past the preacher to shake his hand. Mr. Jennings always put on a good smile for his congregation.

"Great to see you, Johnny. You look great." A thought occurred to Johnny then, and he shot it by the good pastor.

"Hey Mr. Jennings, I know you are busy on Sundays, but I was wondering if maybe you could spare some time after service to sit down and have a talk with me?"

"Of course, Johnny. I always keep a slot open about thirty minutes after each sermon to speak to anyone in my office that desires to converse. Just come on by and we'll chat about any questions you have."

"Okay, then I will see you after church one-a these Sundays?"

"Sounds great Johnny. I'll see you then."

Johnny had never really known what it was like to be unpopular. Popularity was never something he had desired nor had to work for. People were simply drawn to him, and he managed to cultivate affection for their strengths as well as peculiarities. They, in turn, recognized a strength and loyalty in his demeanor that was never feigned. He was the type of guy that would stick up for his friends no matter what the situation.

Since beginning university, Johnny felt he had met more people in a few months than he had in his whole life. There were the Latinos that he played soccer with on a regular basis, the classmates that he helped with homework, and a hundred friendly faces around campus which were growing by the day. His professors had come to recognize a curiosity in him that is far more desirable than intelligence. Dr. Likins greatly enjoyed the intellectual sparring they had kept up since their first meeting. Although they were both a bit burned out afterward, Johnny had learned a great deal from those talks.

But of all the new acquaintances, his favorite was his new buddy, Ahmed. They had three classes together and had started meeting up beforehand to compare answers on assignments. Johnny rarely met people he considered more intelligent than himself. No one knew he thought this, but every person has an opinion about this aspect of themselves. Ahmed seemed to ask more questions than anyone Johnny had ever met. He always seemed to be listening to others, and when he spoke, it took the form of questions more often than statements. You won't hear the ear bragging about it too often, but he is much wiser than the mouth.

"So do Native Americans get more bonus points upon entering university than African Americans, Johnny?"

Johnny and Ahmed were discussing aspects of sociology as they walked to Chemistry class. Johnny wanted to ask Ahmed about a certain stoichiometry problem, but Ahmed was much more interested in some of the nuances of American society and culture.

They were discussing race discrimination and affirmative action, and Ahmed was having difficulty understanding. Johnny was trying to explain how the concept was a good one but it wasn't getting at the heart of the problem. Diversity is beneficial but works much better when encouraged and rewarded, not forced. Affirmative action would be more effective if it gave bonus points for being poor, not just black or brown. Ahmed changed the tack of the conversation as they passed a pretty little sorority girl.

"Johnny, I would very much like to make a date with an American girl. I have asked several but have received no luck. Do you have any advice for me?"

"Well, Ahmed, it's not as important what you ask as how you ask."

"I understand." Ahmed obviously didn't understand as he furrowed his brow and looked down at his shoes. Johnny sought to explain.

"I'll help you get hooked up with some a them hotties one of these days, bro. I dunno about girls in other countries, but American girls tend to be harder to rope than tie down - especially with cliquey little soro *chicas* like that one. Don't ever approach a girl if you won't be able to walk away without caring if you ever see her again. Then you have to let them know you like the way they're put together but kinda smirk when you do it. You've got to be cocky with them but not mean, and you gotta be witty but not too quick with it. But most important of all, bro, you gotta push em when they want to be pulled, and pull em when they want to be pushed."

Ahmed took his mechanical pencil out from behind his ear. Before he could start writing the knowledge in his notebook, Johnny gave him more concrete advice that would be better understood.

"This is just a suggestion, bro, but you also might want to trim up your eyebrows a bit." Ahmed had a thick uni-brow and immediately put his fingers to it. Johnny smiled over at his friend.

"Don't get upset about it, honey." Johnny laughed and squeezed the back of his neck in a friendly gesture. "I'm just lettin ya know what Matt has taught me about the ladies."

"Yes, I have seen Matthew with many ladies. I am very fond of the skills he has. He is very smooth with the ladies. I will make an appointment presently at the salon." Johnny laughed again. He had made a good friend in Ahmed already. He seemed excited to have an American friend and was curious like Johnny. He never needed a pinch of salt with advice, and Johnny liked his humility.

"But you wear nice clothes, and they like that for sure. I've seen the way they look at you in all that *Armani* gear you wear. And you've got really good teeth like me." Johnny flashed them at his friend. "American *chicas* like that."

As they were walking in discussion, Johnny accidentally bumped shoulders with a guy that happened to be black. Being from Egypt, Ahmed rightly considered himself African (albeit the Egyptian hue of African). Johnny and the fella looked up startled as they connected.

Johnny said, "Oh my bad, dude, ma bad."

The black guy drawled, "I's all good, bro - don't worry bout it."

Johnny said, "word," and they continued walking down the hall.

Being from a former British Protectorate, Ahmed loved English and learning American slang. As he and Johnny walked on, he asked his friend about the responses elicited by their bump.

"So that African American man called you bro, right Johnny?"

"Yup", Johnny responded. "It's OK to just call them black, though, man."

"But you just called the black man, dude?"

"Yup", Johnny responded, "but it sounds better to just call him guy, though, man."

"So can you call him bro and he call you dude?"

"Well, he can call me dude, but I can't really call him bro unless he told me somehow that it's cool to do so. It's kinda funny to watch. I'll point it out to you when we eat lunch in the union tomorrow. When a black dude walks up to a white dude and says, "Hey, what's up, bro?" When they slap hands or whatever, if you watch the white guy after the black guy walks off, he'll stick his chest out a bit or talk real loud to his other friends. It's kind of a compliment to most white guys, and they'll think they're pretty cool afterward."

Being from Cairo, Ahmed had a pretty strong Arabic accent. "So... since I am from Africa like their ancestors, I can call them bro, right?"

"If I tell you will you help me with that damn stoichiometry problem?" Ahmed nodded all interested.

"Yup... But here's your personal sociology lesson for the day." Johnny looked at his friend and smiled. "I wouldn't recommend it."

"So how are you likin your new school, Tootsie?"

"It's a really nice school, John. At first it was really hard getting used to, but all the classes are keeping me busy. Calculus is pretty hard, but it always was for me. I really like my American History class. The teacher is super laid-back and even dresses up sometimes. He came to class today dressed like Ben Franklin. He's super goofy, but I like it when teachers act goofy like that. It keeps the lesson interesting, ya know?"

"Yup. I really like my Biology teacher, Len. That dude is cool as hell. We've been meeting up after classes to talk about the lessons and evolution and stuff. I've learned a ton from that guy. He's cool as hell, Laura. You'd like him I think. You really would."

"You been teaching him a thing or two about evolution, John?"

"More like he's been teachin me a thing or two. I've probably asked him a couple hundred different questions, and he fields most of em pretty good. He's been asking me questions about what I believed too. I think that's really helped me come to the truth about some-a the stuff Jennifer taught us in class. I'm gonna have a real heart to heart with her one a these days. A bunch of stuff she was teaching us was pure bullshit, Laura. It really was."

"Oh."

"What? You sound like you're upset."

"No, it's nothing. You just like, kinda talk different nowadays. It sounds like this guy has brain washed you a bit."

"I think I was a bit brain washed before, *chica*."

"Plus, I don't think I've ever heard you cuss so much, Johnny. I mean, it's OK and all. I guess I'll just have to get used to it. I really like talking to you on the phone, though."

"Yeah the phone is OK, but you're more fun to talk to when I can look at you at the same time."

"Why might that be I wonder?"

"Well, I definitely like the way you're put together. I think you've got about the nicest body I've ever seen. I can actually see you in my mind right now. Just like you were that day in my room."

"So, have you like, been with any other girls since that day?"

"Eh-hem, well what do you mean, been with?"

"You know exactly what I mean, John."

"Well, Matt and I went on a double date the other day with some *chicas* from class. We went to some really stupid movie at the dollar theater. Matt and his girl were makin out the whole time. I kinda kissed the girl I was with, but she was the worst kisser in the whole world. She really was. It was like she was trying to inhale my face or somethin. I think she stuck her tongue up my nose for a second. Then she started..."

"Alright! Like, what the hell, John? That's enough. That is so gross I don't want to hear about it. Sounds like you've turned into a real freakin Romeo since I left. Hangin out with nasty sluts!"

"Whoa. Look who's cussin now. You asked me if I'd been with any girls and then you get all hissy fit when I tell you about it. I coulda pulled a Matt and said no to you, but I like you too much to lie to you about anything, Laura. I really do."

"Nice try, John. You like me so much that you go and make out with other girls. Nice try, mister. Real freakin Romeo."

"Well, it's not like we're dating or anything, Tootsie."

"I know we're not dating, Johnny, and don't call me tootsie anymore. I don't like it."

"Okay, fine. Jesus Christ, Laura. I'm gonna hafta start callin you Sassafras you're gettin so goddamn sassy with me. I didn't mean it bad or anything. I meant it like a Tootsie Roll, like kinda sweet and tasty. I meant it kinda endearing like - like in a loving kinda way."

"Speaking of Jesus Christ whose name you just so blatantly blasphemed. Have you been praying to that guy anymore?"

"Come one Laura, you know I don't like talkin about that kinda stuff. I still pray. Don't get all youth group on me now."

"Well, to be honest, I'm kind of worried about you, John. You talk different, and you're acting like you believe evolution now and think we came from monkeys and all that. What the heck's going on with you, John?"

"Nothing's going on with me except you're givin me a bit of a headache."

"OK, ok, sorry. Hey, I know! How bout you give me a compliment, and then we'll both feel better, and I can get off your case. Remember how you used to give me compliments all the time? You'd say things like, 'you smell really nice today, Laura,' or 'your hair looks very pretty today, Laura.' Remember that John? Come on now and tell me something that'll make me feel better. I'm stressed out a bit with all this homework I have. Tell me something that will make me smile."

"Umm, well I just thought about how good it felt grabbin your pony tail that night. I just thought about it in the shower actually. Made *me* feel a lot better for sure."

"Ugh, you have become a real Romeo, John. A real Romeo. Maybe you should take a few tips from someone other than Matthew about how to talk to a girl. It sounds like he's bringing you along real nice."

"Yeah, you're probably right. Hey, I'm really looking forward to seeing you when you come back into town. We'll do something fun."

"Well, we'll see. Maybe I'll have a date or something and won't be able to hang out."

"Aww well, that'd be OK if that's what you want, Laura. Try and squeeze me in, okay cutie? I miss your pretty little face."

"We'll see."

"Alright, well I'm gonna go play some soccer down at the fields. Maybe there'll be someone down there to kick the ball around with."

"Sounds good. Toot-a-loo, Romeo."

"See ya soon, *Sassafras*. Bye."

The open space of the soccer field gave Johnny the isolation he was seeking. There were more than a dozen strung together on campus and were rarely occupied by anyone. He enjoyed the quiet to think while he juggled his soccer ball.

In the time since he had begun his studies at college, Johnny had bitten off a lot to digest. As a senior in high school he felt so much more confident about life. What he knew, he knew well, and he was free in his truth. He had known all of the answers but few of the questions. Now the principles that had defined his life were being assaulted; not by outsiders, but by himself. He was beginning to question what he believed, and some of his conclusions scared him a great deal. The fear was growling in his ear.

"*¡Oye, güero!* You are playing with all your friends?" The friendly voice brought Johnny's reverie to a halt. Johnny smiled back as the approaching Mexican kicked him a ball. There wasn't a soul to be seen, and he liked his sense of humor.

"How's your foot, *güevón*?" Johnny teased back to remind him of his juking months before. They slapped hands and bumped fists in the way of the day as Johnny made the usual salutation - "*¿Qué onda, güey?* means what's up dude, and the Mexican responded the like. Johnny realized they hadn't formally met and introduced himself, "*me llamo, Johnny, güey.*"

"My name is Manuel, but since you are now my friend, you can call me Manuelito." His English was great, and Johnny smiled back disappointed. A language is best learned when both spoken and heard. Manuel seemed to read his thoughts.

"Since my English is already perfect, and I do not need to practice it, we can talk in Spanish for you, *güey*." Johnny lit up, and they laughed together. Manuel's vowels tattle-taled his accent, and his cadence was a little trippy, but perfection is foreign to man. They spread out and passed to each other while Manuel babbled in Spanish. Johnny spoke back as best he could, but Manuel seemed to speak faster than a valley girl, and simply separating his words was difficult. Once his mind translated each word and formed meaning from slang, he was already three sentences behind. The topic seemed to be about *chicas* and *fútbol*, however, so Johnny didn't fret the exactness.

He waited for Manuel to breathe so he could insert a sentence. "You want some Gatorade, *güey*?" They walked to a metal bench and had a seat. Johnny passed the Mexican his bottle before he had a drink.

"What happened to your arm, *güey*?" Johnny wouldn't mar the topic with poor grammar, so he used English for all but the 'dude'.

It is almost pleasing to witness a child confront deformity in a person. Respectful adults have learned that it is bad manners to ask something of another which may cause embarrassment or shame. They will look away from the glaring as if it didn't exist and steal glances to allay their curiosity.

A child's wisdom is not yet sullied with these civil conceptions, and they will march straight up to the strange with some variation of, *what's up with that?*, as if they are proud of the discovery. The experience may be shocking at first, but as soon as an answer has been given they will move right along to other important matters. Those first thirty seconds may raise the pulse, but that sensation is natural and pure. An awkward moment is an adult invention that should have been left in the box.

Manuel wiped the sweat off his brow with his shirt and studied the distant oak trees in silence. He was gathering his thoughts, and Johnny did likewise. "When I was little, I was jealous of my big brother. He wrote with his left hand, and I did with my right. I say to myself, 'I'll show him!' so I started writing with my left hand just like he did. It was really hard at first, but after a while I could write with both hands. I guess it seemed like a waste of time then, but now that I look at myself I am glad that I was jealous." He took another drink and passed Johnny the bottle, pausing even longer this time.

"My family is from a town in Mexico called Rosarito. It is only about thirty miles from Tijuana and San Diego. When I had five years, my father was killed in a car accident." Johnny looked at his new friend but didn't say he was sorry. He had heard the response often enough since the death of his own mother to know it was worth less than the breath it required.

"Since I was a baby, my mother had always wanted the best for my brother and me. She would tell us how much she wishes we could live in the United States and learn English and get a good education. I guess there is nothing special about this, but she is still special." He paused again, and Johnny knew he was thinking about some memory with his mother. He did it all the time, too.

"My father's brother came across the border in the seventies to work in the fields of California. He worked very hard but made a lot of money, too. Sometimes when he gets to drinking his *Tecate*, he says he marched beside César Estrada Chávez, but I think he is full of *sheet* when he drinks."

Johnny chuckled at his pronunciation, and Manuel did at his humor. "In 1986, President Reagan and Congress passed the Immigration Reform and Control Act, and my uncle became a United States citizen, just like that! He is my uncle's favorite president." Manuel shook his head in wonder and laughed all delighted. His look of bemusement was like the friend of one who wins a large lottery - how something so desirable can magically appear without effort.

"Before my brother and me were born, when my uncle still lived in Rosarito, he made a pact with my dad that if one of them ever made it to the United States then they would help the other get there if he could. Right after he got his citizenship, he got offered a job working as a restaurant manager in the Midwest. My mother and father would have a big anonymous sum of money sent to their bank a couple of times a year, but they didn't hear from him. He didn't contact my family for fifteen years. He didn't see me and my brother born or even know that my father had died."

Manuel paused again to reflect, and Johnny studied the trees alongside him. "Then for some reason after September 11th, he called our house, right out from the blue. My mother cried when she heard his voice, and he cried when he heard about my father. They talked for a long time.

"When my mother hung up the phone it rang again a few minutes later. It was my uncle, and he said he hadn't forgot the pact he made with his brother. He came to Rosarito a few weeks later and went straight to the civil registry. The bookkeeping in Mexico isn't that good as I am sure you can imagine. My uncle likes to say that when records are kept in Mexico they are written with a pencil and never a pen. A few pesos in the right pocket can go a long way there."

Manuel looked over at Johnny and said, "I hope you don't mind all the details, *güey*. I guess I am giving the long version of my story."

"Not a bit. I like a good story." Manuel smiled and his eyes said thanks. "My uncle and father obviously had the same last name. He claimed that my brother and me were his children, and we moved here to live with him. My mom got her wish, and we got to go to high school right here in the United States!

"My uncle sponsored us as his children, and we both got our green cards and became permanent residents and worked part time at my uncle's restaurant. The work there was fine, but I have always dreamed to become a citizen. Then I could vote and help my mother to move up here with us.

"My uncle loves the United States so much. He always talks about how it is the greatest in the world and has given him so much to be thanking for. He is a good Catholic, and we always pray before every dinner. At the end he always says, 'Sweet Jesus, Shepherd and Lover of Souls, eternal rest grant your good servant Ronald Reagan, O Lord. And continue to shower love and protect his good wife Nancy. Amen.'" Manuel rattled off the ending with the speed brought from repetition and chuckled.

"He even has a big picture of Mr. Reagan dressed up as a cowboy in the living room. On the bottom it says Señor Reagan. When the census people came a few weeks ago, and my uncle let them into the house, you should have seen the looks on their faces! Here there was a bunch of Mexicans with some mariachi *musica* playing and a big huge picture of Ronald Reagan on the wall.

"The lady kept looking up at it and then at my uncle like he was crazy. I bet they hadn't seen that before!" Manuel's excitement had them both cracked up. He had gone so far off track that Johnny couldn't help but laugh at it all. As Johnny looked over at him his eyes flickered over the arm and brought Manuel back to his question. Manuel caught his breath and continued his story.

"I yet didn't have as much reason as my uncle, but I love this country as much as he does. The day after I got my diploma from high school I went to the office of the Army in the mall and said I want to join the Army of the United States of America." And the conversation sobered up. Johnny didn't know the details yet, but the answer to his question had become clear.

"I completed my basic combat training at Fort Benning, in the state of Georgia. Then I complete my Advanced Individual Training in Fort Bragg, North Carolina. It was the hardest thing I have ever done, but I never been so proud as when I got to wear a uniform for the United States." Manuel's chin lifted at the memory.

"After I had completed my training, I was transported with the 82nd airborne, 473rd Calvary to continue Operation Enduring Freedom in Afghanistan."

Manuel paused again and studied the distance, reliving memories and framing his story. "My platoon was located to this province in southwest Afghanistan called Farah. It is strange over there, man. It kind of looks like Mexico but feels completely different. It smells like dry earth before rain. It smells like burnt gunpowder and pain." What he said didn't make sense, but Johnny understood. He'd smelled the beast before too.

"It is like going back in time when you go there. It's like the Bible times. It's like nothing has changed since the Great Alexander was there. I had been there for about five months, and we were just starting to feel like we were in a groove. We got up early and went on patrol with some Afghan police that were stationed with us.

"When we first got there, I had my head on a swivel every step I took. I knew that any second we could be attacked with RPGs or walk over a bomb. Looking at me now is funny how scared I was about losing a leg from stepping on a bomb." Manuel chuckled, but Johnny just looked at the trees.

"I had a really good friend in the platoon. He was a really big *güey*, and he always stuck up for me in basic training. He was like my brother. His name was Joshua. We were on patrol one day, and he says, 'Hey Manuelito, I have to take a piss, *güey*.'

"The beginning of the day seemed just like all the others before. We walked a few meters off the road and take a piss. As we were standing there, I can still remember the color of the hills that morning, and the sky and that smell, and then I hear it coming."

Manuel closed his eyes and bowed his head as he relived the moment. "It sounded almost like the sound a zipper makes. Only it was so fast and coming right at you. The thump of the bullet hitting Josh in the chest and all his air knocked out of him is a sound I wish I never heard.

"I saw blood explode out of his back right before he looked at me. In that second that we were frozen it felt like someone hit my arm with a sledgehammer. I remember that feeling right then in my head. It was like my arm was screaming the pain, but it felt like a numb pressure in my head.

"As I go down, I lean into Josh. My vision had a black-like border that closed down as my legs gave out. I fell on top of Josh, and the last thing I remember is looking in his eyes before the black took me over. I wish I had not seen his eyes." Looking at Manuel now, Johnny was sorry he had asked about his arm.

"I woke up a long time later with a doctor smiling down at me. I asked him where is Joshua, but he didn't answer me. He told me that I was going to be fine, but I had been hit with two bullets from a sniper. One hit me right on the elbow, and the other one shattered my wrist."

Johnny looked over at Manuel's stump again. It was whiter than his skin and shiny. Gray scars ran up and around his bicep. The marks from where the stitches had been were still visible. A cool breeze kicked up and Johnny shuddered a bit.

"He said he was sorry that they couldn't save my arm. I didn't know it was gone until he said that. I look down, and there was a big bandage wrapped around the end. They had to cut it off... right here above my elbow. I started crying when I saw that my arm was gone. I tried not to cry, but I could not help it.

"Then I remembered Josh. I started screaming his name. I yelled, 'Josh! Josh! Where in the hell is Joshua! I want to know where is my friend! Where in the hell is my brother, Josh! What did you do with Joshua!'" Manuel choked up as he recalled the moment.

"A chaplain ran to me and tried to calm me down, but I was in panic. He told me that Josh died in the day before. I was screaming and crying and yelling at him and at God. I cried and cried until I had no more tears, but I still kept crying... I cried for a real long time."

They both were silent again. Manuel spoke as a man that has felt true loss in his life, but he was not ashamed of the tears on his cheeks. Johnny didn't let his get that far and rapidly blinked away their existence.

"After about a week, they sent me to another hospital in Germany for a while, and then they sent me back home."

Johnny cleared his throat and looked up at the trees. "So are you still in the military?"

"They were really nice and said they could find me a job at a desk or something else that I might like better. I said I wanted to go to college, and they helped me a lot with that. The first thing that I did when I got back here, though, was fill out the paperwork to be a fully naturalized citizen.

"In 2002, President Boosh signed an Executive Order that speeds up the road to be a citizen for those people that were in active service. Now I will be a full citizen of the United States of America in just three months! Can you believe that?" Manuel laughed out loud with his pride.

"You earned it, Manuelito."

"I guess I did," he chuckled again as he looked at his arm. "Of all the things that we use both our arms for the hardest for me is to tie my shoes. It is such a small thing, but it frustrates me more than anything else. I can never get them tight enough." Manuel moved his stump and grimaced as though he were still adjusting to the look and the sensation.

"But I would have to wait a lot longer to be a citizen if it wasn't for President Boosh. I know that a lot of people do not like him very much right now. I get upset when I hear them say bad things about him. I know he makes some mistakes, but everybody makes some mistakes in their lifes. I think that in his heart he is a good man. I like it when he speaks Spanish. His accent sounds funny and makes me laugh, but he is almost as good as you, Johnny." His eyes twinkled at his friend. "I hope that someday I can meet him and shake his hand. I really like President Boosh."

"So I guess you got some awards for what happened in Afghanistan?"

"They gave me a purple heart for losing my arm. I am proud of being in the war with the United States Army, but I am not proud of what happened to my arm.

"I think I would have liked to meet the great General Patton. I like his quote when he said," Manuel put on a gravelly made-up voice, 'Because no bastard has won a war by dying for his country. He has won it by making the other poor bastard die for his country.'" They laughed and looked at the trees again and Manuel said nothing for many minutes. But Johnny could tell he had more to say and let his friend break the silence.

"I have a cousin that has been working at my uncle's restaurant since he was thirteen. His name is Angel, and he is like a brother to me. He crossed the desert with his mother when he was eleven. It was a difficult journey for them. They walked all the way through southwest Texas. They had no drink for two days and it was very hot that year. They went up to a house to ask for water and a bit of food and the rancher shot a gun over their heads and called immigration patrol. They ran away and made it out, but it was very hard for them. Very hard."

Johnny didn't say anything.

"It makes me mad that people can be treated this way, but I understand it. In the south of Mexico, in the state of *Chiapas*, immigrants are treated much worse. They ride on train tops from Central American countries, trying to make it to the United States. They come from *Guatemala y El Salvador y Honduras y Nicaragua*. Many lose arms or legs jumping onto the trains. Many are robbed and raped and beat up real bad by *las pandillas*, the gangs. But some say the police are worse. A girl my cousin knew was raped for three days by *migra* police in a holding cell. She died and they said they found her like that and were never brought charges."

Manuel looked at the trees, and the breeze kicked up strong and cold. It brought goose bumps to their arms and necks and Johnny shivered a bit. Manuel looked over at him. "But all those people know, no matter where they come from, that when they cross into *Chiapas, Mexico*, they are facing the toughest part of their journey north, even tougher than crossing into the United States.

"Most of the Mexicans hate them there. They cannot stand immigrants. They will not help them. They steal from them and call the police on them. They spit on them and throw rocks at them and curse them in the streets. They sometimes beat them because they think the immigrants do the same to them. They think Central Americans are redneck and stupid and they all have a story about a Central American bringing in drugs or murdering or raping a Mexican. They do not like them at all.

"But the immigrants know this. They all know that there is a million things against them there. They all know they could die there. The immigrants call *Chiapas, la bestia...* the beast." A brown leaf slapped into Johnny's face. He had been listening but thinking at the same time. It startled him to attention, and Manuel continued. "But those immigrants also know, no matter where they come from, that once they pass through *Chiapas*, and get a little farther north, the people are loving and generous. *Oaxacans* are good people. They come out to the train tracks and hold out sweaters or soup or tortillas or beans for the immigrants to grab as they pass through on the train. They say prayers for them and let them sleep in their homes and churches. The police are much more nice to them, and the migrants start to feel that there are more good people in Mexico than bad people. *Oaxacans* understand how difficult their journey is, and they just want to help."

Manuel bounced the soccer ball off the ground. He reached down to re-tie his shoe but baulked at the forgotten effort, grimaced, and continued. "I understand why the rancher in Texas did what he did to my cousin and aunt. Americans respect private property and I respect that. I wish I had some property. I would protect it too." Manuel smiled.

"I also understand that the rancher probably did not like Mexicans very much." Manuel looked down and lowered his voice. "I do not like Arab people very much. I had never really seen any before the war. On television and in magazines, but I had never been around them. Any time I see one now, though, I automatically reach for my M4... when I see one." Manuel hung his head and his voice was rough and there was resignation in it. "I fucking hate them. Whenever I see an Arab looking person, I can't help but hate them. I know it is wrong, but I don't know how not to. I do not trust them. I just hate them."

Manuel coughed and looked embarrassed. Johnny just kept looking at the trees.

"So I understand why the rancher did what he did, but I think my cousin deserves a chance at citizenship like me. I do not know when that rancher's ancestors got to America, but they probably just got off a boat with not very much money and wanted to be Americans and wanted to work hard. That is all I wanted. That is all my cousin wants. He would work to be a citizen if he could. He would work construction building bridges or highways or whatever America wanted him to do to work for it. He really would, Johnny. He really wants to go to medical school, though. He wants to be a doctor and help people when he grows up. He will be a good man and he is very smart. Angel just wants to be a citizen, too."

Johnny looked at Manuel for a moment and then up at the clouds for a while. The breeze kicked up again to pull and grow the grass, and all the fallen leaves danced and swirled about. Manuel began bouncing the soccer ball with his good arm. He had a small smile on his face, but his brow had a frustrated set. He got up off the bench, kicked the ball in front of him, and ran after it, bringing his sad thoughts and their conversation to an end.

The two passed the ball around for a long time after their talk. They shared many laughs and stories as the earth turned her back on the sun. The bats seemed eager that evening, and showed up early for the night shift. And the gray doves were dozin, a bit noisy in their nests, sounding like hoot owls blowin through those old wooden train whistles. By and by the waning light brought the kick-around to a close.

J ohnny could smell the gathering as he opened the front door to his house. The living room smelled like a bowling alley. The men were gathered around the television smoking cigarettes and drinking from cans of *Bud Light* tallboys.

"Johnny!" Everyone in town got along with Johnny not only because of his athletic prowess but because of his smarts and humility and wit. He was the type-a guy that only an ass hole would dislike. Johnny could tell they had been at it for a while from the sanguine faces and volume of the greeting. He gave his dad a look that he could have read easily if their eyes had met. Johnny was by no means a teetotalling prude, but he hated that damn smoking smell in the house.

"What's up, fellas? Damn Bob, you're looking portly as hell this evening. Your wife finally get off the sauce and stop milkin that little mouse a yours once a month?" Bob told Johnny to go to hell, but he grinned around the circle like he had just won the lottery. The others loved it and beat the hell out of Bob's back. Mr. Daniels looked proud of his son.

"Hey Long-John, do me a favor and grab me another beer outta the fridge, will ya?"

"You got it, Bobby."

The attention of the ring of gentlemen quickly snapped back to the TV. As Johnny walked into the kitchen, he saw that they were watching Glenn Beck drawing on a chalkboard. They concurred with his irrefutable logic in reverent whispers as if they were in front of the holy pope himself.

Johnny heard someone growl in sympathetic outrage at something Beck said. The gentlemen were not loud but seething and riled. A commercial about buying gold came on, and they all began speaking at once.

As Johnny grabbed a couple beers, he heard his father say, "Now *that* man is a true patriot." Johnny had watched Beck quite a few times with his dad and shook his head. Fear isn't alien to a patriot but the two have nothing in common.

As Johnny walked into the living room, it became obvious that Beck had been discussing the original meaning of the 14th amendment. Apparently it had been designed with regard to Negro slavery, and the recent problem with anchor babies on the border hadn't entered into the drafter's intentions.

It was amazing to hear these men discuss the merits of a constitutional amendment, Johnny thought. After all, it wasn't just a piece of paper, but the bedrock upon which America had been built.

Johnny handed Bob his beer, and the man good-naturedly attempted to bring him into the discussion. "Hell, John, you're smarter than any of us. Can you believe how these Mexicans are takin over our country? I saw some census report just the other day sayin how there'd be more a *them* than there will be of *us* by 2050!"

This made one of the gentlemen on the couch very sad. He looked away all thoughtful and said, "Sweet Mother of God."

Johnny didn't have a chance to respond. A gentleman by the name of Todd immediately picked up the thread and carried it along its natural course. "That fuckin rag head Obama needs to grow a fuckin sack and fuckin do something about this shit. If he had any fuckin guts a'tall he'd string a fuckin fence a fuckin mile high and a hundred fuckin foot deep along the whole goddamn border down there. And fuckin make er electric while he's at it!" Everyone laughed all hearty, and Todd continued to spout his wisdom.

"That Kenyan... Muslim bastard won't do it, though. And you know why he won't? Cuz Hezbollah knows how easy it is to cross that goddamn border down there, and Obama's leavin the door wide open for em. Beck laid it out so clear the other day, guys. I tell you the God's honest truth right now - that bastard O'dumbo won't be happy til this country we love so dear goes up in ashes!"

Johnny Daniels lost his temper on rare occasions. The last time had been eight months previously during a soccer game. A defender had been so frustrated by his onslaught that he slide-tackled him from behind and almost broke his ankle in the process. Johnny had pummeled the man's face until his teammates dragged him off the field.

He had heard his dad's friend, Todd, voice his opinion on multiple occasions at Tea Party gatherings. They had been in much the same vein and always garnered nods and laughs. Todd had bowled a 255 that night and had good reason to celebrate. The beer had made him swilly, and ordinarily, Johnny just would have left the room.

Johnny had heard this thought too often of late, though. He had heard these thoughts much too often lately to let them go. After hearing Manuel's experience, he could let it go no longer.

"Todd! If I hear you call the president a rag head socialist one more time, I swear to God Almighty you'll wish you hadn't." His voice had hardly risen but a fire lit his eyes.

All the gentlemen were instantly flummoxed. No one had thought of Johnny as anything but an accomplice. His silences during these verbal romps had always been taken for youthful shyness. But Todd recovered quickly and stood up to the unexpected challenge.

"Well, well, well! So it seems we have a young bleedin heart in our midst, fellers. Looks like someone's been getting some *edjekation* in college! Whatcha gonna preach to us next, Johnny?" Todd had been double fisting his tallboys and waved them now as if he were conducting an orchestra. "That we should just let all them Mexicans come on up and suck us fuckin dry?"

His point was a damn good one, and his audience concurred with mumbled phrases of "No shit," and "Jesus Christ, Johnny." The man sitting next to Johnny's father had always really liked Johnny. He simply could not believe what he was hearing. He looked away all thoughtful and said, "Sweet Mother of God." Johnny's dad said, "Good God, Johnny, what in the *hell's* gotten into you?"

Johnny took a deep breath to steady himself. "I've never said this to anyone, Todd, and I don't say it lightly, but you're a real racist piece a shit. You know that?" Todd winced as though he had been physically struck. He set his tallboys on the coffee table.

He stepped forward, inches from Johnny. "How dare you call me that you skinny, damned puppy!" He hissed in outrage. "You take that shit back right now. I aint got no problem with blacks er colored people-a any kind." His breath stank of sour hops and cigarettes and Johnny's face showed his disgust, but he flinched not an inch from the bigger man.

"Sorry for using that card, Todd, but I aint sorry I said it. I call em like I see em. I've been watching y'all in your meetings," Johnny glared around at the others. "I've been listening to your rants. I've heard your threats and vows.

The worst part of it all is you don't even got a good reason to hate Mexicans. Most of em just wanna work a goddamn job that you wouldn't touch with a ten foot pole.

"And I'm fuckin done hearin all this birther shit about Obama that you preach every goddamn day. The reason you can't stand Obama isn't just cuz he's black but because he's black *and* liberal. You got no problem with a black Republican in a respectable suit, but a homie with his pants saggin is a different story altogether.

"You got no problem with a English speakin Latino man workin legal and payin taxes in some factory. But if there's a Mexican in a strawberry field speakin Spanish, gettin paid in cash because he's here illegal, well then, by God, that dirty spick should be on the first train south in chains.

"You go to the hospital and see a man from India in a long white coat reading a lab report. Hell, he's alright with you for sure. But if that same man was in some robes on a cell phone in a crowded mall, you'd think twice about not callin homeland security."

"You little bastard! Who in the *hell* do you think you are to talk to me like that? Fuck you, Johnny! And fuck that high horse you rode in here on!" Todd was panting with rage. His breath reeked and his eyes were savage. The vessels in his neck stood out as he ground his teeth. The man was on the verge of violence, but Johnny's chin was lifted and set. The gentlemen on the couches were slack-jawed and silent. The violence was imminent.

But Johnny had held his tongue far too long, and summed up hasty. "No Todd, in my book that's racism alright. It's just multifaceted hate and fear. It's just as politically correct as it has to be. It aint about thinkin or sayin someone's different but hatin em for it. It's brand new, but it never changed, Todd. It's about more than just skin color with you. I'm tired-a hearin it. You can call it what you like you ugly son-bitch, but it's all the fuckin same to me."

Todd was only about an inch taller than Johnny. Right at six foot, he hardly looked down at the boy that had spoken like a man. He was a welder and had the wiry, tattooed arms and thick neck that bespoke his strength. He had fifty pounds on Johnny soaking wet.

It wasn't what Johnny said, but the way he said it that had kept Todd's natural reaction at bay. By this time it had been fully processed, wrath was found and formed, and only divine providence interrupted the ensuing mêlée in the form of an opening front door.

Matthew Ryan had knocked on the front door of Johnny's house a few times. These occurrences took place only when it was locked. Matt considered it uncivilized to knock upon a dear friend's door. As the door opened and he stepped into the living room, he took it all in in a heartbeat.

The gentlemen sitting were utterly dumbfounded. Johnny and Todd were inches apart. Two jaws were locked and four fists were clenched with knuckles drained of color. It wasn't until he glanced at the television that Matthew completely understood.

The golden commercials had long ended. Beck was in a split screen with one of the most beautiful women Matt had ever laid his eyes upon. It was easy for him to unravel the logic of the situation. If there were anything in the world that Matt loved more than a roll in the hay, it was engagement in a violent fray.

And in his experience, there was only one *good* reason why two grown men would physically harm one another - to win the love or affections of a woman. Looking at the angelic countenance on the screen, the two men on their toes with clenched jaws, moments from violence, Matthew let forth his intervention.

"Now, now fellas, let's not lose our heads here. I'm sure there is enough of the gorgeous governor to go around." No one moved a hair; the static tension electrified the air. Matt's quiver was forever loaded, and he tried again.

"I don't know about you guys, but I am in freakin love with that Palin. Just look at them lips and those eyes. And my God, the way she pronounces those o's! I know, right

Bob? I'm all like *Oh! Oh! Oh!* I know she's got a few years on me, but I would definitely do er."

Crickets and Sarah were all to be heard. The tension still crackled like a kindling fire. The standoff was yet undeterred. But Matt had faced tougher crowds and was un-phased.

"Man, I watched an interview with her last night before I went to bed. I had to throw my boxers *and* sheets in the wash this mornin cuz a that little hot potato. Wish I had that dream on tape for you boys. I was just lovin it strong! Now that was some sweet action." Matt put on his *o*-face and started humping the air.

The charm of the third try along with the air-humping finally garnered reaction. Mr. Daniels picked his jaw off the floor and crawled from under the weight of his son's verbal avalanche.

"Jesus H. Christ, Matthew! What in the hell is wrong with you? If we were ever dumb enough to want your opinion we'd ask you for it. As usual your two-cents are overpriced!"

"Well you can have it for free, Mr. Daniels, cuz I aint sellin today." Matt crossed his big arms over his chest and leaned against the door frame. Todd finally took his eyes from Johnny. He glanced over his shoulder at Johnny's best friend.

Matt hadn't the look of a care in the world as he examined his fingernails. The lopsided grin on his big square jaw was pure amusement. A long leg was casually crossed o'er the other. His stance was pure in its nonchalance.

Nobody was fooled.

Anytime Matthew got into a fight the whole goddamn town heard about it. No one had heard about one in months, and it wasn't a poor assumption that he was gettin itchy.

It was an unspoken rule around town that no one could mess with Johnny aside from Matthew. The thought of him losing was almost unfathomable. He had that peculiar trait that big, mellow men possess of going from zero to all out, red-eye-rage faster than a Ferrari. And Matt's full speed was very high, indeed.

Todd didn't take long to make his decision. He spun on his heel and stormed out towards the back door as he yelled at Johnny's dad. "You've got yourself a real pinko there, Jack! Better you than me! You've done one helluva job on that one!"

"Todd!" Johnny brought the man to a halt. Todd turned slow and looked him right in the eyes. He was still mad as hell but would call him a puppy never again.

"I *ever* hear you talk about *any* American president like that again. I *ever* hear you say anything bad about a Mexican again..." Johnny paused and closed his eyes momentarily for emphasis. "I will beat yer goddamn ass like a rented mule. And that's not a promise; that's a good ol fashioned, American made guarantee. Understand, pork-chop?" He hadn't raised his voice, but the fire burned his eyes like Satan's stove.

Todd stormed out the back and slammed the door. The windows shook at the force, and Mr. Daniels looked at his son with sad and confused eyes. "What in the *hell's* gotten into you Johnny? How could you say those things in front of my friends?"

But anger overcame him quickly, and he flung a finger at his son. "Damn your eyes, Johnny! God damn your eyes!"

Johnny was still on fire. "Damn my eyes? Who the hell do you think you are, Dad? Johnny Cash or Sam Hall?"

"Don't you *dare* bring your namesake into this!" he jumped up and screeched with incredulity. He would forever be his favorite. "That is beyond the pale, Johnny!"

Matt knew the situation still had a long hill to slide if left to itself. "Come on Johnny, let's go for a walk, bud."

Mr. Daniels was almost crying from shock. His feelings were sorely hurt. "That's right! Get the hell outta here - right now!" One of the more swilly gentlemen stammered his two-cents just so he could partake in the action. "Yeah! Get the hell outta Dodge, pinkos!"

The man sitting next to Johnny's dad just looked sad. He shook his head and said, "Sweet Mother of God," for the final time and drained his tallboy. Matt steered Johnny out the door and winked at the boys.

T he air was cool, and the ground shed the day's heat as the men strode briskly down the sidewalk. The sun had lashed her tail across the sky, leaving pretty streaks of pink and gold and white in the wake; and the bending breeze through the sycamores and the soft sounds of nature brought Johnny's anger down. Matt hadn't said a word since they had left the house. Sometimes walking is more soothing than talking for a man. He let his friend break the silence.

"Well, that didn't go very well."

Matt scratched his chin and looked up at a little white butterfly that fluttered past them. He smiled for a second. It seemed so aimless as it wobbled away on the wind, up the street and around an oak. He's out late, Matt thought.

And a lone cicada was droning on in a nearby tree. It hummed on and on, not pausing to listen or look around or even take a breath, but calling out to something, all alone on its branch. Strange to hear this time a year, Johnny thought. He tugged on his earlobe and looked at his shoes.

"No worries, dude. That Todd guy is a real chatch. He's probably pissed his name is Todd for Chrissake; real twat-waffle, that guy. I was prayin he wanted to fight. I thought he was gonna go for it, but he wasn't drunk enough, I guess. I could feel the rage rising up, man. It was about to get ugly, but I guess I'm glad he left. Real twat-waffle, that guy," Matt said.

"Yeah man, but I shouldn't a snapped like that."

"Chilax, bro. You've just been watching too much Fox news with those guys. I only watch when I know Sarah's gonna be on. Let's go to my place and watch something else on TV. Hell, you being such a pinko and all, we can watch some Stewart and Colbert." They laughed together.

"Sounds good, man. I hope that Livvy Munn *chica* is on Stewart's show tonight. She's a flat-out fox, dude... Damn I'd like to beat that ass up."

"I had a nightmare about her the other night, man." Johnny looked all skeptical at his best friend. Matt once had a wet dream about a mossy rock. He elaborated to allay Johnny's confusion.

"I got set up on a blind date with her by someone. Well, it was a halfway blind date. I obviously knew what she looked like, but she'd never seen me. She was sittin at the table in a nice restaurant. She was wearin some kinda low-cut, blue silk dress, and damn my eyes she looked fine as hell.

"Anyways, as I was walkin up to her, I was really nervous. She looked up while I was approachin from across the room. When she first saw me and realized that I was her date, I read her lips. She said the worst possible word a woman can say when she first sees her date. I woke up sweating and panting, dude. It was fuckin terrible."

Johnny tried to think of what word it could have been for a few seconds before he broke down and prompted his friend. "Well, what the hell'dja see her say?"

"She said, 'shit,' bro."

Johnny laughed out loud, but Matt was stoic as he relived the nightmare. Johnny helped him along and kind of changed the subject. "So who do you like better, dude, Stewart or Colbert?"

"Hell, I dunno, man. They're both pretty funny. I guess Stewart. Colbert is funny, but he's not pee-your-pants funny. About a year ago Stewart said somethin hilarious that surprised me, and I laughed so hard that some pee came out." They laughed again.

"Plus, I heard somewhere that Colbert is a Canadian spy, dude." Johnny knew Matt was just babbling to chill him out, but he appreciated the effort.

But Matt was serious and sought to explain. "Member when we were watching the Vancouver Olympics a while back and he came out on stage? Member how stoked he was to be in Canada? He had that Canadian pop singer Buble dude on, and they sang Canada's national anthem together. He was pretendin to read it off a card, but he knew it by heart, dude. He was just gushin at Buble the whole time. I didn't buy it, yo. Plus, I heard him say, 'eh' a couple-a times the other day to one a his guests."

They laughed again. Matt could ease the tension before an earthquake. "I don't think Canada has spies in the U.S., dude," Johnny said and thought for a moment. "But I guess the way he says his name is pretty Frenchie, though."

"**M**atthew, this is Ahmed. Ahmed, this is Matthew." The two slapped hands and bumped fists in the way-a the day as they grinned at one another.

"Hello, Matthew. It is very nice to meet you."

"You too, broseph. Johnny tells me you're one smart mutha-fucka." Ahmed still wasn't used to this type of language he heard often from Americans. He had taken English classes since he was a small boy, but this form of address had never been covered by his Oxford trained linguist. But he adapted as best he could and gave it a go for himself.

"Thank you, Matthew. I have seen you with many ladies, and I am very fond of your skills. Really very good. Real fucka of muthas."

Matt belly laughed with delight. "Fucker of mothers. Damn, dude. I've never heard that before." He paused and repeated it slower to himself. As he rolled it around his palate, Matt decided he liked the taste. "You mind if I use that sometime, dude?"

"Of course, broseph. Be my guest."

Johnny smiled at the pair and looked around. It was an unusually warm December day. Winter had shown up in a gradual manner this year - more noticeable in her shortened days than a drop in temperature. The first snow had yet to come around. All the trees, save the evergreens, had shed their foliage to blanket the grass, and a warm southern breeze scattered all the fallen leaves here and there. Although the branches swayed and whispered to one another, the trees seemed dead in the wintertime, Johnny thought to himself. The air had little perfume but smelled fresh and clean, and the low southern sun colored the brown surroundings as best it could.

"So dude," Matt said to Ahmed, "I heard you got a thing for the blonde *femininas*. You been havin any luck with em lately?"

The question would have embarrassed Ahmed if it had been asked a few days previously. He had never been very good at talking to women, but he loved them very much. The way they walked and dressed and smelled was very appealing to him. He had asked thirty-two out on a date since he'd been to the States. Two days ago, the thirty-second had said yes. Ahmed was very proud of himself.

"Yes Matthew, it was very difficult at first, but I think I am getting the hang of things. I asked a blonde girl out to the movies this weekend, and she said yes." Ahmed beamed with pride at the two. It was his first American girl, and, though they hadn't even gone out yet, he considered it a great success.

Matt kicked the ball to Ahmed. "She hot?" he asked all interested.

"I think she is very beautiful." Ahmed hadn't lost his smile, and Matt chuckled at the dreamy look in his eye. "She always wears long dresses and has curly hair and has light green eyes. Her skin is clear and creamy white... and she is very pure."

This last part was confusing to Matthew. He looked at Johnny all confused, and then back to Ahmed. "Very pure? What the hell are you talkin bout, broseph?"

Ahmed smiled again. He was so proud to be discussing his date with an American girl to his two very good American friends.

"I almost did not approach her to invite her to the cinema. I thought she was already betrothed because she wore a ring on her marriage finger. But I am so glad that I did. When I asked her about it, she told me it was a purity ring her father had given her when she was fourteen. She is very pure."

Matt's eyes flew wide, horrified. He looked at Johnny, then back to Ahmed, and then up to heaven. He shook his head all sad and said, "Sweet Mother of God."

Matt rubbed his eyes dramatically and shook his head again. He felt bad for Ahmed. Real bad. He was walking into something he simply did not understand. Purity rings meant no payoff... no hope. Growing up in a Christian school, Matthew had had plenty of experience with those goddamn purity rings. And he hated them dearly.

He had been like Ahmed once, naïve and confident in his abilities to overcome this seemingly insignificant piece of metal. One of the prettiest girls at Almighty Wonders had worn one. She got it when she went to a *Promise Keepers* rally with her father. Matthew had messed around with her a few times before the rally, but afterwards, she would hardly even look at him. His best efforts to make out with her went unrewarded and unappreciated. Every time he tried she would just pull back and smile kinda sassy-like and twirl the goddamn thing around her finger and shake her head and bat her pretty little goddamn eyes like, *but... Jesus is my boyfriend now.*

Matt collected his thoughts for a moment and spit the bad taste of past failures onto the ground. He looked up at Ahmed, and, though he was upset, he spoke to him gently. "Ahmed, listen to me dude. I know it's hard to get chicks to go out with ya sometimes. Trust me, I've had plenty-a bad experiences gettin rejected and shit like that. But dude, just keep tryin and you'll get a better *chica*. Johnny and I'll help. I swear ta God we will. Won't we, John?" Matt had a desperate look in his eyes.

Johnny smiled at him. "Hell I dunno, man. Maybe Ahmed likes this *chica*. Maybe they'd get along well." Johnny laughed at the withering look Matt gave him.

Ahmed could see Matthew was upset and he finally spoke up. "Matthew, why are you so upset about this purity ring? What does it mean to you?"

"It means you aint gettin shit, dude." Matt put on his most serious expression. "You wanna take a chick out to movies and on dinner dates and picnics and shit and not get anything but a pecker of a kiss in return, then be my goddamn guest." Ahmed looked un-phased, and Matt grimaced at past memories. That girl had gotten very good at keeping his tongue out of her mouth. How she could kiss on the lips for so long and not let her tongue loose he'd never understand. But that was in the past. God, she'd been hot though.

"Just let him give it a go, man," Johnny said to Matt. "If he doesn't like her then he can have the satisfaction of telling a girl no for a change. It'll be good for his confidence. Aint that right, Ahmed?" Ahmed smiled again. He was so proud to be discussing his date with an American girl to his two very good American friends.

Matt looked at Ahmed and rubbed the back of his neck in a dramatic manner and finally acquiesced with his hands. He felt bad for Ahmed. Real bad. The poor bastard was way up shit crick and he didn't even fuckin know it; and, judging by the dreamy look in the poor guy's eye, the goddamn paddle was floatin away fast.

Matt was at a loss for words. It didn't happen often, but when it did, it meant he was in some sort of deep emotional stress. He kicked the ball back to Johnny and looked down at his shoes. "I swear ta God," he said all soft and sad, "that *thing* means ya aint gettin shit, man."

Johnny passed the soccer ball to Ahmed and laughed again. He knew they would get along well. Matt and Ahmed were the type-a guys that only an ass hole would dislike. The topic changed quite suddenly to a discussion on the rules of cricket, and Matt seemed interested in Ahmed's excitement about the game.

"Matt, did you know that you can squeeze sandreed leaves between your fingers and it'll squeak?" Johnny said out of the blue.

"Hold up a second, Ahmed. What, dude?" Matt said.

"That prairie grass that's everywhere West River up there. Member we were talkin bout it that one day? It's called prairie sandreed. When you pull on the tips, it'll squeak at'cha."

"What the hell? Jesus Johnny, not now. Can't ya see I'm tryin ta figure this shit out," Matt said back a bit flustered. He turned back to Ahmed. "Where were we, dude? Oh yea, whack it? No... *wicket*? What?" He was learning the vocab.

Johnny walked a ways a bit to enjoy the surroundings. He took a deep breath and smiled around. He had spent a great deal of time on the soccer fields at the university, and he always felt more comfortable in wide open surroundings like these.

He knew where it came from, too. It was a reflection of the peace he found up in South Dakota, just west of the Missouri and a little south of the Cheyenne, where lavender grows wild in the low spots and the wind breaks short of the sun; there on the wavy, gold prairies of the broken lands, where coyotes cry most nights at the moon and prairie chickens cluck and coo at nothin in particular, up there where the muleys stot and the antelope graze and bison dot the distance again, where the ring-necks go to gravel at sunset, where pothole ducks sport all of nature's colors and the smell of burnt gunpowder has plenty of right to exist, up there where the game is tough and the air is good, where the Natives still live and men know what they have. Johnny smiled. No matter where he stood his heart was always there.

"Hey Romeo, quit daydreamin about Laura, and pass me the goddamn ball."

"Yeah, Johnny, please pass Matthew the goddamn ball."

The guys formed a triangle and began passing the ball around. Matt stopped the ball under his foot and smiled. "So, Johnny, I pulled a Davies on my old Comp teacher yesterday."

Johnny's eyes flew wide with horror. He scolded his friend immediately. "Matt, you dumbass! You can't be pullin that type a shit in college, man. They kick people out for that crap, dude. We're not at Almighty Wonders anymore, Matt, seriously!"

Matt looked hangdog at the chiding and passed the ball to Ahmed. Johnny felt bad for snapping at his friend. "What the hell'dja do that for, bro?"

"Cuz she gave me a B *minus* on my comp paper that I spent two hours workin on. I know, right Ahmed? Two freakin hours of hard work, and then she gives me a goddamn B *minus*! God it pisses me off when teachers give you a grade with a minus after it. It's like beatin a dude up and then taking a piss on im while he's lying on the ground. I'd rather a gotten a C *plus* than a B *minus*. You can tell a teacher's got no class when they give their students minuses. What kind of a sick person puts a minus after a grade when they can just leave it as is? Pluses are OK, but minuses are just tacky and unprofessional, bro. Freakin ridiculous."

"Well, I'm guessing you got away with it since you're standing here smilin about it like a dumbass," Johnny said.

Matt's face lit up again. "It was perfect, man. She had no idea. She's like eighty years old. Everyone in there was practically rollin."

"Don't do it again."

Ahmed spoke up for the first time. "What does this mean to pull a Davies?"

"We had this speech teacher in high school named Miss Davies. She was really sweet and nice and pretty good looking. She had the biggest DSLs in the whole world. She was too nice to ever get anyone into trouble, and Matthew tortured the hell outta her our junior year."

"What does DSLs mean, Johnny?"

Matt answered for him. "It means dick suckin lips, bro, and you shoulda seen em. She had the biggest, softest lookin dick suckin lips in the whole wide world. I'd a killed for a blowie from her. You shoulda seen em! *Huge* DSLs," he said.

Johnny smiled as Ahmed absent-mindedly put his fingers up to his ear. He figured he was reaching for a mechanical pencil out of habit to take notes on the new word.

"During speech class Matt would always raise his hand and tell Miss Davies he wanted to put his penis in her mouth. But he muddied up his words big time so you could kinda tell what he was sayin, but she was never sure."

Ahmed started laughing, and Matt took over the telling. "So Mrs. Sanford hands me my paper with a big fat minus on it and kinda pursed her lips at me when she did it. Kinda like she was real disappointed in me getting a B minus. I know, right Ahmed? She's the one that gave me the B minus, and then she looks at *me* like it's my fault that *she* put it on there. Jesus Christ, bro, you shoulda seen it; the minus was bigger than the letter and it just pissed me right off.

"So, she keeps passing out other people's papers, and I could see what they all got on *their* papers and none of em had minuses. I saw a shit ton-a *pluses*, dude, but no minuses. So I just couldn't take it anymore, and I knew it was time for the Davies." Matt beamed with pride at the two.

"So, I raised my hand, and she called on me all bitchy like it was a waste a her breath to even say, 'yes, Mr. Ryan.'"

Johnny was shaking his head but couldn't help laugh at what he knew was coming. The only time he had ever peed his pants outside of infancy was when Matt pulled a Davies for the first time. Matt put on an off pitched, singsong voice that some would say sounded like a mentally handicapped gentleman on crack with a mouth full-a shit.

"I said, 'Merthes Thanfor I wuhna pudda payneth en yuh mawww!'" Johnny started cracking up like old times and Ahmed did too. It really was funny.

"Everyone looked at me like I was retarded, and she said, 'Matthew, what did you say?'

"So I go, 'I said, 'Mertheth Thanfor Iya really kindtha wuhna puddtha paynaaah en dah mawt!' Now all three were laughing all hysterical. Ahmed was grabbing his stomach, and tears were coming down his cheeks. Johnny laced his fingers behind his head and tried to blink his away.

"Well, that's when a couple other dudes got what I was sayin, and they started crackin up big time. Mrs. Sanford looked worried that I was havin a seizure or something - she's like eighty years old. So she goes, 'Matthew, are you all right? What are you trying to say, honey?'

"So I'm practically rollin now, but I held it together, and I cross my eyes and grab my neck, and start shakin a bit and go, 'Mertheth Thanfor Iya wahnnuh kindtha really wuhntha willhya lemme pudd mah paynath ehn ya mawwwwt!'

"Then everyone got it, and they were all laughing their heads off. One dude told me later that it was the greatest thing he had ever seen. Mrs. Sanford thought I was havin some sort of breakdown or somethin, and she looked around at everyone all pissed, cuz she thought they were laughing at my handicap or somethin. So she walks up to me all freaked out lookin and says, 'Matthew, are you alright? Do you need a doctor? What can I do for you honey, just relax.'

"So I go, 'naw Iya nawa nahyda dawktah, budda.. buddha... budda, Iya reallya reallya yah! Yah! Yah! Ya... wahnna yahh! Pleatha, pleeeea, pleeeeeassah!... I wahntha puddahn awhl dah myah payneth en yah mawwwwwt!'"

Matt could hardly talk he was laughing so hard but finally caught his breath. "And that was the last time I did

114

it, cuz I saw a little spark in her eye like she kinda knew what I was sayin. If she had been recordin it she woulda figured it out on the replay. I just kinda shook my head and hands and uncrossed my eyes like I was coming out of a seizure or somethin. She cocked an eye at me, but she bought it. But the class was laughin like crazy. Wish I had it on tape for you boys. It was awesome."

Matt kicked the ball back to Johnny. It took a long while for the three to catch their breath. Every once in a while they would start belly laughing all over again as their thoughts flowed freely amongst them. The conversation danced here and there like all the fallen leaves.

Sometimes the young men were very wise, and would say things like:

"The last time I lost is the last time I won, dude. Seriously, man, think about it - it's deep."

"Ronaldo is ridiculously awesome, man, but he's got nothin on Messi. Messi is a little genius. You can scratch at it, but there ain't no stopping *La Pulga*. The Wee-One is just on fire every game. The difference between Ronaldo and Messi is Messi will pass the ball in front of the goal so that his team can score. Ronaldo passes the ball in front of the goal so he can get an assist. Ronaldo will go down as one of the greats, but Messi will go down as the greatest."

"Man, I'd like to shank that Genesis Rodriguez *chica*. Seriously, fellas, she's got that look to her. Real come hither type look. I just know she's freaky as hell. I bet she talks so filthy in the sack – just filthy. Look at those eyes-a hers next time you see her on TV. I just know she's freaky as hell. She's a flat-out fox, dude. God, she's *rica*. Damn, I'd like to beat that ass up."

"Anytime a chick says somethin bitchy like that to you, just call her a fat ass, broseph. It'll get a rise out of any girl no matter how she's put together. It'll make a fat chick sad, it'll make a skinny chick mad, and it'll make an average chick both. Or you can just call her a cum-dumpster. That'll get a rise outta any chick, too, broseph."

"The darker the berry, the sweeter the juice, dude."

"So I just told him straight up, I says, Jesus Gavin, I don't know why yer braggin to everyone about it so much. It aint that big a deal, man. I gag on my toothbrush sometimes when I'm brushin my teeth and tongue in the mornin. And my toothbrush is small as hell, dude. Just cuz she was drunk off er ass and threw up all over it doesn't mean you're hung like a goddamn mule. That shit's happened ta me like... hundreds a times, dude."

"You've got pretty good skills, man, I'll give ya that. Me, on the other hand, well I don't know if you knew this, but I can make women come with my eyes. And I'm not scared of anyone, man. The only man I fear is myself."

"You gotta pin that one side with your thumb real good then pinch the other side over it with your two fingers, broseph. Unhooking it aint that hard if you plant your thumb good. Most guys try to just pinch it together or unhook it with the thumb. That aint the way, man. You'll end up having to use two arms and reachin around like that will make you look like a real twat-waffle. You gotta plant that goddamn strap between your thumb and her back real good."

"I dunno why, but it completely ruins the whole thing when they don't just swallow it. I told that one *chica* that it would make her hair shinier if she started takin it down the hatch. She cocked an eye at me, but she bought it. I think it's actually workin, too. I saw her in the union the other day and her hair looked super shiny, man. It really did."

"You hafta let the chick know that you're interested, broseph. You gotta let em know that you wanna beat it up."

"You don't gotta own a dog to know what dog shit smells like. Seriously, man, think about it – it's deep."

Sometimes the young men were very curious, and would ask things like:

"Do you have any idea why my eyes cross when I splode, yo? They can't really get stuck like that forever, can they?"

"Man that Governor Palin is pretty as hell. She really is. Don't ya think she's beautiful, man? Do you think I'd have a chance with her if she wasn't married? I don't think I've ever seen a picture of her *be*hind, though. Do you know if she has a nice ass, man?"

"Why do people say that they could care less about something when they are inferring that they do not care about it at all? Should they not say, 'I could not care less?'"

"So, what's your favorite *pa-zish*, man?"

"Do you have any idea why black chicks don't want to have anything to do with me? I wanna know why they won't hook up with me. I really do."

"When exactly do you use the word pretty as a quantitative adjective, broseph? Is it used to say that something is about seventy-five percent? Does kind of hot mean she is fifty percent hot, and pretty hot mean she is seventy-five percent hot?"

"You guys ever accidentally have a wet dream about your aunt when you were younger? Yeah, me neither. That *is* gross."

By and by the conversation moved on to other important matters as they kicked the ball back and forth. Matt noticed Ahmed's cleats for the hundredth time and complimented him on them.

"Damn, Ahmed, those are some nice kicks you got there. Are those *Nike Mercurials*?"

"Yes. I got them at a sale in Cairo. They are very nice. Do you really like them?"

"Course I do. Those things are pimp, dude. That bright orange really pops, man. Those are the same ones Ronaldo wears. I've only seen them on the big boys in the European leagues."

"What size do you wear, Matthew?"

Matt cocked an eyebrow at Ahmed. "About a twelve...why?"

Ahmed bent over and checked the numbers under the tongue of his cleats. He was unfamiliar with US sizing. He lit up when he saw the number 11.5 in the US column. He sat down and began unlacing them. Johnny said, "Ahmed, what are you doin, bro?"

"I am removing my cleats. I want to give them to Matthew."

Matt looked surprised and embarrassed. "Jesus, Ahmed, you don't need to do that, man. I was just saying how cool they are. Hell, they're yours, man."

Ahmed removed the right cleat and began working on the other. Johnny spoke up again. "Ahmed, dude, seriously, that's really nice of you and all, but you don't need to give Matt your boots. Seriously, bro."

Ahmed removed the second cleat and stood up. He walked up to Matt wearing a big smile and handed him the cleats. Matt hesitated but accepted them reluctantly.

"Matthew, what the hell! Give him his shoes back, dude. Those cost a few hundred dollars, man; seriously."

"He wants me to have em though," Matt muttered as he stared all dreamy at the *Nikes* in his hand. He looked up at Johnny as he stroked the soft leather and said, "but he *wants* me to have em, John."

"It is fine, Johnny. Like you said, they are mine, and I want Matthew to have them. They are just shoes." He turned and looked up at Matt. "I will remember the story about you pulling a Davies for the rest of my life. You have very big balls, Matthew, and I would be honored if you would accept the gift." Matt looked like he was about to cry, and Johnny smiled at the pair. Matt grabbed Ahmed and gave him a big bear hug.

"Thanks a lot Ahmed. Damn my eyes, that's super nice of ya. Thanks a lot, man. Jesus, Johnny, you didn't tell me what a good shit this guy was." Matt was almost weepy and tried to coarsen up the situation as Johnny laughed at him.

Ahmed grinned up at Matt again. This was another bit of English his old linguistics teacher had left out of his lessons. He would have to teach *him* a few things when he went back to Cairo.

"Thank you, Matthew. You also, are a very good shit." Matt beamed back and rubbed an invisible bug out of his eye. It was one-a the nicest goddamn things anyone had ever said to him.

"Would you like some gravy with your mashed potatoes Johnny?"

"Nah, thanks Jennifer, I'm good. Dad go to one-a his meetings?" Jennifer nodded at him and smiled. Johnny hadn't spoken to his father since he and Todd had almost come to blows. When he was home for dinner he would eat in front of the TV alone while he watched Fox news.

"I guess Dad's still pissed at me."

"Oh he'll get over it, Johnny." Johnny had always liked his science teacher. She had introduced him to the scientific method when he was in 6th grade and had eventually started teaching high school science. She was very nice and had a chubby little face that smiled a lot. She had started coming over a lot more recently to make dinner for Johnny, and they had been talking more than usual since his father had stopped eating dinner with them.

"So how are your science classes coming, Johnny? I hope I prepared you well." She laughed at such a sarcastic statement, but Johnny just chuckled a little. Of course she knew that she had done a great job preparing him for the rigorous tutelage and common pitfalls of college Biology.

"So I'm sure they started preaching evolution right off the bat to you guys." She looked up with a smirk from her chicken fried chicken and potatoes.

"Yeah, well they teach it a heck of a lot different than you did, Jennifer." She looked back down at her plate but kept the same expression. The warning bells lit up in her head, though.

"What do you mean, Johnny?"

"Well, you always told us you were teaching evolution and the things that were obviously wrong with it. But your version of evolution was pretty wrong, Jennifer." She looked up at Johnny, and her heart beat faster than it had moments previously. Johnny was almost like a son to her. She sort of agreed with him about what he had said to his father's friends, but this was scary stuff he was getting into now.

"I mean, when I was a senior and we had those lessons about evolution. Do you remember that lesson about flightless cormorants on the Galapagos Islands? You taught us that they used their wings in the past, but natural selection favored the offspring of those that had smaller wings or no wings because they weren't using them. It was natural selection, alright, but the result was a loss of genetic material. Winged to wingless is devolution, as you said."

"Of course, Johnny. I still am teaching the lesson."

"Well, first of all, devolution isn't even a biological word."

"Well regardless of whether it is a word or not, we humans did not evolve from bacteria, Johnny. That is ridiculous."

"I think you would rather talk about evolution on a large scale like you do just because it makes it more unbelievable. You can say, 'how can we humans come from bacteria?!' Because that is very hard to believe.

"Evolution isn't some ladder that is being climbed up to more advanced and complex organisms. Heck, a water flea or corn or types of worms have more genes than a human. There is no such thing as 'more evolved'. Evolution is just change. That is all it is.

"You always say you can't add genetic information, but it would be more correct to say that genetic information just changes. The changes in the cormorants on that island you like to refer to were the result of a whole host of factors.

Genetic drift, speciation, mutation, and natural selection - just to name a few.

"You say natural selection can occur, but genetic information cannot be added to an animal's genome. I had to wait til I met Dr. Likins and asked him questions that I realized that evolution isn't some mysterious being that scientists made up to discount God. All it is - is change.

"Organisms don't evolve, populations evolve. We know that a freakin chihuahua came from a wolf. I mean, that is an amazing difference to have occurred by man's selection in so short a time period. You say, 'yeah, but it's still a dog.' You say, 'it is still the same kind like they say in Genesis.'

"But geez, Jennifer, come on and think a little bit. Look at how plastic DNA can be. You say a chihuahua is still a dog just like a wolf is a dog, but your imagination stops there? I mean, there are a few different definitions of species, but the biological definition of a species is the ability to mate in the wild. I'm not saying a wolf might not jump a little bitch chihuahua, but those two sure as hell aren't having puppies together."

"Well, Johnny, you bring up some good points, I suppose. But even Darwin was upset by the lack of transitional forms in the fossil record."

"Well come on, Jennifer. You and I both know that there isn't one single animal that could be observed in a fossilized state that you would say, 'Hey! Now there's a transitional form!' You would just say it is its own species no matter what it looked like. Every single fossil ever found is a freakin transitional form.

"Look at the dog example I was just talking about. Every sire of a chihuahua, all the way back to the wolf, was in transition when observed temporally. Humans steered the change by selecting certain traits like nature does in the wild. Farther back in time, foxes and jackals and coyotes all have a common ancestor with the wolf. We wise humans have a common ancestor with chimpanzees and all other apes, extinct or extant, whether you like it or not – just like foxes and wolves have a common ancestor."

Jennifer picked up her fork and shook her head sadly.

"If I were suddenly fossilized and compared to humans 10,000 years from now, I would be a transitional form. My wisdom teeth I had pulled last year, for example, are vestigial from when our ancestors needed them to grind down plant material. Humans will rarely have wisdom teeth hundreds of generations in the future. We don't need them, so our descendants won't have them.

"Take the specimen found in Germany called Archaeopteryx as another example. Anyone can just look that up on the internet if they'd like to. It's a beautiful fossil and about the size of a crow. Its wing outlines are plain to see, and it has sharp teeth and three fingers with claws and a really long, bony tail. I mean, its skeleton has more in common with small theropod dinosaurs than with birds.

Jennifer kept shaking her head.

"What I mean is that it is an example of the beginning of avian evolution, and you roll your nose up like that, like I'm trying to sell you a rotten fish or something."

Jennifer appeared shocked at the landslide of information coming from her former pupil. She was truly scared for him. Maybe she should speak to his new professor, she thought. Johnny had obviously been brain washed by the man. She squinted at him now and tried to fathom what could have happened to his mind. He had been such a promising student, she thought sadly.

Jennifer pushed her plate away and pouted at her potatoes. She wasn't hungry anymore. She looked up and chided him half-heartedly, but Johnny was just getting warmed up.

"Well, Johnny, there's no reason to get hostile."

"I'm not hostile, Jennifer, I haven't raised my voice."

"Well, if evolution was true, then there would be transitional forms living right now! What about that, mister?" Jennifer raised her jaw and smirked as if she had really deflated the evolutionary balloon with her incisive dart of wisdom.

"Come on, Jennifer, it's the same as what you say about the fossil record. The rates of change vary greatly, but every living thing is a transitional form. Look at the array of life that exists today. You portrayed evolution as a chain of species evolving up and up into one another. It is more like a tumbleweed that shows different species branching from shared ancestors, then becoming extinct, or branching again and again into other species throughout large spans of time.

"You say transitional forms or missing link; like the theory is missing a key piece of evidence that it inherently needs to be true. Those terms are used by people who don't know what the hell they're talking about." Johnny knew Jennifer had a Master of Science, and he finally got a spark out of her as she looked across at her unruly pupil.

"Johnny, I've taken a lot more science classes than you have, and you know that." But her saddened interest quickly turned to dismay as she realized the implications of what she was hearing.

"Gosh, Johnny, I just can't believe this. So you believe in evolution now? What the heck happened to you?"

"I don't *believe* in evolution, Jennifer, I *know* in it. I don't *believe* in algebra or electricity or astronomy, either. Belief implies faith - knowledge implies evidence. What I didn't understand I read for myself. College has taught me that you must question whatever you believe in order to know it. Schools need to teach reading and critical thinking before they teach science."

"Good God, Johnny." Jennifer was so sad. She really was. "I just can't believe you've swung so far away from all we taught you at Almighty Wonders. You've been in college six months, and you've already completely changed your mind on creationism?"

"I didn't change my mind, Jennifer, my mind changed me. All that happened was that I was curious about these things and so I asked Dr. Likins questions. Hell, I prefer a curious man over a smart man everyday but Sunday."

"That's very cute, Johnny." God, this was so sad. It really truly was.

"Evolution isn't some religious march towards perfection, Jennifer. *All it is - is change.* You say that creationists have nothing to defend because it is God's word, pure and simple. You snipe at evolution so you can believe it's not possible. I can do the exact same to you. You would consider yourself a scientist, and you believe that the stories in Genesis are true, right?"

"All Scripture is God-breathed and useful for teaching, Johnny," she sighed. Johnny was getting fired up, but Jennifer's mind had already retired to a reticent peace as she frowned at him in compassion. It is amusing to watch an individual that ascribes to creation argue with an individual that doesn't *believe* in evolution, but simply acknowledges it, debate the topic. The scientist will always get more fired up because he is so frustrated that you aren't listening to his reasoning, and the creationist will be so at peace because you are not listening to his answer.

"Yeah, but you actually believe that a few thousand years ago a man named Noah literally put all the species in the world on his wooden boat after they were summoned there by God."

"I am a Christian, Johnny, of course I believe it."

"Well, Jennifer, I won't even tackle the logistics inherent to such an agglomeration of creation. If I said something about just all the different insects alone not being able to fit on the ark you would say, 'the Lord works in mysterious ways.' Or if I said anything about dinosaurs not being able to fit you would say that God only summoned the babies to trek across continents because they would provide more room than if Noah tried to fit adult brontosauruses and T-Rex's and elephants and giraffes, right?"

Jennifer hadn't ever heard anyone describe the actual process in such a way and simply nodded. Like many Americans, she still believed it, of course. She had to still believe it because her pastor and Sunday school teacher had tied Jesus' message to it, and she was a Christian, after all.

"So let's not even talk logistics. Do you think God had Archaeopteryx go on the ark with Noah or just had it fly overhead while the earth was flooded? Then, after it miraculously survived this deluge, it became extinct from a much less dramatic occurrence? Obviously you know what marsupials are."

"Johnny, you're getting hostile and strident with me and I don't like it. Don't patronize me, and quit talking to me like I'm an idiot."

"Jennifer, an idiot isn't someone that doesn't know, but someone that doesn't *want* to know. And I'm not hostile, I didn't raise my voice. Something like three-fourths of the world's marsupials are found on Australia and New Guinea. Right after they got off the ark do you think this group got together, since they were all marsupials, and said, 'hey, let's stick together and go to Australia. We'll have to cross a massive mountain range and swim across vast stretches of ocean to get there, but we're marsupials, after all, and marsupials stick together. When the swimming gets real tough we'll just stick together and make it to Australia.'

"You first taught me about the duck-billed platypus, Jennifer. Talk about a transitional form! That is an egg-laying mammal called a monotreme. It is one of only a few mammals that is venomous and the only one to use electro-location in its bill. It has a tail like a beaver and feet like an otter. Did that little beaver like animal waddle from Mt. Ararat in Turkey, where Noah's ark landed, all the way across Asia, swim hundreds and hundreds of miles in the ocean to arrive in Eastern Australia and Tasmania?"

Jennifer began re-arranging her cutlery and plates. The tablecloth was really getting old, she thought. And it still had that big wine stain on the corner. She'd have to pick a new one up sometime soon - maybe tomorrow. Light blue would match well with the kitchen curtains. Light pink would too, but Jack would never go for that.

"Did penguins get off the ark and waddle all the way down the African continent a few thousand years ago and then decide to swim thousands of miles to Antarctica? Did you hear about that blind pseudoscorpion they found just the other day in Colorado? It is a cave dwelling spider with venom filled pincers just like a scorpion. It is about as half spider - half scorpion as you can get. If that species didn't change over time into what it is now, then did it migrate a few thousand years ago from Noah's ark, all the way across Asia, across the ice covered Bering Strait, and then make its way down the coast without getting eaten or stomped on along the way? What about the lungfish? Talk about one of your transitional forms. It is a fish that breathes air and has lungs not gills."

Maybe she would cook fish for supper tomorrow night, she thought. Jack loved fish, and she hadn't cooked it in a long time. It would be great to grill up some walleye. (That was Jack's favorite fish.) Darn it, though, they never sold it in stores this far south. Maybe there was some in the deep freeze though. That would be a good way to use up all those lemons in the fridge, too. There might be an extra pack of walleye that had slipped down below everything, but if so it was probably freezer burned by now. Darn it to heck. Oh well, she could always pick up some salmon from *Sam's.* (That was Jack's second favorite fish.)

"Genes from all our common ancestors that aren't used anymore even get randomly expressed *en utero* and even rarely after birth. You don't see this just in humans but in every living thing. Sometimes dolphins and whales are born with hind limbs. Sometimes human children are born with a freakin tail, Jennifer. Atavistic and vestigial features are predicted by evolution, but creationism scrambles to explain them."

Jennifer finally raised her hands to stave off the onslaught. "Okay Johnny, that's enough. You've made your point. Just don't start telling me the earth is some ridiculous number like six billion years old, please." She laughed at the peace offering but Johnny didn't.

"I can't believe you taught us the earth is 8,000 years old, Jennifer. God, your logic is bananas. Do you have any idea how long it takes light from other galaxies to get to us? It takes a *hell* of a lot longer than a few thousand years. It can take *billions* of years!

"The only way science is incorrect about the universe being billions of years old is if God is trying to trick us by constantly dropping light that close to the earth. God, Jennifer, the Milky Way is a hundred thousand light years in diameter! It takes a hundred thousand years for light to travel from one end to the other. And the Milky Way is one of *hundreds of billions* of other galaxies! So you think God dropped that light from other galaxies real faint and real close to us, just to trick us about how far away they are? I don't *really* know the guy, but I doubt he is that devious and capricious.

"And don't even get me started on radiometric dating. You like to denounce radiometric dating by using an example or two about some hack trying to make a point about how unreliable it is. You act like radioactive dating is some kind of scam contrived by evil scientists to discredit your beliefs. You believe that the earth is a few thousand years old just because Moses supposedly recorded his ancestry back to Adam. God, Jennifer, seriously?"

"Yes, Johnny, I believe it because I am a Christian! I don't believe God would lie in His Word! It's MY truth and I'm sticking with it!" Johnny's arguments were really getting through to her.

"Jennifer, scientists try to age things based on definitive scientific data that are repeatedly validated, and you just want to date things because Moses said so. Every single scientific field, from astronomy to geography to chemistry to biology to geology to paleontology, and all those in between, support the fact that the universe and earth are billions of years old. Scientists don't *believe* this. They just observe it by testing their questions.

"But you put more weight in Moses' version of his family history than all of these? These fields aren't out to prove God or Christians wrong like you think in your mind. They would just rather look at empirical evidence than believe yours."

Jennifer had been sitting good-manneredly through Johnny's attempted swaying of her faith, but now she just grinned a bit and looked at him sadly. She looked at him like he was truly lost, and it made her sad. All this was just so sad.

"Well Johnny, I am glad that you are asking questions. That is good, but the fact remains that it is still the *theory* of evolution, and if it is taught in schools, it should be taught alongside creation. Many Americans believe in the creation story, and they have a right to have their views taught in school. The debate and the faults of each should be taught in classrooms, Johnny." It took Johnny but a second to respond to the tired and specious argument.

"Jennifer, you are using the word theory in its colloquial sense, as a guess or unknown. A theory in scientific terms is an enormous body of evidence that repeatedly bolsters a hypothesis. When a scientific theory has been around for a long time it is basically a fact. Like the atomic *theory* that matter is composed of atoms - is a fact, or plate tectonic *theory* that continents drift - is a fact. Evolutionary *theory* is a fact - that is a fact."

Ugh, she had forgotten about how chipped the Daniels' plates were. This one in front of her had been badly chipped a few years ago. That big oaf, Matthew, had done it. She should just throw it away. Jack would never know. Maybe if he saw that the number of plates was dwindling he would buy a new set. Maybe she should just buy them a new set. So domestic, she thought and smiled to herself. But it would be a very nice thing to do. Jack wouldn't get real excited about a new set of plates, but it would be a sweet little thing to do.

"Jennifer, every year there is a poll taken of a large number of Americans. They ask random Americans if the earth rotates around the sun and if that takes around 365 earth days to happen. Every year, about fifty percent of the respondents answer no. They don't believe that the earth moves around the sun and takes 365 days to do so.

"Since so many people believe *that*, do you think that our biology or physics classes should teach that? After all, the heliocentric *theory* that the earth revolves around the sun is a scientific *theory*, ya know."

The dinner had long been finished, and Jennifer ended their frustrating conversation by getting up from the table and collecting the dishes. She had a small smile on her face as she washed the plates in the sink. She would get them a new set this weekend. Jack wouldn't get real excited about a new set of plates, but it would be a sweet little thing to do.

Johnny had made some good points, but nothing would shatter her faith in Jesus Christ. As she smiled and hummed her tune, Johnny stared at the table and scowled.

The best teachers in the world speak less than their students. They realize that the difference between education and brainwashing is the former nourishes questions while the latter nurtures answers. The ultimate purpose of education isn't to supply answers but to spark questions. Being right or being wrong has nothing to do with being happy.

"I tell you what, Ahmed, that freakin Chemistry teacher is really startin to make my blood boil."
"What does blood boil mean, Johnny?"
"It means gettin me worked up and a few other things, too."
"His demands aren't that excessive, Johnny. You are just getting upset because you have so many hours."

"Ahmed, dude, this Chemistry assignment is fuckin ridiculous. I know you did it in an hour and a half, but you're not normal, man. I didn't start taking Chemistry and Calculus in sixth grade."

Johnny was in a rush to get his work over with. Matt had texted him earlier that there was an uncommonly high proportion of ladies at a house party. A lot of girls to Matt really was a lot of girls. It was a Saturday and the word would be out soon. When the fellas heard about it, the see-saw would swing the other way.

"Hey Ahmed, are you a Muslim?" Ahmed had been overly excited about a chemistry problem when Johnny fired the unexpected question. He sobered up quick and looked meekly at his paper. He sighed as he chewed his pencil eraser and looked over his periodic table of elements.

"My family has always been moderately wealthy. We have a library in our house that is full of books in many languages. There are a few books that outline the history of my family. They go all the way back to the 16th century when the Ottomans invaded and took control from the Mamluks.

"I have read these records of my family many times since I was little. Going all the way back to that time and even before then, my family has all been Muslims."

"So you're a Muslim." Ahmed looked away and sighed a bit. He wasn't ashamed of being a Muslim. He never had had any reason to be. But Johnny was the best friend he'd made since starting college in the United States. He wasn't ashamed of what he was, but he didn't know if Johnny's attitude toward him would change.

"Yes, Johnny, I'm a Muslim."

"Well, I was askin because I wanted you to come to this party with me. Matt says there's a ton-a really hot blondes there lookin for some warmth. I reckon you wouldn't wanna come, though, cuz there'd be alcohol there." Johnny was grinning, and Ahmed smiled from ear to ear. Coming from a culture with mostly dark haired women, he couldn't get over that visceral fondness for blondies.

"Blonde American *chicas* make my blood boil, Johnny. I will have *7Up* without the *Seagram*'s." They laughed as they closed up their books. Ahmed had picked up Johnny's habit of calling girls *chicas*. It sounded funny when you knew where he was from.

"Ahmed, I think the Qur'an only forbids you to drink wine if you're goin to prayers. I won't tell yer mama if you wanna have some whiskey tonight." Ahmed had obviously never been privy to this opportunity to imbibe, but his grimace didn't suppose he would take advantage of it. Johnny chuckled at his friend's confusion as they walked outside.

"Your new eyebrows sure do look good, bro." Johnny punched his shoulder and Ahmed smiled.

"Yes, Johnny, I had them waxed at the salon. I must be honest, it was not a pleasant experience. I am not used to them yet, but if you say they look better, I trust your judgment."

"Dang, dude, it must be our lucky day. We're so hot right now we might not even need to go compete with that bastard Matthew."

On the way to the car, a couple of dolled up soro girls had hurried to cross their path and get ahead of them. Staring at their high-slipped skirts and perky shirts, the boys agreed that they had good reason to do so.

The two pairs converged at the T in the sidewalk. Johnny put his arm around Ahmed's shoulder to slow him up and drawled, "Your servants, ladies," while grinning slightly. Ordinarily they would have thought the comment weird, but Johnny's confidence made it interesting. They had never been addressed in such a manner, and they passed one of Johnny's first tests for quality girls - *check*.

Their bubbly giggles most definitely passed the test. Test number two had been the view from the reverse angle as they walked away - *check*. Test three wafted back along their trail with the warm dusk air.

Johnny smelled honeysuckles from his backyard along with flowery lotion and a hint of vanilla vodka. *Checkmate*, he thought to himself.

Ahmed smelled warm milk and honey along with lotus blossoms from his uncle's garden. He smelled a hint of something else, too, but couldn't put his finger on what it was.

"Man they smell nice, don't they, Ahmed," he whispered. "Watch this, bro," Johnny mumbled.

"Please excuse us, ladies." They turned with alacrity to the invisible lasso and the fellas closed the gap. Johnny gave both pairs of eyes his complete attention and put on his best half-cocked smile. Ahmed blushed and immediately took a keen interest in a red line of ants on the sidewalk.

"My good friend and I will be attending a bit of a *soiree* a little later. Ahmed here had the audacity to bet me ten bucks that I couldn't find the most beautiful women on campus to accompany us. I tell ya what. Why don't you *chicas* come along, and I'll buy y'all a drink with my winnin's."

The girls paused in their random thoughts to digest these words. After a few breaths they passed test number one all over again. Ahmed must not have gotten it. He was quiet as a shadow.

"Okay!" The hotter one knew she had sounded too excited and immediately put more poise into her response.

"We're parked in lot C," she said, quite refined.

"What a coincidence, so are we!" Johnny said, quite pleased.

"Okay, well, you can follow us then!" The less hot (but by no means not) of the two responded much too excitedly. The hotter one shot her a wide-eyed *'simmer down'* look as they turned again.

"Trust me; we'd be more than happy to follow you two." Johnny assured them they were interested, and the girls giggled again. Appropriately, they were much more reserved this time.

There was one more crosswalk to pass on the way to parking lot C. It was on a not so busy road on the edge of campus with a speed limit of about forty miles an hour. It had a flashing yellow light on a pole for the benefit of the drivers.

As they approached the road, Johnny and Ahmed were completely absorbed in the great view. A beautiful setting sun was behind them as they walked along the sidewalk, but that view was much more predictable and could wait its turn.

The *chicas* were about ten feet in front of the boys. Johnny had become mesmerized at the clack-clack-clack of the hotter ones heels. He figured he'd have to teach Ahmed a little more sociology about the picker-upper getting first pick. Clack-clack-clack; man she had beautifully shaped calves. And that *behind* was just ridiculous. And how the hell do girls get their hair that shiny and soft-looking, he wondered. God, she was fine as hell. She really was...

All of a sudden he heard tires screeching and saw Ahmed leap forward - fast as a flash.

The dude had had a really bad day. It was about to get way worse. His boss had been on him all day about not getting the goddamn convenience store floor sparkling clean. He had justifiably wondered why in the hell a convenience store floor needs to be sparkling clean; it's a goddamn convenience store floor for Chrissake.

He wanted to drive fast in order to get home to a well-deserved chill session. He couldn't wait to chief some of that new OG he had - it was some serious fire. Sticky as hell, and it had that lemon-fuely funk to it. He could almost taste it as he stared at the windshield. Four tickets in the past year prevented him speeding home, though. As he approached the crosswalk he had approached hundreds of times, he resigned himself to a cigarette.

When God decided to invent bands he probably had *Sublime* in mind. The dude cranked up Sublime's song, *Ain't No Prophet*, as it came on the radio. God that is a good song, and they never play it on the radio. As he pulled a cigarette out of the soft pack he fumbled it loose. He had drunk a lot the night before and was still shaking a bit - needed to cut back on the booze for sure.

As he looked down to retrieve the cig, he heard the scream. His heart jumped into his throat as he glanced through the steering wheel. He slammed on the brakes with both feet.

But it was too damn late. He knew as he hit the brakes that it was too late. For one person it was too late. For Johnny's good friend Ahmed, it was just too damned late.

J ohnny stood frozen in the middle of the street. Ahmed had lunged forward in the blink of an eye. With two bounds he dove full out like a baseball player in a suicide slide. At full reach he hit the girls hard in the back and sent them sprawling - just out of the way of the car tires.

Ahmed's backpack was full of books. There was Organic Chemistry along with the study guide and lab book. There was a hardback physiology book that was very thick and a few calculus books, too. If the tires had hit his back he would have been fine. *God damn it, God.*

The sound of screeching tires along with a woman's scream is an awful sound for those who have never heard it. So is the *crunch, crunch* of your friend's skull being smashed into asphalt. It raked Johnny's spine as he stood there - frozen.

The seconds slowed down. Birds stopped chirping. The sunset was red, and the wind was gone. Johnny's eyes were wide open but unbelieving. Ahmed was gasping and grunting. Ahmed was making the worst sounds Johnny had ever heard. Ahmed was dying. He knew he was dying. Ahmed was dying. Dear God - he was dying right there!

Ahmed's dying. Ahmed's dying. Dear God Almighty - he's fucking dying right there.

Johnny jumped to his friend and cradled him in his arms. The little car was a few feet past them. *Ain't No Prophet* was conspicuously littering the air. The girls were up on their knees, looking back at what had happened in horror. Ahmed's eyes were rolled back in his head and his eyelids flickered electrically. Ahmed was dying. *No God, please...*

His body was convulsing all over. His lungs were pumping - savage and disconnected. The car had rolled right over his head and neck. *Ahmed's dying. Please God, please. God damn it - he's dying!*

There were no last words. There was no lingering eye contact or happy sentiments to relay. He died in Johnny's arms in under a minute.

Men and women cry in completely different ways. There were many tears and flailings as the ladies cried with their eyes - completely uncontrollable.

Johnny was inconsolable.

He hadn't cried in a long time. He hadn't cried at Davy's funeral even though it took all his strength not to. He hadn't cried when Manuel told his story about losing his arm even though he had wanted to. He hadn't cried about losing his mother in a long time, either. But once he opened up, it all came out in a rush.

And so, Johnny paid his dues over Ahmed. And though he cried with his eyes like the girls, his tears came from someplace else. They came from something within him much deeper and personal. They came from a place where men don't always like to go, a place inside yourself where some say God will come and live if you ask him nicely, but it's a place where the Devil lives too, a place where peace and pain can co-exist; and Johnny went there then, to the place where all his fear and hope were kept, and he emptied it all in gut-wrenching sobs.

It is the only time a man is truly inconsolable, when any consolation is simply superfluous, when true sorrow is being given what rightly belongs to it. The beast was racking him. It was a living, breathing thing that invaded every facet of his being. It lashed his guts and squeezed his heart and choked his throat. He couldn't breathe or swallow. The beast was anguish and pain and sorrow.

Johnny cried and cried. He cursed God, and the driver, and the paramedics that came soon afterward. He cursed himself and his reflexes. He cursed everyone and everything he knew. Johnny cried until he had no more tears, but he still kept crying... he cried for a long time.

"How ya doing today, buddy?" Mr. Daniels could tell that Johnny had slept very little as he walked into the kitchen. His eyes were puffy and red. The silent treatment he had been using since his son's outburst had been immediately discarded the night before.

Johnny had walked in the front door with the pale face of a zombie in anguish. He had blood all over his shirt and dirt on his face. His eyes were completely cried out, and Mr. Daniels flashed back to that day long ago when his wife and eldest son had been killed in a car crash.

The only thing that love can gain from loss is the realization of its presence. The loss of that day rushed back to him instantly as he jumped off the couch and ran to Johnny. He hugged his son hard and forgave him without words, realizing again that time is too precious to waste pouting.

Johnny opened a cabinet door and grabbed his favorite cereal. As he poured himself a bowl of *Lucky Charms*, his father spooned oatmeal into his mouth at the kitchen table. He tried to distract his son with conversation. "How bout I put on a little Mozart for ya, bud. Member how your mother used to like to listen to that stuff during breakfast?"

"Okay, yeah, that sounds good, Dad," Johnny mumbled. He sat down at the table and began eating his *Lucky Charms*. Mr. Daniels lifted the lid on the dusty CD player in one of the cabinets. He inserted a CD that had 'classical' written on it. It came over the speakers slowly, and Mr. Daniels sat back down and smiled to himself. Johnny knew he was thinking about his mother. He did it all the time, too.

"You have any good dreams last night, bud?"

The question reminded Johnny of a lesson he and Len had gone over in one of their many office meetings. It was about how men recount their dreams to one other, and the reasons for these strange memories that present themselves during sleep. One of the very first of man's dreams was the terrifying sensation of falling and jerking awake that all have experienced when nodding off. It is one of the useful examples of evolution to be seen in these primal dreams - when dozing and falling out of a tree was, in fact, a real danger. The offspring of those that weren't fortunate enough to have these dreams are now just dust and bones. Johnny grinned to himself. He liked Len a lot.

"Nah, I can't remember any, Dad."

Mr. Daniels began waving his hands up and down like Johnny's mother used to do. He wouldn't have done it in front of anyone else. Johnny smiled at his unusual antics that he knew were for his benefit. "Yer mother used ta love this part, son," he waved his hands dramatically, "right... here!"

And Johnny's eyes flew wide. The floor seemed to tilt underneath him, and he grabbed onto the table with both hands. The dream came back to him in a rush. The song had triggered something in his head that hadn't been there before, but now it was clear as glacier water. His color drained from him, and goose bumps invaded his skin. His breathing came fast and he said, "Holy shit, Pops."

Mr. Daniels was immediately alarmed. Johnny looked as though he had seen a ghost. As the song played, the dream became clearer and clearer, as though it were happening at that moment.

"What's wrong, John? Are you OK? Jesus, Johnny."

"I just remembered my dream. Jesus, Dad, it's clear as a bell."

"What was it son?" Mr. Daniels was worried. Johnny wasn't usually given to drama, and his eyes had a kind of glassy look. He looked sick and pale.

Johnny took a deep breath as the Mozart rang out. It took on a slower, haunting pace, and Johnny sat there trying to sort it all out. God, it was so clear now. He could still hear those voices, as though they were speaking to him at that very moment. They sounded both far away and right next to him at the same time. He could almost feel their breath on his cheek. Their eyes had been clear as crystal and blue as the sky. He could still see their eyes so clearly. God, did that really happen? Johnny looked his father square in the eye, and he told him his dream:

"Last night while I was dreaming, an angel came to me.
He sighed, 'harken to my whisper, my wisdom is for thee;
Tears are shed for you alone, those two have other creeds;
Do not cry for long gone men, they are safe and sound with me.
The homo and the rag head are safe and sound with me.'

Last night while I was dreaming, an angel came to me.
She sighed, 'harken to this knowledge, God's invented love for thee;
Tears are shed for you alone, and spoil fond memories;
If you must remember, please do it joyfully.
The homo and the rag head are safe and sound with me.'

Last night while I was dreaming, an angel came to me.
He sighed, 'if you must remember, I'll tell you what they need.
They do not need your wetted eyes, nor sullen lullabies;
They do not need your thoughtless prayers, nor empty, fragrant deeds;
They do not need your mumbled whispers, nor giddy hopes passed by;
They do not need man's dedication, nor his dainty needs.'

Last night while I was dreaming, an angel came to me.
She sighed, 'the homo and the rag head are safe and sound with me.
If you must remember, please do this thing for thee;
Lift an arm up high to heaven, your eyes to life unseen;
Take a breath of life-God-given, and cheer them joyfully:

Good work, sir, and Godspeed!

> *Good work, sir, and Godspeed!*
> *Good work, sir, and Godspeed!*
> *Good work, sir, and Godspeed!'"*

Johnny spooned some *Lucky Charms* into his mouth and shook his head as though he were coming out of a daze. Mr. Daniels continued working on his oatmeal after Johnny recited his dream. His face did not show it, but inwardly he was relieved. He had done his share of experimenting in college just like anyone else. His son had obviously started chiefin dope in the mornings, 'wakin n bakin' them hippies called it, and maybe that was the source of his newfound liberal thinking.

As long as Obama doesn't go and legalize it in his second term, he almost called him a rag head in his thoughts, but he would never do that again. He had sufficiently recovered from his son's outburst to come to terms with what he had said in front of his friends.

"John, I know you feel guilty about not stickin up for Davy that day in the parkin lot."

Johnny didn't respond and stared morosely at his cereal. He'd broken down and told his father and Jennifer about it a few weeks previously during dinner. There hadn't been a day go by since then that Johnny didn't think about the incident, and how sticking up for Davy then may have prevented him taking his own life. It had kept him from falling asleep quickly on many a night.

"I wish I could take you huntin more often, son. I really do. We used to go all the time when your mother was around. It's just with work and evrathin it don't seem like I get many chances to take off durin the fall. You and me've had some pretty good times up there in South Dakota, though, haven't we, bud? God I love that goose huntin up there on the Missouri. Sittin at Mail Shack up there northa Cow Crick; tall, brown prairie grass wavin in the wind, lookin down at that big blue river. That's heaven, man."

"I'm gonna buy a ranch up there by the river one day, Dad. I swear I am. I like that country West River, though, too. That broken country along the Cheyenne is perfect for a wildlife haven. It'd be really sweet to have a piece out there in Jones County next to Ted Turner's spread though, too. God, I love that wide open prairie. Pheasants, deer, geese, buffalo, and antelope... God, I can't wait to have a ranch up there. I'm gonna get it one day, Dad. I promise ya. I really am."

"Yeah, ol Teddy's got a hell of a nice spread up there, son." Mr. Daniels frowned a bit and nodded. "You've always been a dreamer, bud. You definitely got that from yer momma. Don't ever lose that dreamer tendency a yours. Don't ever stop shootin for the moon, bud. Cuz when you do, yer dead."

Johnny had inherited his father's dream to own a ranch in South Dakota. They often dreamed of the day that they could afford to purchase a nice sized piece of land together. They would raise bison and plant shelter belts with apple trees and be true stewards of the land.

It was good to have dreams, his father thought, but they leave a hole in your soul if they're too big for your means. He glanced up at a yellowed, old picture of a young boy and a big black lab on the wall and changed the subject.

"When I's about ten years old, I wanted a huntin dog so bad. I tortured the hell outta my ol man, and he finally broke down and said I could get one. We drove all the way over to Rapid to get a good AKC pup. I still remember seein ol Muley for the first time. God he was a brute. Biggest pup in the litter by far. He wasn't the smartest pup, but God, that son-bitch had some paws on im. I knew that he was the one. God, he was a brute."

Johnny smiled at his dad's thick northern plains accent. He was awful used to it, but when his dad got excited or talked about old times it really came out in his *o's*. He glanced up at the picture and smiled with his father.

"I worked with him quite a bit but not as often as I could have or should have I spose. He had a hell of a nose on

140

im, though. Hell of a swimmer, too. He coulda swam clear cross Lake Oahe with a twelve pound goose in his mouth. He really coulda. He was never that great at retrieving, though. Oh, he'd go and get the bird or the stick or whatever you tossed, but he didn't like to give it up when he came back. It was a game for im more than a job. Especially when there was people around. If there was other people around ol Muley'd start showing off. He'd bring it right up to ya then jump away and dance around like a big ol dumbass.

"One day I was workin with him down at Capitol Lake. Guess I's about thirteen at the time. He was doing good that day actually. He was really gettin used to the idea of puttin the stick in my hand without dinkin around first. One of our neighbors was walkin by and seen me and ol Muley. He was a pretty good hunter and a hell of a lot better at trainin dogs than I was. So he walks on up and says, 'hey, Jack, lemme see how ol Muley's comin along.'

"Well, that's when I got scared that Muley'd make a fool a me again. I figured with Tom standin there, Muley'd get to dancin around with that stick in his mouth and have me chasin im all over hell and high water. I figured Muley'd make me look like a real dumbass in front-a Tom, and he and my ol man would gimme a hard time bout it later on.

"So here I am with the stick in my hand. Tom was lookin at me. Muley was lookin at me. I could read both their faces. Their eyes were sayin, *throw the stick! Throw the stick!*"

Mr. Daniels looked down and rattled his fingers on the table. "So what do I do? I tell Tom I gotta get goin. I put Muley on his leash and walked back home. I didn't even give ol Muley a goddamn chance. I was too worried about how I'd look if he let me down." Mr. Daniels scowled at the memory.

"You're gonna meet a lot of people in this life that you don't agree with, son. Smart guy like you should have more friends that you disagree with than friends that share yer opinion on evrathin; if you don't, then yer just not working hard enough. There's a lotta opinionated people out there, bud." Mr. Daniels looked up at the photo for a moment and continued, "Every man's got an opinion that's right, but not every man's got an opinion that's correct."

Johnny and his father both looked down at the table. "I guess what I'm tryin to say is sometimes the little things in life are the things that affect us the most. What happened with Davy aint your fault, John. Don't forget about that day in the parkin lot, but don't dwell on it either. We all make mistakes, son. We all do things we wish we could change or take back. I didn't throw the stick that day like I wish I would have, and you didn't stick up for Davy that day like you wish you would have. Learn from it, and the next time you get that scared feelin in yer gut, son... Well, just throw the goddamn stick."

The two finished their breakfast in companionable silence. Johnny picked up the bowls and set them in the sink.

"You bout ready for church, Dad?"

"Johnny, did I ever tell ya that I hate kids?" Johnny had interpreted this common phrase of his father by the time he was six years old. He smiled back at him.

"I love you too, Dad." Being right or being wrong has nothing to do with being happy.

"Romans 1:24-28 says, 'Therefore God gave them over in the lusts of their hearts to impurity, so that their bodies would be dishonored among them. For they exchanged the truth of God for a lie, and worshiped and served the creature rather than the Creator, who is blessed forever. Amen.

"For this reason God gave them over to degrading passions; for their women exchanged the natural function for that which is unnatural, and in the same way also the men abandoned the natural function of the woman and burned in their desire toward one another, men with men committing indecent acts and receiving in their own persons the due penalty of their error. And just as they did not see fit to acknowledge God any longer, God gave them over to a depraved mind, to do those things which are not proper.' If I had the audacity to try, I would not say it any better than that sainted man, Paul himself."

Johnny could tell from the initial Gospel reading that this wouldn't be one of those cheer-you-up types of sermons. But not all sermons are supposed to simply cheer man up. God lies it on each pastor's heart what sermon they decide to preach on Sunday to their congregation; they are simply the vessel through which the God of love gives His broad and gracious message to His children in the most efficient and logical manner that is possible - along the clear and consecrated channel of prayer that was established by God and not priests, but given to man as a merciful gift that is pleasing to both the Giver and the wonderfully unworthy servant, which is abundantly just and proper and righteous and moral and sanctified and exquisitely uncorrupted by the servant and profoundly unpretentious and always unembellished and authentically unassuming and verily lacking the slightest whiff of ostentatiousness and always patient, kind, loving and never boastful and not easily angered and full of rejoice in the truth and not in any way self-seeking and never wayward and always good, beautiful and right in the eyes of the Creator, who, in a very knowable and understandable manner, has performed an extraordinary and amazing miracle that, quite fortunately, resides in the requisite belief that the servant may know the mind, heart, desires and utter will of God (in whose image he has been so unctuously created), while maintaining a very admirable and noble humility... in what are truly mysterious ways.

Johnny wasn't in the mood to hear about damnation on this Sunday but sat in his pew and listened to the good reverend nonetheless. "Everyone in this church has had some encounter with the practice of homosexuality. There are people in these pews right now who have loved ones in their family that consider themselves homosexuals. There are even people in these pews right now that have had homosexual desires themselves. It is a reality of today as it was a reality during the time of the apostle Paul."

Johnny noticed many in the congregation do little things to disguise their wandering eyes. Some scratched their noses to spare a sideways glance. Some pretended to reach in their purses for a piece of gum. Some scratched the backs of their heads in confusion at this possibility. All were glancing around in their own ways to try and identify possible suspects. Though each movement belonged to its individual, their thoughts were singularly: *Good God, I hope it's not contagious.*

"A common theme you will see these days is a constructed effort to defend the legitimacy of a homosexual's committed, long-term relationship with another homosexual." A few scattered snickers of disbelief encouraged the reverend and his message, but he didn't need man's approbation to preach God's truth as he continued on.

"A wise man once said that what the New Testament is against is something significantly different from a homosexual orientation which some people seem to have from their earliest days. In other words, the New Testament is not talking about what we have come to speak of as sexual inversion. Rather, it is concerned with sexual perversion.

"I will tell you all right now that my prayer for us as a church is to find a balance between the clarity that homosexual behavior is sinful and the patient compassion for those of you in our midst, those that experience homosexual desires, or your loved ones that may be homosexuals."

Johnny noticed people look around suspiciously again. Speaking about the sinfulness of homosexuality is one thing, but the realization that there may be a real live one of em sitting next to you actually is pretty goddamn scary when you think about it.

"It is not my aim to drive away homosexuals. Paul told the church in Corinth after mentioning fornicators, idolaters, adulterers, effeminate, homosexuals, thieves, covetous, drunkards, revilers, and swindlers that, 'Such were some of you; but you were washed, but you were sanctified, but you were justified in the name of the Lord Jesus Christ and in the Spirit of our God.'

"Our church should be like the church in Corinth. Where sinners battle together to walk in purity, regardless of our genetic or hormonal disorders that incline all of us to do sinful things. Our church should be a place where any homosexual person can overcome their sexual disorder or find the faith and courage and help and love to live triumphantly and with celibacy, if necessary, to live with their disorder.

"When our lives become disordered, when our sexual lives become disordered, it is most apparent in homosexuality. And in this disordered life of sin, God's judgment upon the human race is most apparent. People often ask if AIDS is God's judgment for homosexuality. Paul's text tells us that homosexuality itself is judgment on the human race because we have exchanged glory for God for glory for man.

"AIDS and every other disease and every other misery in the world is God's judgment for man. They were all spawned from Adam at the fall of man. But those who believe in Jesus Christ are justified by this faith and become God's children. They are given grace to experience God's judgments on humans as the merciful pathway to holiness and heaven rather than sin and hell. When the glory of God returns to its proper place in our lives, the healing of the homosexual soul, as with every soul, will occur."

Johnny began to zone out at the sound of these words. He had known Little Davy for most of his life, and it was difficult for him to imagine such a gentle and compassionate person burning in hell. He had known Ahmed for only a short period but felt the same way about him as well.

It is strange how people come to know other people in such different lengths of time. Sometimes you can know a person for only a short period but truly know who they are. Sometimes you can know a person for a long time and never really know if they'd sacrifice their life for yours if the opportunity arose in a split second. Johnny didn't know Ahmed for a long time, but he knew Ahmed well, nonetheless. After his dream with the angels, his faith didn't irrefutably lead him to think Ahmed and Davy were burning in hell at that moment.

Johnny refocused on Pastor Jennings. He had apparently switched tack during Johnny's daydreaming. It must have been a special Sunday because he was hitting the two main pillars of the present day Christian foundation in one service. There are no two issues more important politically or morally to Protestants and Catholics as of the writing of these words. There are no two issues that will shape the future soul of the United States of America more than these two issues that Jesus forgot to mention while he was on earth.

"Who makes babies? God does. Jesus says that those who deliberately hurt little children will someday face terrible judgment from the Lord. Psalm 139:13-16 says, 'For you created my inmost being; you knit me together in my mother's womb. I praise you because I am fearfully and wonderfully made; your works are wonderful, I know that full well. My frame was not hidden from you when I was made in the secret place. When I was woven together in the depths of the earth, your eyes saw my unformed body. All the days ordained for me were written in your book before one of them came to be.'

"I do not think God could be any more specific about how he feels about the issue of abortion. We choose life because we are Christians. We choose life because we are moral. We choose life because that is what God tells us to do. And we of the Christian faith choose our politicians based on whether they choose life!" Like many well-intentioned preachers, Pastor Jennings couldn't help but insert some politics into his sermon every Sunday.

The congregation gave hearty applause to the good pastor as he closed his message for the day. "Abortion comes from hell itself. The devil himself takes life. Jesus gives life. That is why I hope that you will all join me in our picketing of *Planned Parenthood* downtown this afternoon. My taxpayer dollars will not go to a government institution that kills babies. It is time for us to stand up. We must stand up for what is right. We must make our stand.

"Every man has only so many beats of his heart to make a saintly stand. We will meet there at three o'clock this afternoon after the potluck dinner. God bless you all. And God bless the United States of America. May He grant us forgiveness for our sins."

With a smile and hopeful spirits, Pastor Jennings retired backstage to weigh the offering. The organ struck up a hymn. The congregation stood and sang "His Eye is On the Sparrow," and it was very pretty.

And as they sang the song, they cast their well-worn prayers to heaven. Many were still in rough shape from the recession and needed money, but all wanted something, either for themselves or someone else.

One boy wished for world peace. He wasn't completely sure of the concept, but he figured it was a good move to get on God's good side, for he wanted a brand new bike. Another young man had a brother in Afghanistan, and he prayed for him and all the troops overseas. His younger sister prayed that the climate would stop changing so fast because she loved penguins very much, and she had heard that it would kill them if their home melted.

An older gentleman prayed for a big raise or to hit the lottery. He promised to stop gambling if he did, and he'd even give some of the money to African children. A rich-looking older lady prayed that she would have no egregious side effects from her upcoming *Botox* injections. An elementary girl asked for a new doll and a puppy.

One woman sat forward in her pew, almost shaking with concentration. She wanted a husband more than anything; a husband that would be the spiritual rock in their relationship, one that would give her children and happiness and love. But she was twenty-six now, and she was worried he would never show up. She prayed he would soon. A middle aged woman farther back had loved a husband once, but now he was gone, and she wanted another one to help raise her children.

And there was another young girl in the center of the congregates. She was blonde and had freckles and looked very sweet in her blue Sunday dress. She wore a white hat and had red ribbons tied up in her hair. She asked Jesus to come into her heart for the two-hundredth time in her life that morning. And afterward, she felt poorly for it. For to ask just once and believe was more ensuring, she thought.

And the Good Lord uncrossed his arms and sat back and smiled and listened to all of them call.

Pastor Jennings' office was in the corner of the administration wing down the hall from the chapel. It had a large bookshelf full of Christian literature and a heavy desk behind which he presently sat. He stood with a smile as Johnny knocked politely on the open door.

"Johnny, it is great to see you." Any good preacher has charisma. Pastor Jennings was happy to have such an esteemed member of the community in his office after the sermon. He shook Johnny's hand as they took their seats around his desk. "How is your father doing, Johnny? I saw him at a Tea Party meeting the other day. He looked good."

"He is doing just fine, Mr. Jennings." Johnny asked about his wife and kids as the two completed the standard two minutes of niceties that precedes any important dialogue.

"Well Mr. Jennings, I know you are a very busy man, especially on Sundays. I guess a lot has changed for me since I started goin to college." Mr. Jennings put on a serious face and bowed his head slightly in thought. Obviously he had heard about some of Johnny's new opinions.

"I had this really good friend that I met. His name was Ahmed, and he was a great guy. He was from Cairo and was a Muslim just like everyone else in his family. He was hit by a car just yesterday and died right in front of me. He died saving these two girls that he didn't even know." Johnny didn't cry as he talked about it. His voice didn't crack as he spoke about the recent incident. He didn't need consolation, either. Though the memory would always be with him, his jaw was lifted as he spoke. He had already paid his debt to sorrow.

Mr. Jennings had heard about the accident the night before on the local ten o'clock news. He nodded as he frowned at Johnny in consolation.

"To come to the point, sir, I don't believe that just because he was a Muslim that he is in hell right now. I don't believe that just because Davy was gay that he is in hell now." Mr. Jennings nodded all solemn and clasped his hands together. He made a little sigh as he gave the standard silence that precedes judgment. Of course he understood why Johnny would want to feel this way. No one wants their passed friends to have to experience hell. There is nothing wrong with feeling this way, but there is nothing wrong with delivering the truth to that person, either.

"Well, Johnny, I understand your sentiments. I wish it wasn't so, too." He shook his head sadly. "God gives us all choices, Johnny. Both Davy and Ahmed knew of the redemption Christ gives. In John 14:6, Jesus says, 'I am the way and the truth and the life. No one comes to the Father except through me.' It is not up to me or you to judge, but His Word is very clear about the future of their souls."

Johnny heard the big clock behind him tick off many seconds before he responded to the pastor. "Well, sir, as you know, I went to a Christian school so I can comfortably say I am familiar with the Bible and its words. I know you preach a lot about how Obama has disrespected Israel and how our nation should align itself with the interests of Israel."

"That is correct, Johnny. But it is not my word but God's word."

"Well I support Israel too, sir, so you can stop looking so nervous." They laughed together.

"I agree that Israel has a right to exist. I think you and I may disagree, however, about the future of its people."

"Well, what do you mean, Johnny?"

"You have great concern for Israel and its future, but I'm afraid I don't agree with you about the actual future of its people; the future of Jews." Mr. Jennings was confused and his brow was crinkled. He didn't respond but let Johnny finish his thought.

"If you believe that Ahmed is in hell because he didn't say out loud, 'Jesus, please come into my heart,' then you believe that God's chosen people, Jewish people themselves, the people to whom the entire Old Testament is dedicated to, will come to exactly the same fate."

"Careful, now, what you say, Johnny."

"I'm just repeating your sentiment. This is what you preach, not what I believe. I don't think Ahmed is in hell because I don't think Jews go to hell. How can God send his chosen people to hell and let Gentiles go to heaven?"

"Johnny, Jesus was a Jew, as I'm sure you know."

"Of course I know that, Pastor. I also know that Jews and Muslims are both descendants of Abraham. Abraham's first born, Ishmael, was born from Sarah's handmaid, Hagar, and his second son, Isaac, was born from his wife, Sarah. Ishmael became the father of the eventual Muslims and Isaac the father of the eventual Jews."

"I know this, Johnny. I have read Genesis many times."

"Well Pastor, I don't know if you know *this* but Jews don't ask Jesus to be their Lord and Savior. The concept of God coming to earth as a man is totally unbelievable to Jews."

"Now Johnny, hold it right there. There are plenty of people of the Jewish faith that have come to know Christ."

"I know, Pastor, I've heard of them. They are Jewish people, but their religion then ceases to be Judaism. They are then Jewish Christians or Messianic Jews. Jews that practice Judaism do not pray to Christ or ask Him to come into their hearts. The most holy rabbis in Jerusalem do not believe that Christ is God or that He is the Son of God. Judaism considers it idolatry to believe in the trinity of the Father, the Son, and the Holy Spirit. Are they going to hell just like Ahmed? Why do you care so much about the state of Israel when you think all of its citizens are going to hell anyways?"

The pastor was flummoxed. He didn't respond for a long time as Johnny looked at him. He didn't say, 'well, Jews get a special pass to Heaven' or, 'when the Messiah, Jesus, returns, then Jews will worship Him and be saved.' This reasoning sounds even hollower than it reads, and he just looked at Johnny. Johnny had other points to make and moved on.

"You preach often about morality and the sanctity of marriage, Mr. Jennings." Mr. Jennings looked relieved to be moving onto firmer ground and gratefully nodded his head at Johnny. He was definitely annoyed already, though. "You say that Davy is going to hell because he was morally wrong. Homosexuality is morally wrong."

"The Bible is very specific about that Johnny, in both the Old and New Testaments. Homosexuality is a sin."

"Who is your favorite preacher on TV, Pastor?" Johnny knew it was obviously Hagee, but the young man had a point to make.

Pastor Jennings looked very confused about what was going on. "Good God, Johnny! What's gotten into you? You know who I studied under. Don't patronize me with a hundred and one questions now."

"Do you know who mine is, Pastor?" The pastor rolled his eyes and played along with his hands.

"My favorite TV pastor is Joyce Meyer. Do you know who she is?" Course he knew who she was. She is always on TV in front of thousands of people preaching God's Word.

"Is she going to hell like you think Davy went to hell?"

"Joyce Meyer is a Christian woman, Johnny. She preaches because she was called by God to do so. She has led thousands of souls to Christ. Times have changed since the time of Paul, and she is doing God's work and doing God's work well."

"Paul says in I Corinthians 14 that women should be silent in church. He says that they are not allowed to speak but must always be in submission. If they want to speak they should ask their husbands at home; for it is disgraceful for a woman to speak in the church."

"Johnny, the context..."

"Don't interrupt me, sir." Johnny hadn't raised his voice but a fire lit his eyes. "I assure you that when Paul wrote those words 2,000 years ago, it was most definitely a *moral* issue for a woman to speak in a church. It was inherently and morally wrong.

"It was wrong according to the Old Testament Scripture, and it is wrong according to the New Testament. You are very quick to condemn homosexuality as a moral sin, Mr. Jennings. You will go out of your way to read any mention of it in Paul's writing by annunciating every word exactly as it is written and throwing up your hands to say, 'It is God's word. I am not judging homosexuals, but it is morally wrong; it says so right here!'

"In I Timothy 2 Paul says, 'I do not permit a woman to teach or assume authority over a man; she must be quiet. For Adam was formed first, then Eve. And Adam was not the one deceived; it was the woman who was deceived and became a sinner. But women will be saved through childbearing – if they continue in faith.' When Paul wrote that, it was just as morally wrong for a woman to speak in church.

"Paul also says in I Corinthians that, 'If any person thinks that he is a prophet or spiritual, let him recognize that the things which I write to you are the Lord's commandment. But if anyone does not recognize this then he is not recognized.' That's pretty matter of fact, Mr.

Jennings. Paul says his words are God's, and if Joyce Meyer is preaching to men she is breaking the Lord's command.

"You say Davy is in hell because he broke the Lord's command and didn't change his ways, so how can you say Joyce Meyer won't have the same fate? With all the damn money she makes, I doubt she'll be shuttin her mouth any time soon or threadin any needles in that private jet-a hers. Davy told people about Christ's love and maybe he even led a few people to find love through Christ's message, just like Joyce Meyer. The only difference is he never got paid to do it. Why is he a sinner and morally wrong and goin to hell when Joyce Meyer is just as morally wrong and unrepentant about speaking in church?"

"Context is important, Jonathan. Women weren't educated in those days, and Paul's commands had reasons behind them."

"Well, Joyce Meyer doesn't really strike me as extremely well-educated, Mr. Jennings. And how come I never hear you use your contextual reasoning when it comes to things you disagree with, like homosexuality? I'm sure I could find plenty a context for what Paul wrote to churches about homosexuals."

Mr. Jennings was rolling his fingers on his desk, and his jaw was lifted and locked. "Watch what you're getting yourself into, Jonathan." This is a perfect example of how college leads young people astray, he thought. Johnny had been such a promising student and young Christian. Look at what he's gotten into now – secular humanism and feminist propaganda. Maybe he would have a talk with Johnny's academic adviser at the university. It was very disheartening what had happened to him. It was really quite sad.

"If Paul saw a woman speaking and addressing men in the fashion she does, he most definitely would have considered it a moral issue and forbade it. Why do you ignore such a profound command from Paul and condemn homosexuals so easily?

"I think you do it simply because it is so easy to cherry pick your morality. You have your views that have been shaped by culture and education, and you mold your Biblical message around it. You preach Scripture that agrees with your values and ignore Scripture that doesn't. "

Mr. Jennings looked pretty damn annoyed now. "Johnny there's no need to get hostile about this."

"I'm not hostile, Mr. Jennings, I haven't raised my voice. But I'm not done speaking, sir.

"The church today considers abortion the greatest sin that is under protection of the law. We are doomed as a nation until we reverse *Roe v. Wade* and make abortion illegal again, isn't that right?"

"Now Johnny, you are not going to get me to say that there is anything moral about an abortion. It is murder, plain and simple."

"I understand your sentiment, but do you believe that if you actually were to have your way and make abortion against the law that the consequences would be just and moral? Do you think women would stop having abortions because it was illegal, and our country would finally have righted a moral wrong?"

"It has nothing to do with the implications, Johnny. I believe that life begins at conception. I'm so surprised at everything I've heard today I assume you don't believe that anymore."

"I don't want to argue with you about when life begins, Pastor. I don't think it would change either of our views. I know that life ends when the heart stops beating, or the kidneys stop filtering, or the brain stops telling the body what to do. None of those systems are anywhere near developed when a sperm breaks into an egg."

"Well, that's what I thought. Your views may be more scientific but mine are more clear-cut, and I like that better. Like it or not, life begins at conception, Johnny."

"Life begins at living, Mr. Jennings, whenever that occurs. You may believe that abortion is wrong, and there is nothing wrong with that. But for you to go and picket

Planned Parenthood, which provides a ton of health services to poor women - do you really think that is what the Creator of the universe wants you to do? Do you think that God would really want these services to stop?"

"Johnny, it has nothing to do with what I think but everything to do with what the Bible says." He had finally raised his voice. "Now I will tell you right now, Johnny, you've got a better chance of findin a cotton ball in a blizzard than hearin me say that an abortion is anathin but pure evil!"

Johnny was getting a little fired up now too. "I don't want you to say anything other than what you believe, Mr. Jennings. I don't want you to compromise your beliefs because of what I think or what the Bible says. There are many gay couples that would love to adopt the children you would like to save, but you don't agree that same-sex couples are fit to parent.

"You often tell your congregation to vote for president based on his stance on *Roe v. Wade*, but you never tell them to vote for a president based on his desire to implement social programs for the poor. I just would like you to realize what would happen if that law were reversed.

"Would you really feel so great about your work and so great about the new direction of our country if women had to perform alley abortions like they did before *Roe v. Wade*?

"Just stop and think for a second. Do you know who were some of the most stalwart defenders of a woman's right to choose before *Roe v. Wade*?" Jennings rolled his eyes incuriously and looked at his watch.

"The most compassionate defenders of women in the sixties and seventies were Catholic priests and doctors that saw women who came to them pale-faced and bleeding all over their shoes with a hangar sticking out of them; women that were scared to go to a hospital because they would be thrown in jail; Catholic fathers and doctors that saw the consequences of abortion being illegal.

"They saw the pain that women were going through. The rich ones were fine. They could afford to pay cash to get a doctor to do it off the record. But the poor women that had no one to turn to except the good fathers that cared more for actual people than for their ideals of how women should behave are the ones that got that law passed.

"The doctors that were tired of the shame and anguish that women had to go through, rich or poor, were the ones that helped that law pass. If reversing that law is your ideal state of the United States of America, sir, then you and I sure as hell don't have much in common."

Johnny stood up and looked down at the well-dressed pastor. He looked at him as a man whose definition of right and wrong had defined, for him, man's rights and man's wrongs.

"Maybe instead of picketing *Planned Parenthood* this afternoon, where I'm sure a lot of women will be going to get birth control and pap smears and maybe an abortion, you could do something more Christ like, sir." Johnny turned to walk out, but as he reached the door something occurred to him, and he faced the good pastor.

"If you are still set on taking your congregation to *Planned Parenthood*, may I suggest a Bible verse before you go?" The pastor just stared at Johnny through slitted eyes. The little heathen had completely ruined his day.

"Before you go and stand on the street corner to picket *Planned Parenthood*, please read Matthew 6:1-5. And I'll give you a hint whose command is recorded there - the text is in red." Johnny walked out of the office and did not look back.

Mr. Jennings cracked open his well-thumbed Bible to Matthew. As he read it, a small smile formed on his lips, and he shook his head. It was one of the few times he could remember smiling that day, and he even chuckled to himself for a second.

Mr. Jennings did not go and picket *Planned Parenthood* that afternoon. He went home and had lunch with his family instead. He played catch with his sons and made love to his wife. He even had time to kick the soccer ball around with his kids that evening. He couldn't remember having such a good day. Being right or being wrong has nothing to do with being happy.

T he first thing he noticed was the smell. It smelled of old books and carpet and markers and paint. Johnny had spent hundreds of hours in this room, and he would always smell a memory when he entered here. His old Bible classroom made him feel good.

"Johnny!" Mr. Tyson moved well for a big man. His eyes smiled bigger than his mouth as he jumped up from his seat. He stepped out from behind his desk and wrapped his old pupil in one of his standard bear hugs. He smelled the same too - a mixture of some old aftershave and *Irish Spring* soap.

"It's great to see you, Mr. Tyson." Johnny's voice was muffled as he spoke into the man's shoulder. Mr. Tyson gave a last squeeze and smacked him with his large paw on the back a couple of times for good measure.

"Have a seat Johnny. Man you look good!" Johnny smiled back at his old teacher. He was wearing a button-up white shirt that was frayed around the collar and sleeves. His blue tie still had a stain right under the knot that Johnny remembered. His head was freshly shaved, and his blue eyes sparkled with pleasure.

"So how's college treatin ya, son?"

"Well, I sure have learned a lot, Mr. Tyson." Johnny grinned at the understatement.

"I guess we only see you on Sundays now around here."

"Yeah, I've been pretty busy with school and playin soccer these days. But I usually walk around the halls after church for old time's sake. It makes me feel good bein here."

"Well, we love having you here, Long-John. You're probably the best student this school has put out in its fifty year history."

"That's nice of you to say, sir, but you were always too nice to be a teacher. I bet you'd say the same thing about

Matthew if he were sittin here right now." They both laughed.

"I don't think I would say that to Matthew. I could honestly say that Matthew is probably the most, hmmm, *interesting* student we've put out."

"I think he'd like that, Mr. Tyson."

"So you like all your new classes? Which ones have you liked best, John?"

"I still like science classes the best, Mr. Tyson. Biology is my favorite. Chemistry has been pretty tough but rewarding, I guess. Astronomy is really cool for sure. I didn't realize until college how many other galaxies there are in the universe. Did you know there are hundreds of *billions* of other galaxies like our Milky Way, Mr. Tyson? And that they're all flying apart from each other and every once in a while into one another?"

"Johnny, I definitely did not know that, but it is very interesting!" Johnny laughed. Mr. Tyson would get excited about a doll collection if the person he was talking to were excited.

"What about your other ones, John?"

"I'm taking some b.s. classes like Calc and Sociology and English Comp. That Comp class sure is a pain in my neck, sir. My teacher gave me a *B-* on my last paper because she said my paragraph structure was flighty. I have no idea what that means, and when I went to her office to talk to her about it, she didn't seem to know either. She just babbled on and on about form and composure and fluidity and pace. She's a little out there, but she knows that I want an *A*, and I think I'll still get one."

"That's great, John! I'm sure you'll pull an *A* out of your hat like usual."

"Yeah, well, we'll see, Mr. Tyson."

"Well, I know you've got a lot going on bud, so I don't wana hold you up too long. I called you to come in today because I have a favor to ask."

"Of course, sir. As long as it's not masonry work or skinnin cats." Johnny's brow furrowed after he said it, and Mr. Tyson laughed politely at the weird remark. *God, I'm turning into my dad*, Johnny thought to himself.

"We're having the annual spring choir concert and senior appreciation day here in a few weeks. As you know from experience, the valedictorian is supposed to speak to the student body and congregation. Paul Wright was the man of this year's class, but he told me he didn't want the job. He's pretty shy, and I couldn't convince him for the life of me. I got to thinking afterwards that maybe we could change things up this year. You gave such a good speech last year, I thought maybe you'd like to give it a go again?"

Johnny was caught completely off guard. He'd expected Mr. Tyson to ask him to substitute teach on occasion or run the summer soccer camp. The beast was in his belly again. It was fear this time. It dropped the bottom out of his guts and lifted his pulse uncomfortably. He hadn't expected Mr. Tyson to ask *that*.

"Wow... Umm..." Johnny scratched the back of his head.

"I don't want you to feel obligated at all, son. I thought it may be a good chance for you to talk about what the senior class can expect in college and tell a few stories like you do so well. A lot of them are really feeling the pressure, and it would do them a lot of good to hear some encouraging words from our best alum." He was wheedling a bit now, and Johnny knew he wasn't going to give that goddamn speech. He was worried what he might say. He thought of an out.

"I don't suppose you've talked to Mr. Jennings over the past week?" Johnny raised his eyebrows as a mild warning of what the hell Mr. Tyson may be getting himself into. Of course Mr. Tyson had spoken to Mr. Jennings. His office was just down the hall from where he was sitting. Remarks like that had undoubtedly been repeated and worried among the staff at Almighty Wonders.

Up to this point, Mr. Tyson had been wearing his perpetual smile. The insinuation didn't faze it. "Yes Johnny, I spoke to Mr. Jennings about the little meeting you two had. I know some of your views have changed. I must admit, however, that I know you too well to be worried."

He winked and Johnny bit his lower lip at the parry. He looked down at his lap and frowned in thought. He needed to trim his fingernails. That second fingernail always seemed to grow faster than the others. He would do it tonight after dinner for sure - maybe before. He could bite it right now but this little blonde he had gone out with a few times had said it was a bad habit. She said he should stop doing that. He looked up, and Mr. Tyson was still smiling at him.

Mr. Tyson laced his hands behind his head and leaned back into his squeaky chair. "Do you remember that day with Jordie Brown in the ninth grade? When you two got into a fight on the playground?" He sure did. That was the first fist fight Johnny had ever been in. Jordie had always been jealous of Johnny and said something about his mom.

"I was only about a hundred feet away, and I could have stopped it, but sometimes I think it is best to let boys be boys on occasion. I knew the animosity between you two would be dealt with much swifter that way." Mr. Tyson winked at Johnny again. "He was about double your size, but you still wailed on him pretty good, didn't cha? Jordie was even bigger than Matthew in those days." Mr. Tyson let fly a big laugh, and Johnny chuckled at the memory.

"Matt was standin right there, but he didn't help me out that day. He said afterward that when he saw my face, he knew I could take him." Johnny chuckled again.

"I knew you were a special kid, Johnny, when I saw you helpin Jordie out with his Greek homework just a week later. He may have ended up being closer to you than Matt if his family hadn't moved away." Johnny smiled at the notion and shook his head.

"You've always been a leader, Johnny. I told you that after class one day back then. Do you remember what you said?" Johnny looked at him, then down at his desk. He didn't remember.

"You said that you didn't want to be a leader. You said you didn't care if people followed you. You've always gone your own way and done what you liked to do. People are naturally drawn to you, Johnny. They can sense your strength and purpose, and they just naturally follow that." Johnny winced a bit. He had never been very fond of compliments.

"I don't want you to give a speech at chapel if you don't want to Johnny. I just know that if you did speak and said some things that we weren't used to hearing, you would have good reasons for doing so." Mr. Tyson was using psychology now, and it was working. "Whatever you believe would have good reasons behind it. I have faith in your judgment, son."

Johnny looked down at Mr. Tyson's desk again as he considered his words. It was covered with papers and manila envelopes, but two pieces of cloth caught his eye. They were miniature flags. They sat on square wooden bases and little wooden poles. To the right was the American flag. The left corner had the Christian flag. Both seemed proud and solid. Johnny looked at one, then the other. He nodded his head slowly as he came to a decision.

He looked up and saw the victory in Mr. Tyson's face. The big man knew he had won, and his eyes sparkled like a sun drenched lake. Johnny stood up, and Mr. Tyson did the like. They shook hands like the men they were, and Mr. Tyson winked at him again, still grinning like a bear.

"If I do it, Mr. Tyson," Johnny paused and put on a serious face, "you've got to promise me just one thing." Mr. Tyson looked a bit askance at the unknown request.

"What's that Johnny?"

"You'll be sittin in the front row for the show."

He was still laughing after Johnny left.

"Well, well, well; look who it is. Jayzus H. Christ, I thought I was finally done being tortured."

Johnny entered the office he had come to know so well over the past year. His smile was genuine as he shook Dr. Likins' hand. "No sir, I guess I liked puttin you through the ringer so much that I couldn't stay away." Dr. Likins smiled back at his former student. Although Johnny hadn't a title yet, he had come to think of him as a friend and colleague. They had met dozens of times over the past two semesters and come to know each other very well.

"You got a minute, Len?"

"Have a seat, Mr. Daniels."

Johnny looked at the picture frame on the corner of the desk. "So how's that fine lookin daughter a yours doin, Len?" Dr. Likins chuckled all hearty. Johnny had found one of his soft spots and liked to remind the man that his daughter was put together well. He was afforded such joshin that comes only with familiarity.

"Johnny, I've told you a hundred times, she is too smart, too sweet, and definitely too good-looking for the likes a you." In reality he would have been delighted to see his daughter end up with someone like Johnny. Not only was he handsome and athletic, but Dr. Likins had been truly impressed with his intelligence and wit. It was his curiosity, however, that the old scientist looked most favorably upon.

"Besides, I know if she did happen to go on a few dates with you, that friend a yours would eventually get her scent in his nostrils. I'd have to load up the ol 870 with bird shot if that big oaf walked up to my stoop lookin to take her on a date." They laughed at the thought.

"I reckon you'd need something a little heavier than that to keep ol Matthew away, Len. He wouldn't get the point unless you put some T's in the chamber."

"He is persistent, I'll give him that. I wish he had been more persistent in his studies, though." Len rubbed his chin thoughtfully. "I can tell he's a smart kid, but I was pretty impressed he got an *A* on that last final. That's all that kept him from getting a *D* in my class. I wouldn't say anything to you about it, of course, if you two didn't compare exams *after* the final." Len cocked an eyebrow as Johnny coughed into his hand.

On that day he had noticed Johnny switch places to sit directly below Matt during the test. He had also noticed Matthew's new hat with an unusually large bill. He smiled knowingly and changed the subject for Johnny's benefit. He had a similar buddy when he was in college. He probably would have done the same thing but thought Johnny should know that he was no fool.

"I suppose you've strutted in here to lecture me on the flaws of my lesson on sympatric speciation again. What was it you said to me the other day..." Len rattled his fingers on the desk and looked at the ceiling. "Something about me confusing the mechanism of sexual selection with speciation events." Len smiled at Johnny who looked relieved to move away from discussion of Matthew's final. He almost took the bait but had come to speak about something other than evolutionary biology. Johnny knew once they got to talking about science it would be difficult to move on.

"Well, Len, I know I could rattle your cage pretty good there, so I'll leave that for another day. Actually I kinda wanted to talk to you about somethin else. My old Bible teacher wants me to give a speech in front of the student body like I did last year. I told him I would do it, but I don't really know what I should talk about."

Len responded by looking up again and spoke slowly as if unraveling a great mystery. "If you gave a speech last year... and they asked you to give another speech this year... I would assume they want you to speak in a similar manner that you spoke to them before." Len was smiling as he hashed out the obvious. He could already see what Johnny was struggling with but couldn't help giving him a little shit.

"Well, my Bible teacher knows how my views have changed over the past year..."

"Does he know how much they've changed?"

"He's aware of a few topics upon which my views have changed, but the full extent is unbeknownst to most. As the organizer of the event, I doubt the congregation would consider him a prescient planner if they knew what I was thinking about saying."

Dr. Likins laughed at Johnny's choice of words. "Man, Johnny, you sound like a politician that's been reading too many scientific journals. That'll be the day." He rounded out the laugh and looked at Johnny again. Johnny had chuckled politely, but it was obvious he was looking for serious counsel. Dr. Likins tented his fingers and gave a thoughtful pause before continuing.

"I usually hate even talking about this stuff cuz I'm usually speaking about it to a believer and it's like they just don't listen to ya. They have this deep down belief that the fact of their existence is proof that their God exists. I really think that's what it boils down to. It's like you could give em all this evidence and they don't even have a shred of it and they'll just kinda look at ya real peaceful like, and you can tell they're just thinking to themselves, *of course Jesus is God! I'm here, aint I?*" Len laughed and Johnny did too. He knew what he was talking about.

"I know some things in life are easier when people just tell us what to do. It would be very easy for me to encourage you to give that group of people a science lesson, Johnny. To be honest with you, though, I don't think they want to hear it. It doesn't make them bad people. Most of them aren't bad people. Most of them do a lot of good things in the community; working at the soup kitchen downtown, mowing older people's lawns for free, watching the kids when parents want to have a date night or whatever.

"If you asked any of those people why they do those things I suppose most of them would say they do so because they are Christians. They wouldn't go so far as to say they do it to get on Jesus' good side, but they would probably say they do it for Jesus. What most of them don't realize is that they would still do those things if they were Muslims or Hindus or Buddhists or atheists. Doing good things for other people makes you feel good. When you tell those people there's an evolutionary reason for this, they typically shake their head and give you a knowing smile." Dr. Likins chuckled as if he knew from experience.

"Religion has been a part of culture throughout history, John. It is neither good or bad in itself; it all depends on who's practicing it. Take a two by four, for instance. You can use that piece of wood to help prop up a house for a family or construct a swing set for children to play on. But you can also use that piece of wood to beat a man to death. Religion has been used to build hospitals and give wounded people hope, but it has also been used to justify killing, stealing, and lying. Religion isn't good or bad, only practice makes it so.

"But Jesus didn't invent good, Johnny. That was around long before him; just like forgiveness was. I think he was probably a very good man, but their notion that he never sinned is ridiculous. It is so plain to see if you read some of the things he said in the Gospels. You'll see the God of the Israelites condoning some pretty terrible things if you read the Old Testament. Rape, torture, and genocide are all approved by the Big Guy under appropriate circumstances, but at least he left you alone after you died.

"You had to wait til gentle Jesus meek and mild came along for God's wrath to continue for eternity after death. Jesus did some good things I suppose, but dreaming up and preaching about a terrible place called hell cancels all that out and then some for me." Len shook his head.

"Jesus Christ has scared the shit out of God knows how many people with all that hell talk he was so fond of. That's a wicked lie to be telling children if you ask me. If he really was the son of God and went to heaven after he died, I bet his pa gave him a spankin for that one." Len laughed out loud again, and Johnny winced a bit. He still wasn't used to such language, but he understood where Dr. Likins was coming from.

"I suppose everyone in that congregation believes that the Bible is the word of God, John. No amount of preaching or cajoling from you or me will convince them otherwise because they have been told that their entire lives. If they ask enough questions without reservations, I spose they will realize for themselves that it is actually the word of man.

"What angers me about people isn't what they believe. I really couldn't care less if they believe the tooth fairy craps cotton candy and flosses with unicorn hair. But when they teach their children that some guy named Noah put all the animals in the world on a boat a few thousand years ago." Len's eyes got a bit fiery at the mention of children and Johnny nodded with him.

"When they teach kids the universe is thousands of years old instead of billions. When pastors say God created animals a day before he made Adam and Eve. With all that we know today! When they tie all those lies with the threat of hell and preach it to children is when I get mad. That's mental brain washing and child abuse, and I think our society has tolerated it long enough. It shouldn't be respected and flown under the banner of faith but ridiculed as the Bronze Age bullshit it stems from. It seeps into legislation and is used to stir fear and hate against those that don't believe the same." Johnny smiled to encourage Len, but he thought it was a challenge and continued.

"We're the only animal in the whole damn kingdom to believe such nonsense. Look Johnny, I'll be the first to tell ya that good and evil exist in this world, but they are present in all of nature, not just mankind's tiny corner. They stem from the choices that all life encounters, not God and the Devil.

"You can see killer whales torture a baby seal for hours until they'll kill it in the wild. That seems pretty evil to me, but even a Christian pastor would call it crazy to say the Devil had a hand in it. A male lion will kill a whole pack of cubs if they aren't his. When they're plentiful, a grizzly will kill a salmon for just its skin and waste the rest.

"But there is obviously good in nature, too. Sometimes dolphins will risk their lives to protect humans being attacked by sharks. A loyal dog will knowingly sacrifice itself for its owner. Insects sacrifice themselves for the good of the colony all the time. That seems pretty good to me, but I hope even a Christian pastor would call it crazy to say that God helped em do it," Len said and laughed.

Johnny laughed with him and wondered for a moment if his professor was high. He had heard one of his classmates say something about seeing him smoking in his car one day. He seemed overly talkative and his eyes were kind of glassy. It would be cool to smoke for the first time with my teacher, he thought. He almost said something about it but caught himself at the last moment. Len was getting lively and he didn't want to throw him off.

"Don't get me wrong, though," Len said. "I get why people pray. It is comforting to talk to someone that can maybe help you out sometimes. I sometimes say a few words of thanks or a few *please can ya's* every once in a while to someone or something up there. Sometimes I talk to my gun though too," Len chuckled. "Remember that Quill Lake goose I shot up in Canada?" Len reached into his desk and quickly found the picture he was looking for. He handed it to Johnny. It showed him holding up the ten pound goose with swirling snow and dark skies all around him. There was a beautiful white band across the bird's gray chest, and it had pure white primary feathers on its wings and white stripes up its black neck. It was a gorgeous goose. Johnny wanted one for himself.

"God that bird got me excited. Our guide told me they're pretty rare. I went home that night and cleaned ol Bertha up nice, got her all oiled and smooth, and I thanked her for makin the shot when I needed it. A few other guys' guns froze up that day, but she didn't. I said thanks for holdin up in the bad weather and makin the shot." Len looked a bit embarrassed, but Johnny was a hunter and completely understood. Len had named his gun Bertha.

Johnny had named his twelve gauge Dolly. He nodded at him to continue.

"I guess I don't see anything wrong with talkin to someone in the sky when you feel like you need to talk to someone. There's nothin crazy about that. I guess I don't see anything wrong with talkin to my ol 870 though, either." Len laughed and paused and scratched his chin. "But thinkin ol Bertha talks back to me, though," Len smiled. "I'd hafta call *that* crazy."

Johnny cleared his throat and Len took it to mean, *so, what the hell's your point?* and continued. "Look, if the Devil were a real guy that walks around this earth, I doubt he's *all* bad. I mean, I'm sure he's done at least a few nice things for people down the years. And I know for a fact that if God were real, he sure as hell aint *all* good. Look at all the terrible things that happen to innocent little kids all over the world. He could stop a hell of a lot of suffering in a heartbeat if he wanted to. Just like us, *he* has the choice. He has a billion choices he could make good every day. But he doesn't.

"And ya know why he doesn't stave off the suffering? It's not because Adam sinned in the Garden of Eden and brought evil to the world. And it's not because God gives free will to bad people to do bad things to good people either. You wanna know why he doesn't do anything when he could do something, Johnny? The true reason God doesn't do anything for them is because he isn't really there. A long time ago, people made him up to account for good things they saw, and they made up the Devil to account for bad things they saw. People always say that the greatest trick the Devil ever pulled is convincing people he doesn't exist. Bullshit. Priests and apostles and holy men are the ones that *really* pulled the goddamn trick; and they did it by scaring people into believing that he does.

"Listen, son, good and evil certainly exist, but I've given it a hell of a lot of thought, Johnny, and I'll tell ya the truth right now – the choice to do good or to do bad is ours and ours alone. No one *gave* it to us. It's been with us since our ancestors could think it and do it. The words *good* and *bad* are human creations that came long after man was doing those deeds. Then man invented religion to help him make the choice. Then religion became all this *set in stone*, man-made crap that certain people had heard from this voice in their head they said was God. And nowadays religious people have the damn audacity to say that without *their* particular religion we wouldn't know the difference between good and evil. Gimme a goddamn break!

"Good or bad, watcha gonna do? That's what it boils down to, John," Len said, very animated now.

"We all have some good in us. We all have some bad in us. We can be good or we can be bad, we can help people or we can hurt people, but we all get to choose. You can call the good 'God' and the bad 'Devil', but God's got nothin to do with it and the Devil don't either. The choice is real, but the actors aren't. The only difference between God Almighty and the Devil himself is a scared little species called man."

Johnny was grinning at his science teacher's fire. Len took a deep breath to steady himself. "But what I was trying to say to you earlier, Johnny, is that it is not my place to tell you what you should or shouldn't say to your old student body. Many of these people have their answers and they have become truth to them. You could show them all the proof that we share a common ancestor with chimpanzees, and they would scoff and just stuff up their ears with Scripture.

"They have ceased to exercise the crucial element that separates us from other animals. They stopped asking 'why' a long time ago, Johnny. You can give a man all the evidence in the world, but you can't make him ask questions. And when questions don't father answers, those answers become spoiled brats that think they are always right. They get offended easily and hide under the flag of faith.

Questions must come first, or the answers are meaningless, Johnny."

"Well, Len, I appreciate you not preachin your beliefs to me," Johnny goaded Len a bit after his unusual outburst.

"You're tryin to keep me riled up, and I won't be havin it today, son," Len said and smiled back. "I only believe the evidence. It's not about belief - it's about evidence, Johnny. I just want to know the truth is all, and the best way to get there is by asking questions. Everyone has to find their own path in life, and when you know exactly where you're goin you're a lot less likely to look around along the way. I may not have a slice idea where the hell I'm goin, but at least I know the best way to get there."

Johnny hadn't expected to get so much out of Dr. Likins that day. He was usually much more reserved and preferred listening to speaking. They slowly reverted to the easy chit-chat of friends well at ease with one another. They talked about girls and hunting and college and life.

Eventually Johnny got up and stretched to say he was ready to leave. He held his hand open and slapped palms with his good teacher. As they gripped thumbs in a show of affection, Len held on a little longer than was customary. His eyes kindled a bit.

Then he smiled and gave his student the piece of advice that he knew he had come for - "Give em hell, Johnny."

"I can't believe you're getting all *A*'s, Sassafras. That is just amazing. Have you ever gotten one of those before?"

"Obviously you're giving me a hard time, Jonathan. I always had to work harder than you, but I am doing well this semester. If I were there instead of three hundred miles away, I would punch you in the stomach right now."

"That's fine as long as you kiss it afterwards. So I guess calling me Jonathan is payback for me calling you all those endearing names."

"Maybe…"

"So, prettyface, I was just so happening to wonder what you are wearing at the moment."

"I'm getting ready to go for a run, so I'm wearing running shorts and a tank top."

"Mmm. That sounds nice. Brings back good memories."

"I bet it does, mister."

"So what else is going on with ya, cutie? When you coming back into town?"

"I dunno when I'll be coming back. I've got a lot of moving to do. I'm getting ready to move into an apartment with my roommate. I met her last semester at Wednesday night service. She's really sweet and smart, and she's a really good Christian, Johnny. She's the type of person you can like, really trust without really knowing her."

"I met a guy like that at the beginning of the year. My bud, Ahmed, was like that. He was about a good a guy as you ever saw. He really was."

"Is that the man that was killed in the car accident, John?"

"Yeah."

"Didn't you tell me that he was a Muslim?"

"Yeah."

"Did you ever get a chance to like, witness to him?"

"Uhh, no."

"Oh, well, that's too bad. Do you feel guilty about that?"

"Uhh, no."

"How can you not feel guilty that you didn't talk to him about Jesus?"

"I dunno, Laura. He was already a good person like I told ya. If I started preaching to him it would have been weird. He seemed as though he was doing fine without me reading him Bible verses."

"Well, you didn't need to read him Bible verses, Johnny. You should have like, told him about Christ, though, and about His salvation."

"I guess I could have mentioned it. It just never came up, and I didn't really feel the need to sway him to my religion. His whole family and all his ancestors were Muslims, and I was cool with that. He was cool with all that. He was a good shit, Laura. He really was."

"He may have been, John, but that doesn't help him right now I imagine."

"I don't want to get into that with you, Laura. I really don't. Hey, did I tell you that Mr. Tyson asked me to come and give a speech to the student body? Their valedictorian pussed out, and Mr. Tyson said that since I gave such a good speech last year, he wants me to come and give another speech to all those little rascals."

"That's cool, Johnny. Your speech last year really was good. I guess everything that happened with Little Davy kind of ruined it though."

"Yeah, well, it did kinda overshadow everything I said, I guess."

"Have you written it yet?"

"I kind of have an outline. I'm a little nervous about what I should say and what I want to say. I was thinking about taking a stand up there for some-a the stuff I've learned this year and taking a stand for Davy, too."

"Hmmm... The way you're talking makes me a bit nervous."

"Speaking of Davy, Laura, do you think he's where Ahmed is right now?"

"Yes."

"Jesus, Laura. That is a hell of a thing for you to say."

"It's not up to me, Johnny. That's what the Bible says. Look, I liked Davy just as much as everyone else did, but he was an admitted homosexual, and he killed himself taboot. It makes no difference what you or I believe – it is simply the Word of God."

"Well I think that's bullshit."

"I'm sure you do now that you're into Muslims and believe evolution and all that other crap, John! I mean, my gosh Johnny, what on earth has happened to you this year?"

"Into Muslims? That's a weird thing to say. I was gonna ask you for some advice about some-a the things I was plannin on sayin for my speech. I was thinkin about takin a stand for Davy up there like I said. Maybe take a stand for same-sex marriage up there, too."

"Oh dear Lord Jesus, forgive us our trespasses. I can't believe what I'm hearing, Johnny. I really just cannot! It makes me sad to hear this stuff coming from you. It really does. My God, Johnny."

"So, I don't suppose you believe that homosexuals should be able to get married in the United States?"

"Are you serious, Johnny? Of course I freakin don't. Homosexuality is wrong, plain and simple. It's freakin perverted and wrong, and the United States of America is the greatest country on earth for a reason."

"Geez, Laura. So if Davy were still around, and he found another dude that he liked and wanted to settle down with, you don't think he should be able to get married to him?"

"Uh, no I don't. They can do whatever perverted stuff they want to do together, but the U.S. government shouldn't condone it. It's like, just wrong, Johnny, and I know that deep down you still know that. I'm gonna tell you as a friend right now, Johnny, don't get up there on the altar and make a freakin fool of yourself like Davy did."

"Maybe I will. Maybe I won't."

"Johnny please just listen to me. I know you're hard headed. A lot of times that is a good thing. But you're wrong on this. Homosexuality is wrong. I really care about you, Johnny. I want what is best for you. Just make a good speech like you have before. Don't get like, all political up there, please."

"Maybe I will. Maybe I won't. I haven't decided yet, but you're influencing my decision for sure."

"I hope you're not being sarcastic like you always are."

"I can't believe you think Davy is in hell."

"Like I said, John, it has nothing to do with what I believe but everything to do with what the Bible says!

Maybe I'm wrong about Davy, but I doubt it. If you get up there and start talking about same-sex marriage, you're going to turn a lot of people off, and you probably won't like the way you're looked at afterward. You would really disappoint the student body and congregation. You'll be like, an outcast with some people and friends you've known your whole life. And you need to start thinking about your career and connections, John... Just please let it go. S-o-o-o not worth it."

"Yeah."

"Well, my roommate just got back from youth group, and I think we're gonna go for a run together."

"Youth group, huh? I spose she's in accord with you on what you've said bout everything, huh Laura?"

"Umm, I would assume. She's a good Christian, John."

"Right. *Dyaaaayz*. Well, I'll see you around, Laura. Enjoy youth group."

"Johnny wait..."

"*Adios, amiga.*"

"**M**atthew, would you like some gravy on your mashed potatoes?"

"You betcha, Jennifer. This is some damn good shit. Really good. Really hits the spot." Matt voiced his appreciation in punctuated breaths as he blew on his meal to cool it down. Not to discount Jennifer's cooking, but Matt's spot wasn't difficult to hit at the moment. He was happy as a pig in mud and already on his second plate. Matt would say dirt and insects was damn good shit if he hadn't eaten in a while. He often enjoyed dinner with his best friend and family.

"Jesus, Matthew. Watch yer goddamn mouth at the dinner table. It aint respectful in front a Jennifer." The rebuke hadn't a spark of fire or irony, and Matt smiled and said, "sorry, Jennifer," and went back to his plate.

174

"Oh it's fine, Matthew," she said. "I'm glad you like the meal."

Johnny's dad was back at the dinner table, and the space was pleasantly crowded. "So, Long-John, your speech is at six o'clock tomorrow night?" Mr. Daniels asked.

"That's right, Dad. You guys will be there, right?"

"You bet, bud." Mr. Daniels was proud of his son.

"Man oh man! These potatoes are bomb, Jennifer. Got a bit of a kick to em. You do somethin different this time?" Johnny had seen her add a dash of horseradish to the pot she had been stirring. Matthew liked his food and noticed the difference.

"Well, I did do something a little special tonight." She smiled her secret to the men around the table the way women like to do.

"Johnny, I know your views have changed a lot this past year, but I hope you don't get too political in front-a your old classmates tomorrow. Yer gonna turn a lotta people off if you let em have it all at once like you tend to do. Sometimes it's best to just be patient and let people come to conclusions in their own time. Just try and be a little patient, son."

"My time is too valuable to waste on patience, Pops." He threw a half-cocked smile at his father, and Mr. Daniels couldn't help but let out a big laugh. Charisma never needs to win but always does.

"I know, Johnny, I know." Mr. Daniels acquiesced with his hands. "Just go easy and don't get too political is all I'm sayin."

"What's wrong with that, Dad?"

"Well, son, everyone should come to their own views in their own time. I always encouraged you to think for yourself. My encouragement was just my personal opinion, that's all." Everyone chuckled except Matt. Those potatoes were pretty damn good.

"I know you like Obama and how you feel about his policies. I just truly am concerned for the future of the country, Johnny. It doesn't have anything to do with what kinda person he is."

"Dad, I know you're gonna roll your eyes like it doesn't matter when I say this, but when that man stepped into the job the country was losing 700,000 jobs a month. A president's policies can dampen the sting and length of a recession, but only time will correct it. The most important variable in the equation is time, not policy. The revenue the government was garnering through industry and sales and exports and taxes all were down along with the recession. All of a sudden everyone's a budget hawk. We got two or three wars/country building projects going on overseas that are freakin expensive as hell, and all of a sudden he's public enemy number one."

"I'm not gonna get worked up with you about this, John. We obviously have a difference of opinion on a lot of matters now. Obama shoved socialist health care down the public's throat when we simply can't afford it, and that just isn't right."

"Dad, the CBO said it'll save a trillion dollars for the country over the next ten years."

"Oh those numbers are ridiculous, John." Most days, Mr. Daniels would have been much more fired up at this point in the conversation. Even though Johnny was leaning in a different direction than him politically, he liked the fact that he was showing interest in politics. Maybe if we get that ranch he'll end up becoming a senator from South Dakota, he thought. That would be pretty nice to have a son that was a senator.

"Well you would be all over them if they were the other way, Dad. The moment I knew I would have voted for Obama over McCain is when McCain said health care is a privilege and not a right. This is the United States of America! Health care not being a right for every single American is not my kind of optimism, or policy, or patriotism.

"The public didn't even want it, John. Even the leftist polls showed a clear majority of the country did not want that huge bill forced on them." God, that would be nice if he became a senator, he thought. He's got the looks for it, and he was born there, after all. He'll have to tack back to the right if he wants the job, though. That will come when he gets older and has to pay bills and taxes. South Dakota is a red state, but farmers do lean democrat. All them Natives do, too. Ranchers out west tend to be more independent, but Johnny could win em all over. If he wanted it bad enough, he could win em all over. Damn my eyes, but he really could, he thought.

"Geez, Dad, polls are for pussies."

"Johnny, I know your vocabulary has increased since you went off to college, but please don't use bad words while we're eating. It aint respectful in front-a Jennifer."

"I bet Shakespeare would say the only thing that makes that word bad is you thinkin about it. It's a grown-up word, Dad, not a bad word. Anyways, just imagine if our political leaders only did what a fickle public wanted them to each day. Polls should be used to shape your presentation to the public but shouldn't shape your policies. Leading by public opinion isn't leading at all. That's why everyone is so disgusted with Congress today. When politicians are more concerned about being right than with being correct, they just fuck everything up.

"Hell Dad, if polls had been used to determine whether or not to abolish slavery, whether or not to give women the right to vote, or whether or not to pass civil rights, we might not have made those advances. Simple American rights have nothing to do with polls. We're not a democracy, we're a democratic republic. We elect leaders whose policies and platforms we agree with and let them do what they think is best. If they don't meet your expectations, you vote for the other guy the next time. Isn't that right, Matthew?"

"Yeah man, polls are for pussies." Matt's pace had slackened only ever so slightly. He was on his third plate but had followed the conversation completely. Man those were some good potatoes.

"All we want as members of the Tea Party is a government that doesn't live beyond its means and spend us into oblivion. Our country is flat broke, and we're still spendin like drunken sailors, John."

"I know, Dad, and I think that is well and good. The government should live within its means, but it isn't broke like you say."

"Our deficit is in the trillions of dollars, John, and goin up each second!"

"Broke means you can't even buy a cheeseburger - broke means having to get a root canal in Tijuana when you live in San Diego - after you borrow a couple hundred dollars from someone to do it. Revenue is down from the wars and the recession. We're in the red right now, but we're living on credit.

"When you're living on credit you shouldn't leverage it for consumption but for investment. Most of the spending that Obama wants is for investing in the American people's education, energy research and development, American infrastructure, and American industry. You can't invest without spending, Dad. The economy is more important than the debt. My econ professor says the deficit will always be the little brother of an economy – even if it grows bigger."

"You have to know when to tighten the belt, Johnny. When you grow up, you'll realize that you have to sacrifice sometimes." Johnny smiled to himself. Telling someone to grow up is a very underrated compliment.

"It aint funny, Johnny. It is dire serious. We can't do some-a the things we'd like to for the poor right now not because we don't want to but because we can't afford it. And don't even get me started on how bad inflation's gonna get with the Feds and all this quantitative easing shit. Hell, John, it wasn't that long ago you could go to the gas station and get a pop and a bag a chips for a buck, tops. Same thing costs almost five nowadays." He really is a good looking kid, he thought. God, he looks just like his mother when he smiles like that.

"I understand where you're coming from, Dad. I really do. I don't mind that saying that a social safety net should be more like a trampoline than a spider's web. When I was little you used to always tell me that when a man buys stock, he should buy low and sell high. Wouldn't the best investment our country can make right now be to buy low – help get our poor out of poverty through education, and then sell high? Sell the poor when they become rich or middle class and then buy new poor ones!" Johnny was the only one to laugh. He had been joking when he started the reasoning, but after it came out it didn't sound like that bad of an idea.

"Let's say you gave me two million dollars of American tax-payer money. With half of that let's say I bought... twenty-five pounds of gold. And with the other million, I financed the trade school or university tuition of twenty-five low income high school graduates. Ten or fifteen years after my purchase, I *guaran-damn-tee* you the investment in the American student's education would yield higher returns for the American taxpayer over the course of their lifetimes than a pot of gold. That's not just a good patriotic policy, but a good investment policy, too."

He's living in a dream world, Mr. Daniels thought to himself. He smiled at his son and tried to remember what it had been like to be so young and optimistic and naïve. He'll grow out of it someday, he thought and smiled at Johnny.

"Okay, okay son, but how bout our foreign policy? Johnny, you have to understand what is going on in the world right now. China is growing at an exponential rate. They're expanding their military muscle in the Pacific every day. Their economy is on track to overtake ours in five to ten years. The world is a better place when the United States is on top."

Jennifer was cocking her head in amazement at Matthew Ryan. She had never seen anyone eat so much in one sitting. Every once in a while he would give a little grunt or snort of delight and shake his head at how good the meal was. She giggled a bit and shook her head as she looked at him go. It made her feel good.

"Well, I agree Dad, but I learned in class the other day that China has had the largest economy in the world for eighteen of the past twenty centuries. The United States will still be number one in the world in most things even when China's GDP is larger than ours. They have over four times our population which makes their *per capita* income way lower.

"Their GDP growing is a good thing for the United States. The more wealthy their middle and upper classes become, the sooner they can start buying more of *our* stuff and giving us our money back that they're holding. It won't only create jobs in the U.S. but help get us back in the black.

"And look at the two countries' allies, Dad. We have the strongest most democratic allies in the world. They've got Iran and North Korea and Syria and Zimbabwe. As long as the Chinese government keeps locking up scientists and artists and professors for speaking their minds, I'm not too worried about China being better than the United States at anything except a few statistics."

"Listen, Johnny, I know you're wide-eyed right now and very bright, but government intervention isn't always a good thing. Government intrusion into the free market is not good for business or investment." Mr. Daniels rolled his fingers on the table and grinned a bit at his son. Senator Daniels – damn that had a fine ring.

Matt gave another little snort, and Mr. Daniels looked over at him. "Jesus, Matthew; breathe son, breathe! You can slow down a bit, bud. No one's gonna take yer food from ya." He and Jennifer laughed, and Matt smiled real big and took a drink of milk. "Whew. Man, these potatoes are bomb, Jennifer."

"You know, that's my problem with your Tea Party, Dad. They act like the word government is leprosy or something. The government is the law, not some monster. If the Tea Party had been around in the mid-thirties, they woulda said Social Security was bad for America. If the Tea

Party had been around in the early sixties, they would have said Medicaid and Medicare were socialism. They can call Obamacare socialism all they want, but when it's as popular as Medicare they'll be claimin it as their damn idea. They'll tweak it, and then they'll claim it. I'm sick and tired-a hearin your Tea Party whine about socialism when they don't even know what the hell it is. And the rest of the good ol boys in the GOP way out-number em, but they don't got the balls to stand up to em cuz they're afraid of losin their seats in primaries. They're scared a bein called moderate by commentators on Fox news for Chrissake. They're scared of the wild ones in the party and not bein 'conservative' enough. I think Reagan would be disgusted if he saw the GOP today. Their leaders aren't actin like leaders at all; they're actin like a buncha scared little wishy-washy limp dicks."

"It aint that bad, John. Relax, bud."

"Some of the shit I've heard at those meetings is bad, Dad. It borders on sedition, and there's nothing patriotic about it. The Tea Party is full of Jingoes, but the scariest thing about them is that their enemy is domestic. Their enemy is Washington and Obama and the Union, and that's why I can't stand em. Most Tea Partiers claim to be Christian but don't support any type of welfare or school lunch programs that help America's poor kids. Jesus, Dad, those programs aren't perfect, but they just want to get rid of them entirely. They may be zealots, but they sure as hell aint Christian... Christian my ass.

"God, John, I just can't believe you support that Pelosi and Reid crap." Ordinarily, Mr. Daniels would have been very fired up by now. Talking about his Tea Party in a pejorative manner usually made him defensive and upset. But he had just gotten a hell of a raise the week before. Plus, right before dinner, he and Jennifer had... well, the man was in a damn good mood.

"Well Dad, I do like Nancy Pelosi even though you guys can't stand her. I lost a lot of respect for Harry Reid when he said they shouldn't build that mosque in New York City."

"But, John..."

"But nothin, Dad. It was an old *Burlington Coat Factory* and blocks from the old trade centers. It was surrounded by peep show joints and bars. This is America for cryin out loud."

"That was the only thing I ever liked about Reid," Mr. Daniels mumbled as he pouted to his potatoes. This role reversal was very strange at the dinner table. As Johnny had grown up, he was always the one listening to his father, but now his father was listening to him. Johnny liked this version better.

Mr. Daniels just shook his head a bit and rolled his fingers on the table some more. He looked over at Matthew again. He was grinning like an idiot as he looked at his best friend. He hadn't actually been listening to the conversation very much. He had a full stomach and a session planned with a girl later that night. It's kind of hard to get upset when there is a big oaf like Matt just smiling away right next to you.

"What in the hell are you always grinning at, Matthew?" Mr. Daniels sought easier prey. "How come we never hear your opinions about any of this stuff?"

"Well, I don't really like politics very much, Mr. Daniels. My dad says politickin is dirtier than dirt."

"Well, how come I've never heard you talk about religion or any serious stuff at all?"

"I dunno, Jack. I guess I just don't have much to say about it. My mom doesn't really care for the institution of religion too much, and I guess I kinda take after her. She always says, 'God healed a thousand lepers but can't crack the common cold.'" Matt chuckled to himself and burped. "Sorry, Jennifer."

"My mom says that I don't need religion to be a good person. She wrote me a poem a few years ago and said that was all I needed to live a good life."

"Let us have it, bud."

"Huh-uh. No way, Jack. You'd think I was a Nancy."

"Don't be scared, Matt," Johnny prodded his friend.

"I'm not scared-a nothin!"

"Oh just tell us, Matthew. I promise I won't call you a Nancy. It can't be any worse than Johnny's from that day. God, that one was a real sparkler; the homo and the rag head." He laughed a bit and looked at his son. Johnny looked down at his plate, and he felt a little bad. "Hell's bells, it's like a meetin of the poetry guild in this goddamn house nowadays - out with it, Matthew."

"Well, I aint gonna read it out loud, Jack. I'd look like a little sister. Here's a copy that I keep in my wallet. It's not one of those fancy-schmancy poems that doesn't rhyme or anythin like that." Matt dug his wallet out of his back pocket and unfolded the thick brown paper. "My mom wrote it a few years ago and gave me this copy to keep."

Mr. Daniels put on his reading glasses that were sitting in front of his plate. He read the poem out loud so everyone at the table could hear. *

Matt looked at his empty plate and rubbed the side of his nose. Johnny smiled big at his best friend. Mr. Daniels handed the little slip of paper back to Matt and looked up at the ceiling as if to say, *'Dear Lord, help us.'*

Matt was by now getting pretty bored.

"You wrote that speech yet, dude?" he asked Johnny.

"I didn't have to write this one, man. It's all up here, yo."

"Sweet, man. Let's go down to the pitch and play soccer with those Mexican *güeys*."

"Sweet."

The fellas stood up and put their dishes in the sink. Johnny wiped his hands on a towel and looked over at Jennifer. She was looking down at her new dinner plates all happy. Johnny smiled at her. "Hey Jennifer," he said, "no matter what I say tomorrow, don't take it to mean I don't love ya." Mr. Daniels looked up at his son and smiled and nodded. It was the first time he'd heard Johnny say that to her.

Jennifer smiled back at him. "Oh that's fine, Johnny. I love you too," she said and giggled.

They turned to leave, but as they were about to walk out the door, Mr. Daniels brought them to a halt.

"Johnny!"

His voice was stern, and both Matt and Johnny whirled around. He wasn't facing them, but they heard him drawl, "About that speech tomorrow, Little Man..."

"Yeah, Dad?"

Mr. Daniels rattled his fingers on the table and said, "throw the goddamn stick."

Johnny smiled. "OK, Big Boy."

"And as for you, Matthew..."

"Yeah, Big Boy?"

"Did I ever tell ya that I hate kids?"

Matthew smiled and everyone else did too. "Love you too, Mr. Daniels!"

The soccer field was about two miles from Johnny's house. Johnny and Matt walked side by side down the familiar sidewalk. Matt was throwing the soccer ball up and down while Johnny looked down and tugged on his ear lobe. Matt looked over at him and smiled.

"I've got a little confession to make, John."

"Oh yeah, what's that?" Johnny replied absent-mindedly.

"Well, when I went to the bathroom at dinner I saw some papers on your desk that I happened to peruse." Johnny looked up sharply, and Matt smiled at him.

"I thought you didn't need to take notes for this speech." Johnny continued to look down and put his hand in his pocket. Matt let him break the silence.

"Yeah, well, I just said that to impress my dad. He acts like I've got a photographic memory or somethin. I think he thinks I'm smarter than I actually am." Johnny cleared his throat. They both knew that Matt was referring to the content on those notes more than just their presence.

"What in the hell are you always grinning at Matthew?" He borrowed his father's line as he lifted his chin. Johnny chuckled out of embarrassment and Matthew out of fondness.

They covered another block before Johnny couldn't take it anymore. "Well, dickhead, what the hell'dja think?" Matt never gave advice unless it was asked for. Johnny usually admired the trait, but sometimes it was frustrating as hell.

"There's some pretty heavy stuff in there, *amigo*. You sure you wanna go all out on this?" Johnny continued thinking to himself. The pace had quickened considerably, and they covered another block before Matt continued.

"We've never talked about it, John, but do you remember that day last year after basketball practice? When we went to my house to get a sandwich and found my mom on the floor."

"Yeah, I remember," Johnny mumbled. "What about it?" That day had been embarrassing for both of them. Her dress was rucked up to her waist, and a plastic handle of vodka was lying next to her on the floor. Plates were broken, and a cabinet door had been torn away from its hinge. She was snoring into the kitchen tile.

"God I was mad at her. I did a lotta thinkin that night. She was still sick the next day, but I had to tell her how I felt about everything, and I sat her down after dinner to talk. She knew what I wanted to talk about, and she looked really sad, but I had to do it. I sat her down in the living room and talked to her like I've never talked to anyone in my whole life.

"I said, 'Mom, you know I love you more than anything, but this drinking stuff has gotten completely out of control.' I said, 'if you don't stop drinking – like completely stop drinking, I'm going to drop out of your life after high school. You've been a hell of a good mother to me, and I know everyone has their weaknesses, but I won't sit by anymore and let you drink yourself to death. It's gonna kill you someday if you don't stop now, and I don't want that to happen. If you continue like this, you won't be seein me much after school.'"

"Geez, man, you said that to her?" Johnny was surprised. Matt was a very let live kinda guy and never much trespassed into other people's decisions.

"I had to get amped up before I told her. She can read me like a goddamn book, and I knew if I wasn't one-hundred percent serious, it wouldn't work. I had to commit to it myself before I told her. It almost made me nauseous to think about not talkin to my mom, but somethin had to be done, and that was all I could really do."

"Your dad was being kind of a dick to her that day, though, wasn't he?"

"Yeah, well, he's not the nicest guy in the world sometimes, but she always had an excuse for drinkin like that. It was either the neighbor's dog shittin on our lawn or not bein able to get new cabinets or curtains or whatever. When she didn't have a reason to drink, she found one, and I didn't want her to deal with her problems like that anymore. She started goin to them meetins, and she hasn't drank since."

"I knew she was going down to the club, but I guess I just assumed she decided to do that on her own."

"She *did* decide to do that on her own, goddammit." Johnny was surprised at Matt's emotion. "I didn't threaten her as much as I just told her. It wasn't a goddamn game no more. We both knew that she could play hide the bottle and keep it from me for a while. I think she saw in my eyes that it wasn't about me, though. It wasn't about right and wrong or accusations and guilt. I didn't tell her that I knew best or what she was doin was bad. It was about her, not me. I just told her I loved her and put the ball in her court. It was a chance worth taking, I guess. I gave her the choice because I knew that she was the one that had to make the decision. I had to take the chance for her sake." Matt hadn't choked up, but Johnny could hear the emotion in his voice.

"Member when I got this scar?" Matt pointed to his eyebrow and smiled away his watery eyes. "I think we were six or so. Your mom took us to the park like she always did on Sundays. We had just watched Superman that day, and I thought I could fly." They both laughed.

"I can still kinda remember that feelin. I really thought I could fly, dude. Somethin inside a me deep down just believed it. I climbed to the top-a that slide and looked down at evrathin like I was king-a the world. It's kinda weird because I was still scared to dive into the pool. But that day was different. I spread my arms and went for it. I think I knocked myself out, cuz the next thing I remember is your mom's face lookin down at me and her wipin the blood away with her dress."

"I remember her screaming, 'Oh good heavens, Matthew!'" Johnny smiled at the memory of his mother.

"I've got a lotta memories of your mom actually; some that you probably don't even remember. I remember her that day the best, though. After she had calmed down, she looked at me kinda impressed and said, 'you almost scared me to death, you little devil.'"

Johnny chuckled. "She always called you a little devil."

"When we got into the car she said, 'Matthew, don't you ever do anything that crazy ever again! But I know you thought you could fly, and I guess that's pretty admirable.' I can still see her face when she put that ice pack over my eye. Do you remember what she told us then?"

Johnny smiled with his eyes as Matt told the story. His father usually found it too painful to speak more than a couple of sentences about his mother. As Johnny aged he found his memories coalescing around big events and places. Details were fuzzy and felt made up. When Matt talked about his mother this way, he could see her eyes sparkle more clearly and hear her voice more closely. The little things were fresher and vivid.

"She said, 'you've got to take chances in this life because it's the only one we get. This world is full-a people that don't take chances, and no one will remember them.' She said, 'You took a chance today, Matthew, and it didn't work out, did it honey? And it looks like you'll have quite the scar to remember it by. When you take chances you're just bound to lose, and you've got to live with the consequences. But you have to take chances if you're ever gonna really win.' Then she said somethin about spankin the hell outta me if I pulled that crap again." They laughed.

They were getting close to the soccer fields, and Matt started throwing the ball up and down as they paced on. "I guess what I'm tryin to tell you, Johnny, is what your mom was tryin to tell me that day. If you say half-a what I saw in that speech tomorrow," Matt paused and grinned at his friend, "you'll be taking one hell of a chance, bro. And I don't think it will go over so well with the crowd." He grinned again. "It will really piss them off. I mean *really* piss them off. You'll be tellin em a lotta shit they don't want to hear. But that's not what's gonna get em. What's gonna get em is who they're hearin it from." Matt shook his head.

"If you take that chance, you better be prepared for the consequences, dude. People are gonna look at you different. A lotta people won't think so highly of you anymore. You'll stop gettin smiles and handshakes and start gettin stares and whispers. A lot of em will think you're gay, or you're goin to hell, or you're possessed maybe." Matt laughed at the thought. "You aren't gay, right?"

"Matthew, I know I'm smaller than you, but I could knock you out in a heartbeat." Matt feigned fear with hunched shoulders as Johnny lifted a fist. Johnny laughed again. They could see the lights of the field now.

"But you've got my back no matter what I say tomorrow, right bro?" Matthew's eyelids drooped along with the corners of his mouth. His voice was stern.

"That is a hell of a thing for you to say to me." Johnny smiled at his buddy's show of loyalty. It made him feel good.

"So, you don't think they'll like the speech?" Johnny asked sarcastically.

Matt grabbed his crotch and spit. "No. No I do not, bro," he said, all serious. "The younger ones might. The students might. I know I woulda liked tuv seen some shit like that when I was goin ta school there. But the teachers and older people aren't gonna take too kindly to it, man. Most of em are already pretty set in their ways and just aint gonna change for nothin. You'll get a few students and younger people to listen, though... But still," Matt said, "I dunno if you should do it, man. I just don't know if it's worth it."

Johnny frowned and pulled on his earlobe. "You think gay people should be able to get married?" he asked quietly.

Matt grabbed his crotch and spit. "Jeez Christ, Johnny. I don't fuckin know."

"I didn't ask you if you fuckin know, dumbass, I asked watcha think." Matt cocked an eyebrow at his friend. Johnny was the undisputed leader, but Matthew still rough-housed him into submission on occasion. He obviously needed to do it again soon - maybe tonight after the game.

"I haven't really ever given it much thought to be honest. I think if I hadn't known Little Davy, I'd think no. But Davy was a good guy, and if he wanted to get married to another dude, that would be cool with me, I guess. Davy was a good shit, man." Johnny nodded, but his expression did not change. Now they could hear the Mexicans on the field. Matt continued.

"I had a dream bout Little Davy a while back."

"A wet one?" Johnny returned Matt's earlier jibe with a smile. Matt just grinned back all sly. He'd definitely do it tonight.

"He was standin up on the altar again behind the podium. There was no sound. There was like a kinda breeze in the room, but it wasn't movin anathin – hell, I dunno. Anyways, he was wearin the same sweater and jeans. He wasn't really movin. No one was. He was just lookin at everyone in the audience. His head was movin back and forth as he looked at everyone. I could see those blue eyes a his so clear. Member how scared he looked that day? He didn't look like that anymore. He didn't look happy or sad. He just looked kinda peaceful. He looked good, man. I bet I know what he would say up there if you asked him what you asked me."

Johnny looked over as Matt closed the conversation. He spoke more to himself than he did to Johnny. "I bet he'd lift his chin a mile high and say, 'I am a goddamn American – *your* rights are mine too.'"

They both looked down and thought about their old friend. They stepped onto the pitch and were spotted by the Mexicans. Matt chipped the ball to them as they approached.

"You know what, John?" Matt looked over at Johnny, and his eyes twinkled at his friend. And although he was smiling away, Johnny could see that he was serious as hell. "Take a chance for Davy tomorrow. I think he woulda done it for you."

Then he summed up hasty before running onto the field. "Give em hell, Johnny."

Johnny wore dark slacks and a polo shirt for his speech. The shirt was fresh from the dry cleaner and very crisp and white. He hadn't slept a wink the night before. Every time he dozed, the fear of the morrow would jump into his heart and raise his pulse. He knew he could use the outline of the speech he'd used the previous year, and everyone would be happy and content.

But he wouldn't.

The beast had whispered all the consequences of honesty into his thoughts. The ostracism, the mean looks, the disappointment were all at the forefront of his mind. Johnny had been scared like never before in his life. He had wavered until this point. But standing where he now stood; where Davy had stood that day a year ago, he knew what he had to do. Johnny shook the fear off his shoulders, and he let them have it.

"Almost every day for the last dozen years I have been coming to this church and this school. Every day as I pull into the parking lot, I notice those same two flags on the flagpole out front. Both give me a swelling pride every time I see them. That American flag that represents my country, and that Christian flag that represents my faith."

Seemingly everyone from Almighty Wonders was there. The large auditorium was packed to the gills with humanity. The overflow rooms on the sides of the main auditorium were full. The high ceiling echoed his voice and the dampening murmurs of those in the back. Every pew was crowded, and most wore their Sunday best. There are probably over a thousand people here, he thought. God, there were so many people there. He could see his old coaches, old teachers, friends of friends, and relatives of students that he didn't know. Even his first grade teacher, Mrs. Smith, was there. God, why did Mrs. Smith have to come? he wondered uncomfortably. There was to be a choir performance after Johnny's speech, and most of the people expected to attend had come to watch the opening performance.

"At my home we have the American flag in our front yard, too. And in my bedroom I have a miniature Christian flag that my mother gave me a long time ago. I love them both a great deal. I remember the night that she gave it to me very well. She had just read me a bedtime story and was tucking me in. I can still see her smiling at me in the lamplight as she gave me the little flag. She said, 'this flag is yours, Johnny. It represents a faith that no one can take away from you. It is yours to keep and treasure, too.' I've prayed with it next to my bed ever since that day. It belongs to *me* and is mine to keep. It represents *my* faith, and no one can ever take that away from me."

In addition to the high school, many elementary and middle school kids were seated as well. Others were standing at the back, and some were even sitting in the carpeted aisles. There were so many people there. All the murmurs had evaporated. Only Johnny was speaking now.

"About a week ago, my dad was talking about the American flag out front of our house as we pulled up in the truck. He looked up at it with a contagious pride and smiled at me and said, 'treasure that flag forever, Johnny, for it represents something far greater than those that fly it.'

"Both of my parents were right. I treasure both of those flags outside a great deal. The Christian faith that I am so proud of belongs to me and is mine to keep. But that American flag out front doesn't belong to me, or to you, or to anyone for that matter. The stars and stripes that are a symbol of our nation don't *belong* to any American, but all Americans belong to her." The audience came to their feet and applauded all hearty. Johnny heard his father roar his approval from the back of the auditorium. Mr. Tyson was smiling up at Johnny and gave him a little wink.

Johnny knew he was about to give the folks something they hadn't heard before. He also knew that the only thing worse than unsolicited advice is repetitive unsolicited advice; Johnny was about to break one of his few rules and give unsolicited advice. He doubted it would be repetitive, though.

"I have had the privilege to know you all for the greater portion of my life. I think most of you would agree that I have led a life marred with my share of sin, but it's been a life in which I have been happy and content. This school, where I have spent much of my life, has been a second home to me. It has given me more than I deserve throughout the years, and I will always treasure this place and the people that come to school here and the people that come to worship here." Hearty applause broke out again.

"Through this place I have come to know Christ and His love and acceptance, and for that I will always be grateful. I held a girls hand for the first time under this roof, had my first kiss under this roof, won awards and honors under this roof, and made great friends under this roof. I have studied the Bible many times under this roof, but what

I gained under this roof has nothing to do with the building, but the people I have come to know under it.

"We are all Christians because we love our Lord Jesus Christ. We are Christians because we honor His teachings and His love. We need to remember that it is His life we honor through our own actions. We are not obligated to follow letters written by a man named Paul, or commands written by a man named Moses, but the life of a man named Jesus.

"Why do we tolerate sermons that have nothing to do with love but everything to do with hate? Why do we exclude God's benevolence from anyone that does not follow the exact same pathway to love? Why do we hate our enemies not with words, but with hateful thoughts of hell and damnation? Why do we insist on humanity mumbling a specific prayer for heaven that ultimately denies the descendants of Abraham?

"Jesus told us repeatedly not to judge others or we will be judged. I challenge you to find a Sunday sermon that does not condemn Muslims or Hindus or any other group that does not say Jesus was God. I challenge you to find a minister that will say Muslims aren't going to hell. If that is his conviction, then that is his prerogative. Ask him if God's chosen people, the Jews, are not going to hell based on his reasoning. If he tells you no, then he is a liar. It strikes me as a bit presumptuous and ill-advised to condemn the children of God to eternal hell, so I'll not condemn his children of other faiths to hell while I'm at it."

A susurration went up from many in the congregation. This rhetoric was not over the line, but it was certainly unexpected. Many were whispering to each other what they thought he meant here, and though it was understood, there were many furrowed brows and confused expressions.

"The best missionaries for Christianity; those who do the most to represent Christ and His love, all have one thing in common when they go overseas or just down the street to do so. In order to best represent Christ and Christ's love, they first ask the person if he is hungry, and if so, they give him food. Then they ask him if he is thirsty, and if so, they give him drink. Then they ask him if he is sick, and if so, they give him medicine and aid. Then they ask him if his family is well, and if not, they do the same for his family. They give him whatever he needs to live and give him whatever his family needs to thrive. And if the person asks him why he does all these things, they tell him why, and let him decide if he'd like to do the same.

"As most of you know, I am majoring in Biology and Chemistry at the university here in town. I wish I could express to you all how much I have learned in the span of just one year, but I would bore you half to death, and possibly convince you not to go to college after all." Many of the seniors laughed as Johnny hoped they would.

"I know about the hostility you are taught here towards evolution and its perversion of creation." Mr. Daniels and Jennifer were in the back of the auditorium standing behind a pew. Jennifer began chewing her fingernails.

"Evolution is taught here as some sort of evil scam conjured up by a man named Darwin to discount God in nature. I wish that weren't true, but that sentiment is common in our entire country right now. I know that most of you all probably won't be majoring in sciences during your years at university. I know that it is easy to just believe what you are taught, and when what you are taught comes straight from God, there should be no questioning it.

"With regards to evolution, I ask you to think for yourselves without fear. If you are interested in science, then please study it when you go to college. Ask your professors questions - that is what they are there for. If you will not be studying science but are interested in the controversy over evolution, I ask that you read about it and form your own opinions. If you are curious enough to do this, I only ask that you read books on evolution by actual scientists that don't seek to solely discredit it, but actually define it.

"Books by so-called scientists that try to convince Christians that evolution doesn't occur, and that the earth is very young, are written by complete and total perverts. These people act as though they are God's messengers and doing His work, but they are nothing but cowardly hucksters sullying truth. They are incurious perverts and cowards that know nothing of God. If demons truly do possess men, then they are well at home within these individuals and their like.

"The great scientist and founder of taxonomy, Carl Linnaeus, was heavily criticized by theologians and the public when he classified humans as primates in his *Systema Naturae*. Based on anatomy, he found that the main difference between humans and other animals was speech. There was no tangible difference of being more God-like.

"When Galileo Galilei constructed the telescope, and supported Copernicus' theory that the earth rotates around the sun, he was considered a heretic by the Roman Catholic Church. Psalm 104:5, which says, 'The Lord set the earth on its foundations; it can never be moved,' or Ecclesiastes 1:5 that states, 'The sun rises and the sun sets, and hurries back to where it rises,' were all used against Galileo in his trial on suspicion of heresy in 1633.

"He was found vehemently suspect of heresy for believing that the sun lies motionless at the center of our solar system, and that the earth is not at the center, but moves. He was ordered by the church to curse and detest those opinions, and sentenced to live under house arrest, which constituted the rest of his life. Galileo is known today as the father of science, the father of modern physics, and the father of modern astronomy. Galileo Galilei was a great man.

"People are wont to choose their most hated group of individuals and say the hottest place in hell is reserved for them. If there is a hell, cowardly men and others who say that Christians shouldn't acknowledge the truth of evolution have a first class ticket there for sure. The men that seek to discredit evolution because of Biblical Scripture are the inquisitors of today. If Satan is the prince of lies, then these men are his wolves in creationist clothing.

"They deceive like their master. They feast upon ignorance and fear. They pervert God's glory that He has provided in nature. They cash in on fear and shame and lies. Wherever they end up, I wouldn't even spit on them to cool em down." Matt was in the far back next to Jennifer and Jack. He had a big grin on his face. Jennifer did not.

"The evidence for evolution is overwhelming in its entirety and simplicity. It is found in biology and chemistry and geology and anthropology and genetics and every other field of science. It is simple, observable change, nothing more. You do not have to discount evolution to believe in Jesus' love.

"Science and religion have always had a contentious history. As science seeks to explain mysteries of the universe that men have pondered for ages, there is a seemingly concerted effort to discredit God. Why does science have to explain everything? Why does science say that a rainbow is a refraction of light through water droplets between the observer and the light? It is God's covenant to man that He will not flood the earth again.

"In your defense, I imagine if God came down to earth in person, split the clouds, and descended down to mankind, the scientists would say, 'look! It's E.T.!'" The audience clapped all hearty at that. Everyone was nodding and wagging their chins at one another like come on, Johnny, throw us a bone here. They were obviously very surprised at what they were hearing from their golden boy.

"Why must we insist on taking the story of Noah's ark in Genesis literally? Why must we insist that dinosaurs were made a day before humans, only a few thousand years ago? Why must we take these great stories literally when we know as a matter of truth that it isn't so? Why do we preach the stories in Genesis as truth and ignore the entire book of Leviticus? The hundreds of commands that regulate the composition of our clothing, or food we ingest, or cattle we raise are ignored; even though they are God's sanctified word, just like Genesis.

"A brilliant astronomer & physicist named Lawrence Krauss has said, 'Every atom in your body came from a star that exploded. And, the atoms in your left hand probably came from a different star than those in your right hand. It is really the most poetic thing I know about physics: *You are all stardust.* You couldn't be here if stars hadn't exploded, because the elements – the carbon, nitrogen, oxygen, iron were created in the nuclear furnace of stars.'

"I can stand up here and tell you about all the different reasons that evolution is true. I could tell you about all the evidence that the universe and the earth are billions of years old. I could tell you about the millions of different species that live and have lived upon this earth in order to justify scientific reasoning. I could tell you that mankind right now has more evidence for the *theory* of evolution than he does for the *theory* of gravity or the *theory* that the earth rotates around the sun. This isn't just a matter of fact, but also a matter of truth.

"We don't debate the controversy of these theories in the classroom, and we shouldn't debate evolution either. The argument seems to be an obligatory one and has nothing to do with empirical evidence. Even the Holy Pope, John Paul II himself, realized that denial was not in the interests of the church - but acknowledging evolution was.

"There are people in the world today that deny the germ theory of pathogenic disease. There are people that deny the Holocaust occurred. There are people that believe man and dinosaurs roamed the earth at the same time. When denial can endure in the presence of overwhelming evidence, it becomes obvious that, for some, answers are more valuable than truth. And that's why truth never has anything to fear. It takes a hell of a lot more guts for a man to stand corrected than to lie in faith. Truth doesn't need man to exist, but answers always will.

"I could give you all the answers, but they would mean very little if you do not ask the questions yourselves. If you don't have the desire or the guts to even question how ridiculous the concept of a man named Noah putting all the millions of species on earth into a wooden boat a few thousand years ago, then you and I have little in common. If you don't ask any of the questions, then all the answers mean little. The truth doesn't belong to man, but the questions were his invention and his answer to life. And only through questions can man find the truth we should all be looking for."

The crowd was not expecting anything like this, and people were definitely annoyed already. A few of the older people had already walked out. Some of the less serious students were smirking and enjoying the unexpected show, but as Johnny looked down at them, he thought he saw a few questions kindle their eyes. They were on their way.

"Many of you had the privilege to know Davy Jones." Johnny looked around for a moment at all the eyes on him. "Davy was a friend of mine, and he was gay. I would like to say that I have known a kinder soul than Little Davy, but that wouldn't be true. He was probably the kindest person I'll ever know, and I've thought about him every day for the last year since he took his life. And I've thought a lot about how we treated him as a church, as a student body, as human beings..." Johnny lowered his voice and looked down for many seconds. "And I've thought a lot about how I treated him too."

"You and I could argue about whether or not Davy was born gay until tomorrow and the next day, but that would be missing the point. Many of you would say that Davy is in hell as we speak because he was gay and because he took his own life. You and I could argue about that until tomorrow and the next day, but that would be missing the point. But if your love for Christ obliges you to say that Davy is in hell right now because he was gay, then I am afraid that you alone are missing the point.

"Homosexuality is mentioned in the Bible a handful of times. It is considered a moral issue by many Americans, and it is considered a sin by many Americans." Johnny smiled at the audience. "It is so easy for a heterosexual to condemn a homosexual. Isn't it? It is so easy for a teetotaler to condemn a drunk. It is so easy for a prude to condemn a carouser. It is so easy for a sinner to judge another sinner... It's so easy to say someone *else* is goin to hell.

"All these things are *so* damn easy, that sometimes you just can't help but wonder - if that high road you're walkin, just may be a little too easy goin. You wonder if maybe it's time to stop for a second and look around and ask yourself where in the hell you're *really* headed. What road you're *really* on. Many things in life are easy - sometimes suspiciously so.

"When Paul wrote many of his letters that make up the New Testament, he very specifically said that a woman speaking in church was an abomination. He said that a woman teaching a man was morally wrong. Because of our culture and our education and our knowledge, we see the fallacy in this and do not preach it nor expect it. But homosexuality continues to be a moral issue for a heterosexual preacher these days, even when that preacher is a woman.

"Believe it or not, homosexual behavior is common in the animal kingdom. Swans and giraffes, dolphins and monkeys and bison, lizards and dragonflies, and thousands more species display homosexuality in nature. If you believe that animals go to heaven, do you believe all the homosexual ones go to hell?

"When Paul wrote his letters, a woman speaking in church was most definitely a *moral* issue; and it has taken us as a civilization almost 2,000 years to realize that it was not. Animals don't consider sexuality a moral issue. I hope that our society will not take another 2,000 years to realize that sexual preference isn't a moral issue either."

And the susurration was there again. It was louder now, but still respectful. Surprise was turning to anger in many, however.

"In the United States of America, we believe that every American should have the same rights. Conservative-minded individuals are very fond of Thomas Jefferson's words, 'The government is best which governs least.' I like that quote, too, but he has another that I like even better - 'We hold these truths to be self-evident, that all men are created equal, that they are endowed by their Creator with certain inalienable rights, that among these are life, liberty, and the pursuit of happiness. That to secure these rights, governments are instituted among men, deriving their just powers from the consent of the governed.'

"I believe that the Constitution of the United States and all her amendments is the greatest script ever written. It is often said that this document is great because of the rights it gives to the people of the United States. The right to practice your religion, the right to speak freely, the right to freely print your views, the right to a fair trial, and the right to bear arms are a few of the greatest rights acknowledged in the Constitution.

"Any democracy that does not allow and protect the rights of her people is a shell that will eventually crack without their protection. But the Constitution does not *give* the people of the United States any of these things. Every man and woman born anywhere in the world is entitled to these same rights. The Constitution of the United States does not *give* her citizens any of these freedoms - it simply acknowledges and protects them.

"But what is a right? The word gets thrown around a lot, but I don't know if people really think about what it actually is. I didn't know what it really was until I knew Davy was gay and started to think about it.

"In the 1860's, our country went to war against itself because of men's rights. We did not have our civil war because black people were entitled to something special; they were entitled to the same thing white people had. In the early twentieth century, women fought for their right to vote and hold office in the United States. They didn't want anything special; they simply wanted the same thing men had. In the 1960's, Martin Luther King Jr. headed a revolution that led to our country passing the Civil Rights Act. Minorities didn't want anything special; they just wanted the same thing white people had. The most wonderful thing about rights is that there is nothing special about them.

"As of the speaking of these words, there is another group of people in the United States that don't want anything special; they just want what heterosexual people have. Can a citizen of the United States say with a straight face that all men truly are valued equals when there are Americans right now that don't want anything special; American men and women that only want what heterosexual people have?

"It was just over forty years ago that laws preventing marriage between a black man and a white woman were finally repealed by the Supreme Court. In 1965, before the acknowledged unconstitutionality of these ridiculous laws, a trial judge named Leon Bazile defended the law by writing, 'Almighty God created the races white, black, yellow, Malay and red, and he placed them on separate continents. And but for the interference with his arrangement there would be no cause for such marriages. The fact that he separated the races shows that he did not intend for the races to mix.'

"The name of God is often invoked in order for men to oppress one another. No government in the history of mankind that aligns itself against the equal treatment of its citizens has ever been on the right side of history. And any man that purports his right is greater than another man's right has never lived lacking objective judgment and justice.

"Rights have nothing to do with polls. Did slavery or women's suffrage or civil rights have anything to do with a silly survey called a poll? How much longer will heterosexual Americans cherry pick the words of Thomas Jefferson and cherry pick their Biblical morality?

"As far as the government is concerned, marriage is a legal contract between two consenting adults. The Equal

Protection Clause of the Fourteenth Amendment to the Constitution secures all citizens' rights to equality and fair treatment. A congressman from Ohio named John Bingham drafted this equal protection clause in 1865. I wonder if he would think that some people's religious views should trump equality in America.

"In the midst of this battle, many have said that same-sex marriage should be left up to the states. I'd never call them wrong, because that's a terrible argument - I'd just call them incorrect. The Constitution of the United States is the supreme law of the land, for no other law may trump it. And when American citizens are denied liberty - that is a Federal issue, for it is unconstitutional. When American citizens are denied equality - that is a Federal issue, for it is unconstitutional. When American citizens are denied justice - that is a Federal issue, for it is unconstitutional. When but one American citizen is denied these fundamental values, my friends, all Americans are ultimately denied them. And damn my eyes for temper, but when someone denies me liberty I can't help but get a little fiery; because I am an AMERICAN - your rights are mine too.

"The argument will immediately fall into a moral one because it cannot stand as a legal one. Those who oppose equal rights for gay Americans will say it is immoral and that is that. I tell y'all what; they have every right to cast their morality stones, but Jesus and I will hang on to ours.

"The subjectivity of morality will always be lesser than the objectivity of equality. That subjective smirk of superiority to which every man is entitled may last him a lifetime or a day, but the objective countenance of equality that America defends as her own will always be Her saving grace."

Almost everyone in the congregation was shaking their heads and frowning at Johnny. It reminded him of how he used to shake his head during Len's Biology lessons. Johnny wondered for a moment if he'd be shaking his head at this speech a year ago, too.

"I am well aware, ladies and gentlemen, that the Bible does not condone homosexuality. You often hear that the sanctity of marriage must be preserved. I didn't actually know what sanctity meant, so I looked it up the other day. It is definitely a pretty word, and it's so pretty I am surprised I haven't heard of a girl named Sanctity before. Sanctity means godliness, holiness, or saintliness.

"The next time a person tells you that they believe marriage should only be between a man and a woman because of its sanctity, ask them a simple question. *'Do you believe in the sanctity of genocide?'* or *'Do you believe in the sanctity of slavery?'* Slavery is condoned repeatedly in the Old and New Testaments of the Bible, and it is therefore sanctified. But even if it weren't, the Bible has nothing to do with our law. American law has nothing to do with man's right and wrong, but everything to do with man's rights and man's wrongs.

"Fear will immediately be employed by the threatened individual. God's wrath will undoubtedly come upon the wayward America that would condone such a thing. What we must come to recognize is that allowing American citizens to marry whomever they choose isn't an erosion of goodness and decency, but simple acceptance that comes from freedom."

All of a sudden, a man jumped up from the pew in the middle of the auditorium. It was Johnny's old English teacher. He looked flushed and wild-eyed angry. As he sidled toward the aisle he began yelling at Johnny. "I've seen a lot of things in my day but none as disgusting as this, Johnny! You've slid *way* off the path. Disgusting! Absolutely disgusting!" He reached the aisle and began shaking his fist in the air. "You should be ashamed of yourself, Johnny Daniels!" he shrieked. He stormed out the back doors, and more people followed him out.

And the susurration was back, louder than ever. Surprise was gone, and anger had filled the void. A murmur of agreement went up throughout the audience, and many began clapping. Hundreds of people were shaking their heads and cursing him with their eyes. Johnny had been expecting something like this, but it stung more than he thought it would. He looked down at his Bible teacher, Mr. Tyson, then. He winked and smiled in an unforced manner, and Johnny nodded his thanks. He took a deep breath, and continued on with his speech, in a voice more determined than it was before.

"Men will say, 'This is *scary* stuff.' They will say this is dangerous ground, and *they* will want *you* to be afraid. You are well within your rights to do so - but I wouldn't recommend it. I can stand before you all and confidently say that the only man I fear is myself - and I recommend that attitude. Any man that tells another man to be afraid is nothing but a coward. If any man tells you to be fearful, it is because he wants you to share his own.

"The decision of marriage does not need anyone to defend it. It does not need mankind's pedantic definitions and self-righteous morality. My mother always said that there is only one thing any marriage needs to be successful. Marriage makes only one request of the couple that seeks its solace. All it needs - is love.

"Satan is a seasoned warrior, my friends. He has been fighting for a long time and has many weapons at his disposal. But his favorite weapons; those weapons with which he has had his most success and most effect on mankind, are his arrows of oppression, his bow of insistent exclusion, his sword of fear, his spears of shame and hate and lies, his shield of right and his armor of wrong.

"God, however, in his infinite wisdom and wonder, has chosen his weapon with infinite wisdom and care. His weapon has more power than anything that rascal named the Devil can wield. God's weapon is simple love. God's shield is simple truth. No line in the sand is necessary for you to choose your side. No creed, nor oath, nor dedication is needed to wield your weapons. They are all at your disposal. They are all right in front of you. They are all at your mercy. The purity of a man's life is measured not by what he accomplishes in it, but by the weapons he uses during it. Choose your weapons wisely, every single day, my friends.

"A wise man named Learned Hand once said, 'The spirit of liberty is the spirit which is not too sure that it is right.' The most wonderful thing about liberty is that there is nothing special about it. I don't need to be a homosexual to believe that homosexuals have a right to get married. Abolitionists in the nineteenth century did not have to be black to believe that all men are equal. Feminists that believe women are entitled to the same rights as men do not have to be women. I believe what I believe because I am an American. I believe that all Americans are equal and have the same rights, whether they are accorded them or not.

"The oppression has continued to this day not because of religious sanctity but because of personal comfort. It is uncomfortable for many Americans to think about two men or two women getting married. It was uncomfortable to have a white woman marry a black man not so long ago, too.

"George Orwell said that, 'Mankind is not likely to salvage civilization unless he can evolve a system of good and evil which is independent of heaven and hell.' I know that my words today may make you all uncomfortable, but I swear I'd rather be on the wrong side of comfort than on the wrong side of justice. And justice has nothing to do with man's right and wrong, but everything to do with man's rights and man's wrongs."

The congregation appeared uncomfortably astounded. This was not the Johnny they knew, nor the Johnny they loved. No one had spoken to them this way before, and they didn't seem to be enjoying themselves very much. Johnny was rolling, though, and hardly paused in his speech.

"Over the past year, I have heard many different men described as true patriots. I have heard the creeds of these men, and I have come to form my own definition of a true patriot. A *true* patriot - a true American patriot isn't just someone that wants what is best for his country, but someone that just wants what is best for his country's people.

"Every man is confronted with a myriad of ignorant ideas and beliefs throughout his life. Some of these ideas are tied to religious dogmas - some assumptions get weighed down with misconceptions - some are smothered with fear - still others become saddled with hate. In order for a man to fill his mind with knowledge, he must first discard his ignorant fears and fearful assumptions. In this life, the acquisition of knowledge is far more valuable than the knowledge itself. In this life of ours, the prize is never the true reward."

Johnny had never written a poem before. He definitely did not consider himself a poet. Up to this point, he hadn't decided whether he would recite the poem he had composed in his mind throughout the past year. It cut to the soul of who he considered himself to be. It reflected all that he had learned at university and his love of science and humanity. Looking down at the audience now, he looked them square in the eye, and Johnny let them have it...

'It wasn't his fire,
that struck from the sky.
Nor was it his answers,
that boom'd from on high.

It wasn't his writing,
It wasn't it his cries.
It wasn't his buildings,
nor airplanes that fly.

It wasn't his weapons,
as strong as they are.
Nor was it his mirrors,
that gaze oh so far.

It wasn't his ships,
for space and for sea.
Nor was it when he,
planted food with a seed.

> *It wasn't his wheel,*
> *(though momentous indeed).*
> *Nor was it when he,*
> *tamed the beast and man freed.*
>
> *I tell you the truth,*
> *because I never lie -*
> *Man's greatest achievement,*
> *is the day he asked why.'*

"One of my favorite stories took place on a pretty Sunday morning in June of 1865. The war which has killed more Americans than any other had just ended. The South was in tatters, her morale was shattered, and her sentiments were poor. At St. Paul's Church in Richmond, Virginia, a very uncomfortable situation happened to take place.

"It was communion day at St. Paul's. The minister was about to administer Holy Communion, and an unforeseen eventuality occurred. As he called his flock forward to take communion, a tall, well-dressed black man stood up and approached the communion table. Everyone was completely shocked. The audacity of the man was unbelievable. The war had just ended, and he had the nerve to take Holy Communion along with white folks.

"The pastor was embarrassed. The congregation was wide-eyed and whispering to themselves. No one could believe it. No one moved a hair; the static tension electrified the air. After some tense moments, a man stood up, self-assuredly walked down the aisle, approached the chancel rail, and took a knee next to the brave black man.

"That man was one of the best generals this country has ever produced. That man was none other than the commanding general of the Confederate army, General Robert E. Lee. The congregation looked to his leadership and followed suit. General Lee realized that the past is related to the present, but the two have nothing in common. He realized that acknowledging a man's rights has nothing to do with agreeing with him. General Lee understood that a man's circumstances never discount a man. I believe he knew at that moment, that every man is allotted only so many beats of his heart to make a manly stand. General Robert E. Lee rolled away his stone that day... Will you do the same?

"My favorite quote was written in the 1920's by an American writer and naturalist named Dr. Henry Beston. This wise man once said, *'We patronize them for their incompleteness, for their tragic fate of having taken form so far below ourselves. And therein we err, and greatly err. For the animal shall not be measured by man. In a world older and more complete than ours, they move finished and complete, gifted with extensions of the senses we have lost or never attained, living by voices we shall never hear. They are not brethren, they are not underlings; they are other nations, caught with ourselves in the net of life and time, fellow prisoners of the splendour and travail of the earth.'*

"I know some of you remember my old dog Spunky. We got Spunk when I was in the second grade. My mom's friend said she had a litter of Shih Tzus and was selling them. When we arrived, all of the pups had already been purchased - all of the pups except Spunky. He was the runt of the litter and had a bad right eye that made him undesirable for breeding. All of his brothers and sisters had been taken, and he was left all alone, shivering in the corner of the big cage. She had been charging 200 dollars, but she said we could have Spunk for twenty bucks. We most definitely got a good deal. Spunky became a great dog and a great friend to me and my father.

"During the summertime my friends and I would go out to a friend's property that had a creek running through it. We would run down to a swimming hole in the crick every day. The side that we could park on had a steep mud bank, and we had to jump from it into the swimming hole. Spunky always came with us but would never take the plunge. It was twelve foot high if it was a foot, and the water was usually moving pretty fast.

"Every day for I don't know how long, Spunky would stand on the edge of the bank and bark down at us playing in the water. He loved the water, but wasn't thrilled with the manner in which he'd have to get to it. Every day we played in the swimming hole and would call to him to jump to us. We'd say, 'Come on, Spunk! Good boy, Spunk! Come on, buddy! Jump, Spunky, jump!'

"But he wouldn't do it. He didn't know how high he was, just that he was really high, and fear made him even higher. No matter how much we called to him though, he would just bark in frustration and paw the dirt like the little Shih Tzu bull he was." Johnny got his first giggle out of the audience in a while.

"Finally, towards the end of the summer, we gave up on Spunk and stopped callin for him to jump. Day after day he came along, but he never got farther than the lip of that ol mud bank. He could see we were having a blast, and one day Spunk just couldn't take it any longer. All of a sudden, he stopped barkin, and my buddy, Matt, muttered, 'dude, look at him!' He wouldn't say his name out loud because Spunky was deep in concentration, and he didn't want to throw him off. He was totally focused on the water as he backed up slowly - step by step, step by step.

"We were all staring at him. Nobody flinched an inch or said a word. Nobody wanted to distract Spunk-Dog. After he had enough distance in front-a him, he paused and bounded forward - fast as a flash. I'll always have that snapshot in my memory of Spunky in mid-air; shaggy ears back in the wind; little legs stretched full-out like a greyhound; fearful eyes big as silver dollars. He hit the water with a splash!

"He surfaced faster than a fishin bobber, snortin like a Shih Tzu, and swam to us on the other side. He got a hero's welcome from all of us and proceeded to pee on every tree in the woods. We were very proud of Spunk that day. But as he snorted and strutted around on that side of the crick, no one was prouder of Spunk than Spunky was. From that day on, no one ever hit the water faster than Spunky. No one could get to the lip of that bank before him and take the plunge before he did.

"On that day, that little dog did what most men fail to do in their lives. *He went for it.* And it taught me that when fear is overcome, it does not disappear, but becomes a springboard to unimaginable heights. Spunk taught me that when you are ready to look at it, fear will always lose a staring contest. He taught me that one has no greater tests in his life than those which fear provides. He taught me that when fear is beaten, it cannot help but catapult you to freedom and glory. Spunky rolled away his stone that day... Will you do the same?"

As Johnny came to the close of his speech, he looked down at the audience. Some were laughing, a few were crying, others were looking at their laps. The majority, however, were cursing him with their eyes. And Johnny Daniels looked down at them all, took a deep breath, and told them why he was a Christian.

"Jesus Christ is the greatest physician to ever walk the face of the earth. He healed the blind, he cleansed lepers, he healed a paralytic man, he cured a bleeding woman, and he healed a deaf mute. Jesus performed many other miracles and healed many, many more people. And the one thing all these people had in common was that they all believed He could do it.

"I have scoured the Gospels, and I can say as a matter of fact that Jesus healed all these people. And before he did so, he never once asked them if they had a health savings account or health insurance." Johnny had hoped for a laugh here but didn't get it. Matt and Mr. Tyson were the only ones smiling in the whole damn auditorium, but there was nothing real special about that.

"We are all Christians here. We are Christians not because of wise men's commands and proverbs. We are not Christians because of letters written by men like Paul. We are all Christians because we believe in the love of Jesus Christ. His sole command to man was love. His purpose for mankind was love. His reason for existence was love. He was simple love, and He was a great man.

"If any of you has a preacher that doesn't preach about that love, every single sermon he preaches, then I am afraid that he has completely missed the point. If there is a single instance that your preacher doesn't preach simple love and the simple works that must follow it, I ask you to do this. Get your congregation together and approach the good pastor. Ask him politely if he would please re-read the Gospels of Matthew, Mark, Luke, and John. Tell him to pay extra special attention to the red text. That text is in red because it is the very words of Jesus Christ, himself.

"If the pastor happens to slip up again and preaches a sermon that isn't about love, get your congregation together and approach the good pastor. Ask him politely if he would please re-read the Gospels of Matthew, Mark, Luke, and John. Tell him again that you all would appreciate it greatly if he paid special attention to the red text.

"If the good pastor happens to slip up again, and preaches a sermon that isn't about love, get your congregation together and approach the good pastor. Ask him politely if he would please get the hell outta Dodge, and help him pack up his things while he is doing so. If any so-called Christian pastor ever preaches hell and damnation he shall himself be damned, and good riddance, good sir - for there is no more convenient a place for the devil to reside than under holy robes.

"Modern day conservative Christians have hijacked Jesus' message and tied it to Paul's statement that the wages of sin is death. You get what you deserve, you sinful being - unless you mutter this special sentence. Jesus taught us that love is in actions, not words. Jesus taught us that the poor and downtrodden are the best investment a society can make, because the highest returns on an investment reside in its potential and not its present circumstances.

"And this investment is not a part of some moral obligation that lends itself to the sanctity of the giver, but a tangible affirmation of love that is never wanting or conserved. You shall reap what you sow was never meant to be taken as some judgmental justification for the subjugation of the unfortunate but as a simple command to love.

"There is nothing conservative about love and forgiveness. The poor youth with a meth addicted mother and absent father is purported by many to have all the same opportunities as any other American child. What a perverted mindset, indeed. Love and conservative have no business being in the same sentence or sentiment. Christ's sole command was love. Real Christians don't run around blindly collecting heaven's souls but walk around this earth giving love. If more Christians would just repeat the words and actions of Jesus there would be more Christians in the world right now.

"I don't know positively that there is a Heaven that we Christians all go to when we die. I hope and believe there is, but I do not know for sure. An afterlife full of everlasting joy and harmony is a wonderful thing to believe, but we can never be sure of what we believe until we come to terms with what we know.

"I know that there are billions of people on this earth that are hungry right now. And instead of worrying about their souls, let's worry about their stomachs. I know there are a billion people that don't get clean drinking water. I know there are countless people that are sick and poor and lonely and flat broke on this earth right now. Let us quit worrying about their souls and start worrying about their circumstances.

"For Christ's sake, let us stop talking about eternity and souls and things we believe and get to working on those things which we know. For Christ's sake, let us bridge the gap of superiority over those of other faiths. For Christ's sake, let us stop preaching to people and just start helping people. For Christ's sake, let us quit scaring children with evil and perverted talk of hellfire and damnation.

"I know that there are a lot of you in the audience that disagree with the things I've said today. I know that there are a lot of you who will look at me different. I know that I have changed a great deal over the past year, but I reckon the reasons why I've changed are more important than what I've become. If you remember just one thing from what I've said today, I ask you to remember that man's greatest achievements all stem from questions; without them we just float through life, looking around and wondering a lot less often than we should.

"And finally, please remember that a man's trail to truth is walked by him alone. And when your trail is unknown, or difficult, or winding - just keep on walkin to find *your* street. Jesus gave enough lessons to last a lifetime. He taught us that the best advice is seen, not heard. He taught us that the greatest love is given to those with the least. He taught us that love and lines can't co-exist. He taught us that fear was never ours to give; righteous stones were never ours to throw.

"Above all, He taught us that the only thing easier than loving love, is hating hate. There is definitely other good advice in the Bible, but none is better than Christ's best. Jesus rolled his stone away... that we may do the same."

As Johnny looked down at the students and teachers and friends at Almighty Wonders from the altar, he thought about Little Davy Jones. Johnny was looking down at the same people Davy had been looking down at when he made his confession. Davy had been standing exactly where Johnny was now standing, and Johnny realized that Davy had, in fact, been a brave young man.

And as Johnny looked down at the congregation then, he did not think of them as sheep. He did not think of them as dim-witted or wrong or mean. He thought of a story he once heard told by a wise man named Jiddu Krishnamurti, who believed truth is a pathless land.

One day the devil was walking through town with a friend. Ahead of the pair, there was another man walking down the street. All of a sudden, the man stooped down and picked something up off the ground. He studied it for a while, carefully put it into his pocket, and continued walking down the street. The friend asked the devil, "What did that man just pick up?" The devil responded, "The man has just picked up a piece of the truth." The friend responded, "Well that is very bad news for you then, I suppose?" "Oh not at all," the devil replied to his friend, "I am going to help him organize it."

As Johnny looked down at the congregation then, he did not think of them as sheep. He did not think of them as dim-witted or wrong or mean. They knew all of the answers but few of the questions, for they had not been organized to question, but to believe.

Johnny stepped down off the altar. Everyone's shock was displayed in lifted eyebrows and slack jaws. No one said a word. It was as quiet as if no one were there. He glanced at his old Bible teacher, Mr. Tyson, again. The big man smiled one of his carefree smiles and winked at Johnny. It wasn't uncommon for him to do that, but it meant a lot this time.

Johnny walked slowly down the aisle - shoulders back and chin proud. He walked by the congregation and the students as he made his way toward the back door. He saw Lisa in a floral dress near the back of the auditorium. She looked at him sadly. She looked at him just like she had been looking at Davy in the parking lot that day one year ago. She looked at him like he was truly lost, and only Christ could show him the way back.

Lisa was the type of woman whose eyes cursed more often than her mouth. At that moment, her eyes said, *'someday you will grow up. Someday you will know Christ again. Someday you will understand.'* Most people will tell you that the worst words in the English language contain four letters, but they are very wrong indeed.

'Someday' is the vilest word man has ever created. It is meaningless, and full of half-assed intentions that harbor only sadness and dismay. There is simply nothing filthier, than telling someone - someday.

The young man looked right back at her. Johnny was the type of guy whose eyes cursed less often than his mouth. Most days his eyes never cursed - but today was not one of those days. At that moment, as he looked at Lisa, his eyes said, '*go to hell, devil woman. And fuck that high horse you ride around on, too.*'

And he continued towards the back doors. He noticed Davy's mother standing in the back corner of the auditorium. They had spoken only a few times over the years. He did not know her well, but he knew how much Davy had loved her. She had aged a great deal since Johnny had last seen her. Her hair was much grayer, and there were wrinkles where none had previously existed. She had tears on her cheeks, but they were feminine tears of happiness. She didn't say it out loud, but her eyes said, '*Thank you, Johnny.*'

He came to the end of the long aisle, and he looked to his right. He saw his father as he opened the back door. He had his arm around Jennifer and a tear on his cheek. He didn't say it out loud, but his eyes said, '*Did I ever tell you that I hate kids?*' Johnny nodded to his father as they smiled at one another. Being right or being wrong has nothing to do with being happy. Johnny loved him too.

Then there was that big oaf Matt, standing at the back of the auditorium, not a care in the world, grinning like a big ol dumbass at his best friend. As Johnny walked out the doors, Matthew followed him out.

"Sweet Mother of God, bro. Here comes Pastor Jennings, and damn my eyes he looks freakin pissed," Matt mumbled to his friend. "I got your back, bro, I got your back."

Pastor Jennings did appear upset as he cut off the pair. There was a wildfire in his countenance. His eyes said... well, let's just say his eyes would have scared the hell right out of Satan himself.

"That was one heck of a speech, Jonathan. I think my favorite line was the part about the most convenient place for the devil to reside being underneath holy robes."

"Well, sir, that part wasn't actually meant to be directed *right* at you. The part on preaching about love and forgiveness may have been meant as a bit of advice for ya, though."

"I didn't ask you for any gosh darned advice, Jonathan. And the next time you get up on that altar, you had better ask my permission to speak to my congregation in such a manner. If I wasn't a preacher, I'd have half a mind to tan your hide right here and now for all that crap you said up there!"

Johnny and the pastor stared at one another for many moments through slitted eyes. Pastor Jennings was taller, but they weighed about the same. Four fists were clenched with knuckles drained of color. Matthew cleared his throat respectfully. Only one person was allowed to tan Johnny's hide, and that person was *not* Pastor Jennings.

Johnny opened his fists and took a deep breath before he spoke. "Well, Pastor. I understand why you're upset, but that altar is mine, too, and it was Davy's altar, too. I hope when you cool down a bit you can try to see where I was comin from. If you're just *that* upset with me though," Johnny said real slow, "I guess there's only one thing left for a man in your position to do."

Johnny thought he was gonna go for it then. His eyes were still wild and his breathing was shallow and rapid. The son-bitch actually lifted his fist like he really was gonna go toe-to-toe with Johnny right there outside the goddamn auditorium.

Johnny just smiled and said, "Forgive me."

The pastor stared down Johnny for a few moments longer, and then he seemed to deflate a bit. He lowered his fist. A small smile formed on his lips as he shook his head, and he even chuckled to himself for a second. He gingerly offered his hand, and he and Johnny shook like the men they were.

As they squeezed hard he said, "In the future, I would appreciate a little warning before you tell me to get the hell outta Dodge, by the way. But for now..." he bit down hard and shook his head like he couldn't believe what in the hell he was saying, "thanks for the advice, John." They all smiled together, and Johnny and Matt walked on.

T he two young men walked out of their old school into a beautiful spring sunset (if you would like a beautiful description - well, there's the damn door.) As they paused to enjoy the view, a spunky little breeze scampered in from the west. He carried an old message from Nature's chest that man doesn't always hear; a superficial revelation of what flows from her nickel-iron core with a harmony and understanding deeper and more everlasting than any language we so pitifully lob its way. The breeze whispered it to the leaves as he tickled the blades of grass. He held it loose as he ruffled the men's hair and swirled the fluffy clouds.

As he carried spring's perfume to every living thing, Matthew looked over at his best friend. Johnny had a smile of satisfaction on his face and the raised jaw of a man that knows his fears - but isn't scared of them. Both pairs of eyes were naturally drawn to the big flagpole in the parking lot. To the Christian flag they knew so well, flying *below* the American flag they loved so dearly. Both looked proud and strong as they fluttered and danced with the breeze.

Clang! Clang! Clang! hit the halyard.

"So Matthew, what do you think they thought a my speech?"

Matt grabbed his crotch and spit. "Well, bro, I think they liked yer speech a year ago much better. You definitely gave em hell, though!" they laughed hard. "But it was a pretty good speech, man. I reckon you and Davy are all squared up."

"Reckon, huh?"

"Yeah man, I like that word. Cowboys used to say it all the time. John Wayne said it all the time, too. He was a good shit, man."

"Yes he was, Matthew. Yes he was." Johnny looked over at his friend and said, "You also, are a very good shit, bro." Matt puffed up a bit.

"Isn't it good to be alive, Matt?"

"Hell, I dunno, man. I've never been nothin different."

"You know, Matthew, that's why I hang out with you. Not because you'd wail on anyone that screws with me, your good looks, or even your way with the ladies. It's because you're just so wise."

Matt put his arm around his buddy. "I've got skills you haven't even heard of, bro. Hey, what's that thing Manuelito always says that I like the sounda?"

"He says, *pura vida, güey* all the time," Johnny said.

"Yeah, he says that all the time, but naw, man, it's what he always says when he's leavin."

"Oh," Johnny said, "he says, *que le vaya bien.* Guess it kinda means go in peace."

"Yeah man. I like the way that shit sounds," Matt said, "kay.. lay.. viya.. byen."

Clang! Clang! Clang! hit the halyard.

The two men did not realize it, but at that very moment they were being watched. There was a wise old tree standing next to them. And in that tree a butterfly slowly raised his wings and lowered them; back and forth, back and forth - nature's quiet lullaby.

The butterfly had the prettiest, deep blue wings that were outlined in a lighter shade of the like. He had a little pink mark on his left wing, and two long furry antennae that danced and moved with the wind. And as he sat he watched the men with round chocolate eyes.

Once more the breeze kicked up to pull and grow the grass; playing down the leaves and branches, he pushed the butterfly away. He hovered for a moment, then caught the squirrely wind, escaping the leafy shadows.

Now, people will tell you that butterflies are not curious animals, but they are very wrong, indeed. The men were walking away from him, but the butterfly could see they were talking, and he wobbled off that way, pretty on the breeze – up and down and all around. He got a little nudge when he strayed off course, pushing him toward the pair.

It was not easy, but he *just* managed to flutter over them as they walked home upon the grass. He was straining to hear, and the breeze was at play, but as he flew over Johnny, he heard the young man say:

"God, that butterfly is pretty... *Good work, sir, and Godspeed...*"

And the men did not look back that day to worry right from wrong, while the flagpole saw them homeward with a song.

Clang! Clang! Clang!
Clang! Clang! Clang!
Clang! Clang! Clang! hit the halyard.

That's all he wrote *

Give your soul to Goodness, it will never push you down;
Give your soul to Kindness, purest remedy for a frown.
Give your soul to Gritty, that gutter aint your home;
Give your soul to Dreaming, those shackles are your own.

Shield your soul from rightness, it poisons many things;
Shield your soul from ego, man's servant and his king.
Shield your soul from fearing (it has a thousand names);
Shield your soul from boredom, life runs it's never lame.
Give your soul to Patience, and you'll get there soon enough;
Give your soul to Gentleness, but you can still be tough.

Give your soul to Hopeful, and luck will look your way;
Give your soul to Mercy, it may come back one day.
Give your soul to Questions, answers never try;
Shield your soul from answers, questions cannot lie.
Shield your soul from doubting, just hope and you'll do fine;
Shield your soul from cruelty, its deeds will never shine.

Give your soul to Joyful, it's free and can't be sold;
Give your soul to Forgiveness, let go before you're old.
Shield your soul from contentment, it slowly turns to pain;
Shield your soul from envy (for dreams cannot be vain);
Shield your soul from someday, man's vilest thought and word;
Shield your soul from worry, just like Marley's little birds.

Give your soul to Wisdom, which doesn't always speak;
Give your soul to Courage, born and bred to teach.
Give your soul to Creative, it can't be taught so learn;
Give your soul to Loyalty, true friends will never spurn.
Give your soul to Acceptance, and those scary walls will fall;
Give your soul to Loving, the best and brightest of them all.

If all these things you try to do, and pure life eludes you still,
Then give your soul to God whichever.
(I hope he'll pay your bill.)